Sebastian ...y best-selling ps... ...ny. His unique, mi... ...over five million copies around the world and have been translated into

Sebastian Fitzek is the number one internationally best-selling psychological thriller writer from Germany. His unique, mind-bending thrillers have sold over five million copies around the world and have been translated into twenty nine languages.

THE CHILD

SEBASTIAN FITZEK

Translated by John Brownjohn

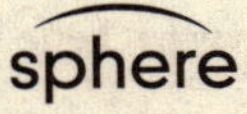

SPHERE

First published in the English language in
Great Britain in 2014 by Sphere
This paperback edition published in 2015 by Sphere

Originally published in German as *Das Kind* in 2008 by Droemer Knaur

1 3 5 7 9 10 8 6 4 2

www.sebastianfitzek.de

The book is published by agreement with AVA International GmbH,
Germany (www.ava-international.de)

A CIP catalogue record for this book is available from the British Library.

ISBN 978-0-7515-5687-2

Typeset in Sabon by
Palimpsest Book Production Limited, Falkirk, Stirlingshire

Printed and bound in Great Britain by Clays Ltd, St Ives plc

Papers used by Sphere are from well-managed forests
and other responsible sources.

Sphere
An imprint of
Little, Brown Book Group
Carmelite House
50 Victoria Embankment
London EC4Y 0DZ

An Hachette UK Company
www.hachette.co.uk

www.littlebrown.co.uk

For my parents and Viktor Larenz

The Meeting

Out of the mouths of babes and sucklings hast thou
ordained strength because of thine enemies,
that thou mightest still the enemy and the avenger.

Psalms 8:2

1

When Robert Stern agreed to attend this unusual meeting a few hours earlier, he hadn't known he was making a rendezvous with death. He'd been even less aware that death would barely come up to his chest, be wearing jeans and trainers, and enter his life with a smile on this derelict industrial estate.

'No, she isn't here yet, and I'm beginning to lose patience.'

Stern, staring through his car's streaming windscreen at the broken windows of the old factory a hundred metres away, silently cursed his secretary. She had forgotten to cancel the date with his father, who was fuming on the other line.

'Call Carina and ask her where the hell she's got to!'

He punched a button on the leather-covered steering wheel. A crackle of static, then he heard his old man coughing over the loudspeaker. Seventy-nine and still a chain smoker. He had even lit up while waiting to be put through.

'I'm sorry, Dad,' said Stern. 'I know we were having supper tonight, but we'll have to make it Sunday instead. I've been called to a completely unexpected meeting.'

Please come – you must. I don't know what to do.

He had never heard Carina sound so anxious on the phone before. If she was play-acting, she deserved an Oscar.

'Maybe I should pay you five hundred euros an hour like your clients,' his father snarled. 'Then I might get to see you sometime.'

Stern sighed. He looked in on his father regularly, but there was no point in mentioning that now. Nothing had ever taught him how to win an argument with his father, neither his scores of courtroom successes nor the lost battles of his wrecked marriage. As soon as he locked horns with the old man he felt like a child with a bad school report, not forty-five-year-old Robert Stern, senior partner of Langendorf, Stern & Dankwitz, Berlin's leading defence lawyers.

'To be honest, Dad,' he said, trying to inject some levity into the conversation, 'I haven't the faintest idea where I am at present. If I didn't know better, I'd say I was somewhere in Chechnya. My satnav had a hard time getting me here.'

He turned on the car's headlights. They illuminated an expanse of unpaved forecourt piled high with steel girders, rusty cable drums and other industrial waste. Paints and varnishes had once been manufactured here, to judge by the stacks of empty metal drums. Seen against the dilapidated brick factory building with the half-demolished chimney, they looked like props in a post-apocalyptic movie.

'Let's hope that gizmo of yours can find its way to my funeral when the time comes,' the old man said between coughs. Stern wondered if this embitterment was hereditary. He'd had the makings of it himself for ten years or more.

Since Felix.

Stern's traumatic experiences in the neonatal ward had brought him closer to his father outwardly as well. He had aged before his time. The man who used to spend every spare minute on the basketball court, improving his shooting, could scarcely hit his office wastepaper basket with an empty Coke can.

Most people who met him were deceived by Stern's tall, slim figure and broad shoulders. The truth was, his perfectly cut suits concealed a physique that had gone to seed, the dark smudges below his eyes were camouflaged by a naturally swarthy complexion, and skilful haircutting prevented the sparse patches above his temples from showing through. It took the better part of an hour to scrub the fatigue from his face each morning, and he left the bathroom feeling more and more of a sham. Like the sort of showy designer furniture the hidden defects of which don't become apparent until they're exposed to the merciless overhead lights in your living room.

There was a click on the line.

'Sorry, I'll be right back.' Stern escaped any further paternal reproaches by taking his secretary's return call.

'Let me guess: she cancelled the appointment?' That would be typical of her. Carina Freitag was a reliable and efficient nurse, professionally speaking, but the structuring of her personal commitments was as chaotic, erratic and uncoordinated as her love life. Although their relationship had broken up after only a few weeks three years ago, they still phoned each other regularly and even met for an occasional coffee. Both forms of contact tended to end in a row.

'No, afraid I couldn't get through to her.'

'OK, thanks.' Stern flinched as the autumn gale spattered the windscreen with a sudden flurry of rain. He started the car and turned on the wipers, his eye briefly caught by a russet-coloured maple leaf stuck to the glass beyond their reach. Then, looking back over his shoulder, he slowly reversed the car, its tyres crunching on the loose chippings.

'If Carina calls, tell her I couldn't wait any—' Stern broke off just as he faced the front and was about to engage first gear. Whatever was racing straight towards him, emergency lights flashing, it certainly wasn't Carina's decrepit little car.

The ambulance was making its way along the approach road as fast as the potholes permitted.

For one brief moment Stern genuinely thought the driver meant to ram him. Then the ambulance veered off and came to a stop beside his car.

He switched back to the other line after telling his secretary goodbye. 'Dad? I'll have to sign off, the person I'm meeting has just arrived,' he said, but his father had already hung up. A gust of wind blew the Mercedes saloon's heavy door as he opened it and got out.

What the hell is she doing with an ambulance?

Carina opened the driver's door and jumped out, landing in a puddle, but she seemed heedless of the muddy splashes on her white nurse's uniform. Her long, auburn hair was gathered into a severe ponytail. She looked so good that Stern was tempted to take her in his arms, but something in her expression deterred him.

'I'm in big trouble,' she said, producing a packet of cigarettes. 'I think I've really messed up this time.'

'Why all the drama?' Stern asked. 'Why not meet at my office instead of on this . . . this bomb site?'

No longer in the comfort of his car, he could feel the unpleasant chill of the freshening October wind. He hunched his shoulders and shivered.

'Let's not waste any time, Robert. I only borrowed this bus – I have to return it as soon as possible.'

'All right, but if you've messed up, can't we discuss it in more civilized surroundings?'

'No, no, no.' Carina shook her head and made a dismissive gesture. 'You don't understand – this isn't about me.'

She strode briskly around the ambulance, opened the rear door and pointed inside.

'Your client is lying down here.'

Stern gave her a searching, sidelong look. To a man of

his experience, the sight of a bank robber with gunshot wounds, or a victim of gang warfare or some other shady character in urgent and, above all, anonymous need of his help would have been nothing new. What puzzled him was where Carina came into the equation.

When she said no more he climbed aboard. His attention was immediately drawn to the figure lying motionless on the stretcher.

'What is this?' He swung round and looked back at Carina, who had remained standing outside the vehicle and was lighting a cigarette – something she seldom did, and only when extremely nervous. 'You've brought a boy out here. Why?'

'He'll tell you himself.'

'The little shrimp doesn't look as if . . .' *he's capable of talking*, Stern was going to say, because the pale-faced youngster appeared almost lifeless. When he turned round again, however, the boy had sat up with his legs dangling over the side of the stretcher.

'I'm not a little shrimp,' he protested. 'I'm ten! My birthday was two days ago.'

Beneath his cord jacket the boy wore a black T-shirt with a death's-head transfer. To Stern his brand-new patchwork jeans looked far too big for him, but what did he know? Maybe it was fashionable for kids that age to turn up their trouser legs and draw on their trainers with a felt-tip pen.

'Are you a lawyer?' the boy asked rather hoarsely. He seemed to have trouble speaking, as if he hadn't drunk anything for a long time.

'Yes, I am. A defence lawyer, to be precise.'

'Good.' The boy's smile revealed two rows of surprisingly white and regular teeth. His long lashes and rosebud mouth would have been enough to melt any granny's heart, even without the addition of a gap-toothed grin.

'That's fine,' he said. He got off the stretcher, briefly turning his back on Stern as he did so. His curly light-brown hair was shoulder length and freshly washed. Seen from behind, he could have passed for a girl. Beneath the hair Stern noticed a plaster the size of a credit card on the back of his neck.

The boy was still smiling when he turned round.

'I'm Simon. Simon Sachs.'

He held out a slender little hand. Stern hesitated for an instant, then shook it.

'And I'm Robert Stern.'

'I know. Carina showed me a photo of you – she keeps it in her handbag. She says you're the best.'

'Thanks a lot,' Stern mumbled rather awkwardly. As far as he could recall, this was the longest conversation he'd had with a child for years. 'What can I do for you?' he asked just as awkwardly.

'I need a lawyer.'

'I see.' Stern turned his head and shot an enquiring glance at Carina, who was impassively smoking her cigarette.

Why was she doing this to him? Why had she dragged him out to a demolition site and introduced him to a ten-year-old? She knew how hopeless he was with children and how he had avoided them ever since tragedy had destroyed his marriage and then nearly him.

'What makes you think you need a lawyer?' he asked, suppressing his annoyance with some effort. This absurd situation might at least provide an amusing topic of conversation during breaks between court appearances.

He pointed to the plaster on Simon's neck. 'Is it because of that? Did someone attack you in the playground?'

'No, it isn't that.'

'What, then?'

'I'm a murderer.'

'What?' Stern had paused before asking the question, firmly convinced that a ten-year-old couldn't have said that. He kept looking from Simon to Carina and back like a spectator at a tennis match. But only until the boy said it again loud and clear.

'I need a lawyer. I'm a murderer.'

A dog barked somewhere in the distance. The sound mingled with the incessant hum from the nearby dual carriageway, but Stern was as deaf to it as he was to the raindrops beating an irregular tattoo on the ambulance's roof.

'OK, so you think you've killed someone,' he said after another moment's disconcerted silence.

'Yes.'

'May I ask who?'

'I don't know.'

'Ah, so you don't know.' Stern gave a mirthless laugh. 'And you probably don't know how, why or where it happened either, because the whole thing is a silly practical joke, and—'

'With an axe.' Simon whispered the words, though for a moment it sounded like he'd shouted them.

'*What* did you say?'

'With an axe. A man. I hit him on the head with it. That's all I can remember. It was a long time ago.'

'What do you mean, a long time ago?' Stern blinked nervously. 'When was it?'

'The twenty-eighth of October.'

Stern glanced at his watch. 'That's today,' he said, looking mystified. 'You just said it happened a long time ago, so when was it? Make up your mind.'

He wished he always had such easy witnesses to cross-examine – ten-year-olds who contradicted themselves within a minute of taking the oath. He was soon disabused.

'You don't understand.' Simon shook his head sadly. 'I killed a man. Right here!'

'Here?' Stern repeated. Bewildered, he watched the boy push gently past him, get out of the ambulance and survey his surroundings with interest. As far as Stern could tell, his attention was focused on a derelict shed beside a clump of trees some hundred metres away.

'Yes,' Simon said, taking Carina's hand, 'this is it. This is where I killed a man. On the twenty-eighth of October. Fifteen years ago.'

2

Stern climbed out of the ambulance and asked Simon to wait for a moment. Then he grabbed Carina roughly by the wrist and led her behind his car. The rain had eased somewhat, but the day had grown darker, windier and, above all, chillier. Neither she in her thin nurse's uniform nor he in his dark three-piece suit was suitably dressed for such lousy weather, but unlike him Carina didn't look cold at all.

'Quick question,' he whispered, although Simon was too far away to hear him above the sound of the wind and the dual carriageway's monotonous, surf-like roar. 'Which of you is the crazier?'

'Simon is a patient of mine in Neurology,' said Carina, as though that explained everything.

'He might do better in a psychiatric ward,' Stern hissed. 'What was all that nonsense about a murder fifteen years ago? Can't he count, or is he schizophrenic?'

Stern opened the boot with his car key's remote control and turned on the interior light, dispelling some of the gloom.

'He has a cerebral tumour.' Carina demonstrated its size by forming a ring with her thumb and forefinger. 'They give him a few more weeks. Maybe only days.'

'Good God, and it has *those* side effects?' Stern took an umbrella from the boot.

'No. I'm to blame.'

'You?'

He looked up with the brand-new designer brolly in his hand. The way it worked escaped him. He couldn't even find the button that opened it.

'I told you, I messed up. The boy is highly intelligent, incredibly sensitive and remarkably well educated for his age. Which is almost miraculous, if you ask me, considering his background. He was rescued from his chaotic mother's squalid flat at the age of four – they found him half starved in the bathtub with a dead rat for company. Then he was put in a home, where he stood out from the rest because he liked reading encyclopedias more than playing with kids of his own age. The supervisor thought it only natural that a child who did so much thinking should have a permanent headache, but then they discovered this thing in his brain. Simon has been a patient on my ward ever since. He doesn't have a soul to care for him apart from the hospital staff. Well, only me, really.'

Carina was obviously feeling cold now, too. Her lips had begun to tremble.

'I don't see what you're getting at.'

'It was Simon's birthday two days ago, and I wanted to give him a special treat. I mean, he's only ten but his experience of life and his illness have made him so much more mature than other children of his age. I thought he was old enough.'

'Old enough for what? What did you give him?' Stern, who had finally abandoned his attempt to open the umbrella, was pointing it at her chest like a gun.

'Simon is afraid of dying, so I arranged a regression for him.'

'A *what*?' said Stern, although he had recently seen something about it on television.

It was, of course, typical of Carina to subscribe to such an esoteric fad. People of all ages seemed to be fascinated by the notion of having been on earth before. This hankering after the supernatural provided fertile soil from which shady therapists could sprout like weeds and charge substantial fees for 'regressions': journeys into the antenatal past during which their clients discovered, usually under hypnosis, that they had occupied the throne of France or been burned at the stake six centuries ago.

'Don't look at me like that. I know what you think of these things. You won't even read your horoscope.'

'How could you expose a little boy to such mumbo-jumbo?'

Stern was genuinely horrified. The television programme had warned of the possibility of severe mental damage. Many unstable personalities couldn't cope when a charlatan persuaded them that their current psychological problems stemmed from some unresolved conflict in a previous existence.

'I only wanted to show him that it isn't all over – when you die, I mean – and that he mustn't be sad to have lived for such a short time because life goes on.'

'Tell me you're joking.'

She shook her head. 'I took him to Dr Tiefensee. He's a qualified psychologist and gives courses at the university. Not a charlatan, whatever you may think.'

'What happened?'

'He hypnotized the boy. Not a great deal happened, actually. Simon couldn't remember much under hypnosis. He just said he was in a dark cellar and could hear voices. Voices saying nasty things.'

Stern grimaced with discomfort. The cold creeping up his

back was becoming steadily more unpleasant, but that wasn't his only reason for wanting to get away as soon as possible. Somewhere in the distance a freight train was rumbling past. Carina was whispering now, just as he himself had at the start of their conversation.

'Tiefensee initially failed to rouse Simon from his hypnotic trance. He had fallen into a deep sleep, and when he woke up he told us what he told you just now. He thinks he used to be a murderer.'

Stern felt an urge to wipe his hands on his hair, but it, too, was wet with rain.

'The whole idea is nonsense, Carina, and you know it. All I'm wondering is, what's it got to do with me?'

'Simon has a profound sense of right and wrong. He insists on going to the police.'

'That's right, I do.'

They both swung round. The boy had stolen up behind them unobserved. The wind was stirring the mass of curls on his forehead. Stern wondered why he had any hair at all. He must surely have had to undergo chemotherapy.

'I'm a murderer, and that's wrong. I want to turn myself in, but I won't say a thing unless my lawyer's present.'

Carina smiled sadly. 'He picked that up from television, and you're the only defence lawyer I know.'

Stern avoided her eye. Instead, he stared at the muddy ground as if his hand-sewn Oxfords could tell him how to respond to this lunacy.

'Well?' he heard Simon say.

'Well what?' Stern raised his head and looked straight at the boy, surprised to see that he was smiling again.

'Are you my lawyer now? I can pay you.'

Rather awkwardly, Simon fished a little purse out of the pocket of his jeans.

'I've got some money, you see.'

Stern shook his head. Almost imperceptibly at first, then more and more violently.

'I have,' Simon insisted. 'Honestly.'

'No,' said Stern, glaring at Carina now. 'This is all beside the point, am I right? You didn't get me out here as a lawyer, did you?'

Now it was her turn to stare at the ground.

'No, I didn't,' she admitted quietly.

With a sigh, Stern tossed the unopened umbrella back into the boot of the car. Pushing a briefcase aside, he opened the first-aid locker and removed a torch. He checked the beam by shining it on the tumbledown shed Simon had indicated earlier.

'All right, let's get this over with.'

He patted Simon's head with his free hand, unable to believe that he was really saying this to a ten-year-old boy:

'Show me exactly where you say you killed this man.'

3

Simon led them around the back of the shed. A two-storey building must have occupied the site many years ago, but it had been destroyed by fire. All that now jutted into the overcast evening sky were isolated sections of soot-stained brickwork resembling mutilated hands.

'You see? There's nothing here.'

Stern played the beam of his torch slowly over the ruins.

'But it must be somewhere here,' said Simon. He might have been talking about a lost glove, not a dead body. He too had come armed with a light source: a little plastic rod that emitted a fluorescent glow when you bent it.

'From his box of magic tricks,' Carina had explained to Stern. The boy had evidently been given some normal birthday presents as well as the regression.

'I think it was down there,' Simon said excitedly, stepping forward.

Following the direction of his outstretched arm, Stern shone his torch at the old stairwell. They could see only the entrance to the cellar now.

'We can't go down there, it's too dangerous.'

'Why not?' the boy demanded, scrambling over a pile of loose bricks.

'Stay here, sweetheart, it could all cave in.' Carina sounded uncharacteristically anxious. During her brief affair with Robert Stern she'd been the soul of exuberance, almost as if she were trying to compensate for his permanent melancholy with an overabundance of *joie de vivre*. Now she was agitated, as if Simon were behaving like a disobedient dog let off the leash. He plodded on.

'Look, we can get down there!' he cried suddenly. The other two were still protesting when his curly head disappeared behind a reinforced concrete pillar.

'Simon!' called Carina. Stern blundered after them across the rubble-strewn floor, nearly twisting his ankle a couple of times and tearing his trousers on a rusty piece of wire. By the time he reached the entrance to the cellar, the boy had made his way down some twenty charred wooden stairs and turned a corner.

'Come out of there at once!' Stern shouted, immediately cursing his ill-considered choice of words. The memory triggered by them was worse than anything that could happen to him here, he realized.

Come out of there, darling, please! I can help you . . .

That wasn't the only lie he'd called to Sophie through the locked bathroom door. In vain. They'd tried everything for four long years – every technique and form of treatment – until at last they received the longed-for phone call from the fertility clinic. Positive. Pregnant. On that day, over a decade ago, it seemed to him that a higher power had totally reoriented the compass needle of his life. It had suddenly pointed to happiness in its purest form, but only, alas, for as long as it took him to transform the ceiling of the new nursery into a night sky with stick-on fluorescent stars and go shopping for baby clothes with Sophie. Felix never wore them. He was cremated in the sleepsuit the nurses had dressed him in.

'Simon?' Carina called the boy's name so loudly, it jolted him out of his dark reverie.

Simon's muffled voice came drifting up from below. 'I think there's something here!'

Stern swore. He tested the first step with his foot. 'It's no use, I'll have to go down there.'

Those words, too, reminded him of the worst moment in his life. The moment when Sophie took refuge in the patients' bathroom with their dead baby in her arms and wouldn't give it up. 'Sudden infant death syndrome' was the diagnosis she refused to accept. Two days after giving birth.

'I'm coming with you,' said Carina.

'Don't be silly.' Stern took another cautious step. The stairs had supported Simon. He would have to see whether they could support more than twice the boy's weight. 'We've only got one torch and someone'll have to call for help if we aren't back in a couple of minutes.'

The rotten treads creaked at every step like the rigging of a ship. Stern wasn't sure if his sense of balance was playing tricks, but the stairs seemed to sway more violently the lower he got.

'Simon?' He must have called the boy's name at least five times, but the only response was a metallic clang some distance away. It sounded like someone hitting a central heating pipe with a spanner.

Before long he was standing at the foot of the stairs. He looked around with his heart pounding. It was now so dark outside, he couldn't even make out Carina's silhouette at the top of the stairwell. He shone his torch over the underground chamber on his right. Two passages led off it, both ankle-deep in stagnant water.

Incredible of the boy to venture into this industrial swamp of his own free will.

Stern opted for the left-hand passage because the other was obstructed by an overturned fuse box.

'Where are you?' he called. The water closed around his ankles like an icy hand.

Simon still didn't answer, but at least he made a sign of life: he coughed. The sound came from not far away but beyond the range of Stern's torch.

I'm going to catch my death, he thought. He could feel his trouser legs absorbing the moisture like blotting paper. Just as he made out a wooden partition some ten metres away, his mobile rang.

'Where's he got to?' Carina called. She sounded almost hysterical.

'Not sure. He's in the next passage, I think.'

'What's he been saying?'

'Nothing. He's coughing.'

'Oh my God, get him out of there!' Her voice broke with agitation.

'What do you think I'm trying to do?'

'You don't understand. The tumour. That's what happens!'

'What do you mean? What happens?'

He heard Simon cough again. Closer at hand this time.

'Bronchial spasms are a prelude to unconsciousness. He could pass out at any minute!' Carina was shouting so loudly, her voice reached him direct as well as over the phone.

And he'll fall face down in the water and suffocate. Like . . .

Stern set off at a run. In his mounting panic he failed to see the beam sagging down from the ceiling, so black and charred as to be almost invisible. He hit his head on it, but the shock was even worse than the pain. Thinking he'd been attacked, he threw up his arms defensively. By the time he realized his mistake it was too late. The torch flickered underwater for another two seconds, then died where he'd dropped it.

'Damnation!' He felt for the wall with his right hand and groped his way along step by step, trying not to lose his bearings in the darkness. That was the least of his worries, however, because he hadn't changed direction. What concerned him far more was that Simon had not made another sound, not even a cough.

'Hey, are you still there?' he shouted. His ears clicked suddenly, and he had to ease the pressure on his eardrums by swallowing several times, like an airline passenger coming in to land. Then he heard another faint cough. Ahead of him. Beyond the wooden partition and around the corner. He had to get there – had to get to Simon in the side passage. Although slowed by the water, he was still going fast enough to trigger a disastrous chain reaction.

'Simon? Can you hear . . . Heeelp!'

The last word was uttered as he fell. His foot had caught in an old telephone cable that had formed a sort of poacher's snare in the stinking, stagnant water. He clutched at the wall beside him in an attempt to stop himself falling, only to break two fingernails on the damp mortar as he pitched forwards.

He must have reached the end of the underground passage, he realized, because he didn't fall headlong into water. Instead, his outstretched hands were brought up short by an expanse of plywood or a door. With a groan – like, but far louder than the one caused by his foot on the first stair – it gave way. Panic-stricken, he saw himself plummeting down an old mine shaft or bottomless pit. Then his fall was brutally checked by solid, hard-packed mud. The only favourable part of this new situation was that the water hadn't reached this corner of the cellar. On the other hand, unidentifiable objects dislodged from the ceiling and walls were falling on him.

Oh my God . . . Stern hardly dared touch the sizeable,

roundish object that had just landed in his lap. His initial, nightmarish certainty was that, if he did run his hands over it, they would touch blue lips and a bloated face: the face of his dead son Felix.

But then, gradually, the darkness began to lift. He blinked, and it took him a moment or two to realize where the light was coming from. Not until she was standing right beside him did he see that it was Carina, whose mobile phone's greenish display was dimly illuminating the underground chamber into which he'd blundered.

He saw the scream before he heard it. Carina opened her mouth, but there was an instant's silence before her piercing cry reverberated around the cellar's concrete walls.

Stern shut his eyes. Then, summoning up all his courage, he looked down at himself.

And almost vomited.

The head in his lap was attached, like the knob on the end of a curtain rod, to a partially skeletonized body. With a mixture of disbelief, disgust and utter horror, Stern registered the gaping cleft the axe had made in the victim's skull.

4

Tears welled up in Inspector Martin Engler's eyes faster than he could blink them away. He groaned with his mouth shut, tilted his head back, and groped blindly around the interview room's table until he found what he was looking for. At the last moment he tore open the pack, fished out a paper handkerchief and clamped it to his nose.

Aachoo!

'Sorry.' The homicide detective blew his nose, and Stern wondered whether he hadn't uttered an almost imperceptible 'Arsehole!' as he sneezed.

That would have figured. Having secured acquittals for several of Engler's personal collars, Stern wasn't exactly one of the inspector's closest friends.

'Ahem.'

The policeman seated beside Engler had cleared his throat. Stern glanced at him. An overweight individual with an enormous Adam's apple jutting from beneath his double chin, he had introduced himself, on entering the windowless interview room, as Thomas Brandmann. No rank, no clue to his function. He hadn't uttered another word, just emitted a guttural grunt every five minutes. Stern didn't know what to make of him. Unlike Engler, who after over twenty years' service was almost part of the murder squad's furniture, this man mountain had never crossed his path before. His manner could have signified that he was heading the investigation. Or the exact opposite.

Engler held up a packet of aspirins. 'Like one too? You look as if you could use one.'

'No thanks.' Stern instinctively fingered the painful, throbbing lump on his forehead. His brains were still scrambled after that fall in the cellar, and he resented the fact that, bloodshot eyes and runny nose apart, the inspector made a livelier impression than he did. Sessions on a sunbed and jogging in the woods were more beneficial than long nights at the computer in an office.

'Right, then I'll summarize.'

Engler picked up his notebook. Stern couldn't hide a grin when Brandmann, who still hadn't uttered a word, cleared his throat again.

'You discovered the body around five-thirty this afternoon. A boy, Simon Sachs, led you to the spot, accompanied by Carina Freitag, a hospital nurse. The said boy is ten years old and suffering from a cerebral tumour. He is currently' – Engler turned over a page – 'undergoing treatment in the neurological ward of the Seehaus Clinic. He claims to have murdered the man himself in a previous life.'

'Yes,' said Stern, 'fifteen years ago. I haven't been counting, but I reckon I must have told you that a dozen times already.'

'Possibly, but—'

Engler broke off in mid-sentence. To Stern's surprise he tilted his head back again and compressed his nostrils between his thumb and forefinger.

'Take no notice,' he said in a Donald Duck voice. 'Goddamned nosebleed. Always happens when I get a cold.'

'You shouldn't take aspirins, then.'

'Thins the blood, I know. But where were we?' Engler

was still addressing the drab grey ceiling. 'Ah yes . . . You may well have spouted this crazy yarn a dozen times, and each time I've wondered whether I ought to submit you to a drugs test.'

'Feel free. If you want to violate a few more of my rights, be my guest.' Stern held out an imaginary tray on his upturned palms. 'I don't get much fun out of life these days, but taking you and your outfit to court would certainly make an amusing change.'

'Please don't upset yourself, Herr Stern.'

Stern gave a start. *Amazing*, he thought. *Engler's hulking great companion can speak after all.*

'You aren't under suspicion,' Brandmann went on.

Stern seemed to hear an unspoken 'yet'.

'Just to dispel any doubt,' he said, resisting the temptation to clear his own throat, 'I may be a lawyer but I'm not insane. I don't believe in reincarnation, the transmigration of souls, and all that hogwash, nor do I waste my spare time digging up skeletons. Speak to the boy, not me.'

Brandmann nodded. 'We will as soon as he comes to.'

Simon had been found unconscious. As luck would have it, he hadn't blacked out as suddenly as he had two years before, when the tumour in his frontal lobe first made itself felt. Then he had collapsed in the middle of the classroom after hitting his head on the teacher's desk on his way to the blackboard. This time he'd managed to slide down the wall and wind up sitting with his back to it in the flooded side passage. He had fallen into a deep sleep but seemed all right in other respects.

Carina had driven him back to the clinic in the ambulance as quickly as possible, with the result that Stern was alone at the scene of the crime when Engler turned up with his people and the forensics team.

'Better still,' Stern advised, 'get hold of the psychologist.

Who knows what that man Tiefensee planted in the boy's mind under hypnosis.'

'Hey, good idea! The psychologist! Thanks, I'd never have thought of that in a thousand years.'

Engler grinned sarcastically. His nosebleed had stopped and he was once more looking Stern full in the face.

'So you say the murdered man had been lying there for fifteen years?'

Stern groaned. 'No, *I* don't say so, the boy does. He may even be right.'

'Why?'

'Well, I'm no pathologist, but the cellar was damp and the body was in a dark wooden cubby hole like a coffin, where it wasn't exposed to a direct supply of oxygen. For all that, some parts of the body were almost completely decomposed. They included the head, which I had the dubious pleasure of holding in my hands. And that means—'

'That the victim wasn't dumped there yesterday. Correct.'

Stern swung round in surprise. The man leaning against the door frame in a studiously casual pose had materialized without a sound. With his frosted black hair and tinted, gold-rimmed glasses, Christian Hertzlich looked more like an ageing tennis coach than a chief superintendent of police. Stern wondered how long Engler's immediate superior had been listening to them sparring.

'Thanks to modern forensic medicine, we shall very soon learn the approximate date of death,' said Hertzlich. 'But no matter whether the man died five, fifteen or even fifty years ago' – he took a step forwards – 'one thing's for sure: the boy can't have killed him.'

'My view precisely. Is that all?' Stern stood up, shot his cuff and ostentatiously glanced at his watch. It was nearly half past ten.

'Of course you're free to go. In any case, I have a far

more urgent matter to discuss with these gentlemen.'

Hertzlich had been holding a folder clamped beneath his arm the whole time. He presented it to his subordinates like a trophy.

'There's been a truly surprising new development.'

5

Martin Engler waited until the lawyer had closed the door behind him. Then, unable to control his annoyance any longer, he got to his feet so abruptly his chair fell over backwards.

'What was all that crap?'

Brandmann cleared his throat. He actually seemed about to say something, but Hertzlich got in first. He deposited the folder face down on the table.

'What do you mean? It went perfectly.'

'The hell it did, sir,' Engler retorted. 'That's no way to conduct an interview. I'm not doing it again, not ever.'

'Why so hot under the collar?'

'Because I made myself look ridiculous. Nobody falls for the good-cop bad-cop routine any more, least of all a lawyer of Robert Stern's calibre.'

Hertzlich looked down at his highly polished shoes. He shook his head in surprise.

'I thought you'd grasped our methodology, Engler.'

Methodology . . . What garbage! Engler was seething with rage.

Since Inspector Brandmann had joined them, barely a week had gone by without him having to take part in at least one seminar on psychological interviewing techniques.

The youthful giant had been loaned to them three weeks earlier by the Federal Police Bureau, under the auspices of a training programme for which he worked as a psychological profiler. He was officially assigned to Engler's team as an adviser, but it very much looked as if his status had just been upgraded to that of special investigator. In any event, Engler was even compelled to tolerate his presence during interrogations.

'I'm bound to say the chief superintendent is right.' Brandmann's amiable tone only made the prevailing tension worse. 'Everything went according to plan.' He cleared his throat. 'First, we frayed Stern's nerves by keeping him waiting. Then my silence prevented him from knowing which side I was on. That, incidentally, is the difference between our own technique and the obsolete tactic you've just described, Inspector Engler.'

Brandmann paused for effect. Engler wondered why he had to add such a stupid grin to his lecture.

'Just because I *didn't* play the so-called good cop, Stern's nervousness turned to bewilderment and he tried to get at you. When he failed he lost his temper.'

'OK, perhaps I would have got him to talk in the end if that's what we'd been aiming at. But all I can ask myself is, what's the point of this?'

'Angry men make mistakes,' said Hertzlich. 'Besides, we needed Stern to experience mood swings in order to evaluate his optical reflexes.'

Optical reflex analysis. Eye-tracking. Pupillometry. Newfangled crap, all of it. For the past week, the bleak interview room had been wired for experimental purposes. One of three concealed cameras was focused on the faces of those being questioned. In theory, guilty parties gave themselves away by increased blinking, pupillary contractions and changes in angle of vision. In practice, Engler accepted that these were significant but believed that an experienced interrogator had no need of any technological refinements to tell when someone was lying.

'We can only pray that Stern never discovers we were filming him secretly.' Engler pointed to the wall behind him. 'He's one of the ablest lawyers in the city.'

'And a potential murderer,' said Hertzlich.

'You don't believe that yourself.' Engler swallowed, trying briefly to remember if there was a late-night chemist on his route home. He badly needed some kind of spray to anaesthetize his throat. 'The man's got an IQ higher than Mount Everest. He wouldn't be stupid enough to lead us to the remains of a man he'd murdered himself.'

'It could be a clever ploy.'

The chief superintendent raised his heavy tinted glasses a few centimetres and massaged the marks they'd left on the bridge of his shiny nose. Engler couldn't recall ever having looked straight into his boss's eyes. It was rumoured in the building that he even went to bed in those monstrous shades.

'Or perhaps he's simply flipped,' Hertzlich mused aloud in Brandmann's direction. 'In any case, his story of the reincarnated boy doesn't sound very kosher to me.'

'He does make an emotionally unstable impression,' the psychological profiler agreed.

Engler rolled his eyes. 'I'll say it again: we're wasting our time on the wrong man.'

Hertzlich turned to him with an air of surprise. 'I thought you disliked him.'

'I do. Stern may be an arsehole, but he's no murderer.'

'What makes you say that?'

'Twenty-three years' experience. I've got a nose for these things.'

'And we can all see and hear how well it's functioning.'

Hertzlich was the only one who laughed at his little joke,

and Engler had to concede that Brandmann hadn't yet crawled all the way up the chief superintendent's fundamental orifice. He did not, unfortunately, get to explain why he considered Robert Stern incapable of slaughtering a man with an axe, because he was suddenly afflicted with another torrential nosebleed. His paper handkerchief turned crimson and he was once more compelled to tilt his head back.

'Oh not again . . .'

Hertzlich eyed him suspiciously. 'Earlier on I thought these nosebleeds were part of the show. Are you up to heading this investigation?'

'Yes, yes, it's only a slight cold. No problem.'

Engler tore two clean strips off his handkerchief, rolled them into balls and plugged his nostrils with them.

'I'm fine.'

'Excellent. Then round up your team and come to my office in ten minutes.'

Engler glanced at the clock and groaned inwardly. It was a quarter to eleven. Quite apart from his own state of health, Charlie urgently needed his walkies. The poor dog had been shut up in his cramped little flat for over ten hours.

'Don't look like that, Engler, it won't take long. Read the file, then you'll understand why I want you to keep after Stern and give him a hard time.'

Engler took the folder from the table.

'Why?' he called after Hertzlich, who was just leaving the interview room. 'What's in it?

'The name of an old acquaintance.'

Hertzlich turned.

'We know who the dead man is.'

6

Stern was greeted by a mournful voice on the answerphone in his hall when he came home shortly after 11 p.m. the following night. Carina had tried to contact him several times in the previous twenty-four hours but had left only one message. She had also been interviewed, and that morning the hospital's medical director had suspended her until further notice.

'Simon is doing well. He's asking for you. But I'm afraid you now have two clients in need of a lawyer,' she said in a weary attempt to be humorous. 'Can they really charge me with kidnapping because I took Simon out of the hospital?' She gave a nervous laugh before hanging up.

Stern pressed 7 twice to delete the message. He would call her back tomorrow, Saturday, if at all. He really wanted nothing more to do with the whole business. He had enough on his plate already.

Clamping the mail under his arm, he went into the living room without removing his overcoat. He surveyed the room after turning on the overhead light. It looked as if a well-organized gang of thieves had turned up with a van and driven off with all the decent furniture and anything of value. He stood there without moving for a moment longer, then turned off the light again. Its unforgiving glare reminded him of the bleak room in which Engler and Brandmann had questioned him last night. After all that had happened in the past week, the sight of his neglected home was more tolerable in semi-darkness.

Stern's footsteps on the cherrywood parquet re-echoed from the bare walls as he made his way over to the sofa past an overturned chair and a desiccated pot plant. No bookshelves or curtains, cupboards or carpets, just an unshaded silver-grey lamp standing askew beside the sofa. Even if it had been on, it wouldn't have illuminated the cavernous room properly because three of its four bulbs were missing. What usually functioned as Stern's light source was the decrepit old valve TV in front of the empty fireplace.

He sat down on the sofa, picked up the remote control and shut his eyes as the screen filled with snow and white noise.

Ten years, he thought. He ran his hand over the bare expanse of rough leather beside him, feeling for the burn hole the sparkler had made at that New Year's party. Sophie had been laughing so much she'd dropped it. Over ten years ago. She was two weeks late at the time.

Unlike him, Sophie had managed to escape from herself after Felix's death by taking refuge in a second marriage. It had produced two children to date – twins. The little girls were surely the only reason why Sophie hadn't drowned in her own depression.

Unlike me.

Stern severed the skein of memory by opening his eyes again. He removed the cork from the neck of the half-empty bottle of red wine that had been languishing on the floor for days. It tasted horrible, but it fulfilled its function. He never expected visitors, so there was nothing in the fridge. Even if one of his colleagues did turn up unannounced, he wouldn't let them in.

There was a good reason why he regularly employed a security firm to fit all his doors and windows with the latest burglar-proofing devices. He was well aware that the technicians thought him crazy because there was nothing worth stealing.

But he wasn't afraid of burglars, only of observers: of people who might see through his carefully constructed façade of expensive suits, shiny cars and smart offices with a view of the Brandenburg Gate. If they did, they would discern the empty husk that was Robert Stern's soul.

He took another swig from the bottle, clumsily spilling some wine on his white shirt. As he looked down wearily at the spreading stain, he was involuntarily reminded of the birthmark. Sophie had been the first to notice it on the baby's shoulder when holding him in her arms, freshly bathed and denuded of the warm blanket in which he'd been wrapped immediately after his birth. They'd been worried at first that it might be a malignant skin condition, but the doctors had reassured them. 'It looks like a map of Italy,' said Sophie, laughing as she rubbed Felix with baby oil, and they'd made a solemn resolution to spend their first family holiday in Venice. In the event, they got no further than the woodland cemetery where the urn was buried.

Stern put the wine bottle down and went through his mail. Two flyers, a parking ticket and a statement from his bank. The most personal item was a DVD from his Internet library. He no longer patronized the video library at weekends now you could get films sent by post. He opened the cardboard envelope without looking at the title. He'd probably seen the film already. He made a point of ordering pictures that didn't feature children and had a minimum of sex, so his selections were pretty limited.

Having inserted the DVD, he removed his jacket and tossed it carelessly on the floor before slumping back against the cushions. He was dog-tired, so he wouldn't last more than a few minutes before falling asleep on the sofa as he so often did at weekends. Luckily there would be no one around to find him still there in the morning. No family, no friends. Not even a housekeeper.

He picked up the bottle again, pressed 'Play' and waited for the ridiculous, unfastforwardable warning notice that threatened you with imprisonment if you illegally copied the ensuing film. Instead the image jumped several times like a badly exposed holiday video. Stern frowned and sat up. He had suddenly recognized the scene, and it jolted him out of his stupor. From one moment to the next, everything around him seemed to dissolve. He was unaware of the wine bottle escaping from his grasp and emptying the rest of its contents over his shirt. At a stroke every external stimulus had faded out. Only he and the television remained. Stern himself had changed, too. He was no longer looking at a television screen but through a dusty window into a room he'd never wanted to enter again in his life. When the camera zoomed in, he was afraid he'd lost his mind. A heartbeat later, he felt sure he had.

7

The greenish image of the neonatal ward freeze-framed just as the distorted voice uttered its opening words:

'Do you believe in a life after death, Herr Stern?'

Although it was coming from the loudspeakers, the metallic voice possessed such weird immediacy that Stern was fleetingly tempted to turn round and see if its owner was standing just behind him, clothed in flesh and blood.

After a moment's shocked immobility he slid off the sofa and crawled towards the television on his hands and knees. Incredulous, he touched the electrostatically charged screen and ran his fingers over the digital time-and-date line like a blind man reading Braille.

But even without that information he would have been in no doubt as to when and where the film had been made: ten years ago, in the hospital where Felix had come rosy-cheeked into the world and left it only forty-eight hours later, blue-lipped and cold.

Stern's fingers groped their way to the centre of the screen, where his newborn son was lying in a perspex cocoon surrounded by several other babies in cots. *And Felix was alive!* He was waving his puny little arms as if trying to touch the cloud mobile that Sophie and Robert Stern had made for him out of cotton-wool balls, long before his birth, and suspended above his cot.

'Do you believe in the transmigration of souls? In reincarnation?'

Stern shrank away from the television set as though the ghost of his son had just addressed him personally. The blurred image of the infant in the pale-blue sleepsuit had monopolized his senses to such an extent he'd almost forgotten about the voice.

'You have no idea what you've got yourself involved in, have you?'

He shook his head like a man in a trance, as if he could genuinely communicate with the anonymous speaker whose voice resembled that of a glottic cancer patient condemned to speak through a throat microphone.

'Unfortunately, I cannot reveal my identity for reasons that will soon become apparent to you. That's why I considered this the most sensible way of getting in touch. You've transformed your home into a fortress, Herr Stern. With one exception: your mailbox. I trust you won't resent my having disrupted your Friday night ritual by substituting this DVD. Believe me, though, what you are about to see will prove far more gripping than the wildlife documentary you actually ordered.'

A tear detached itself from Stern's eye as he continued to stare at Felix.

'However, I must now ask you to concentrate with particular intensity.'

As the camera zoomed in on the baby's face, Stern felt he'd been kicked in the stomach.

Who filmed this? And why?

An instant later he was beyond formulating any more questions in his mind. He wanted to turn away and dash to the bathroom – to bring up his meagre lunch and all his memories with it – but an invisible vice held him fast. So he was compelled to endure the sight of the grainy images that showed his son opening his eyes. Wide, staring and incredulous, they seemed to convey a presentiment that his tiny body would soon lose all its vital functions. Felix gasped for breath, started to tremble, looked as if he had choked on far too big a morsel, and suddenly turned blue.

At this point Stern couldn't stop himself any longer. He vomited on the parquet floor. A few moments later, when he turned back and stared at the screen with one trembling hand over his mouth, it was all over. His son was gazing at the camera with eyes blank and lips parted. The whole of the neonatal ward was once more in shot: four cots with four occupants, but one of them unbearably still.

'I'm very sorry. I realize that these last pictures of Felix must be very distressing for you.'

The grating voice was as sharp as a razor blade.

'But it was unavoidable, Herr Stern. I've something important to tell you, and I want you to take me seriously. I assume I can now rely on having gained your full attention?'

8

Robert Stern felt he would never regain the ability to think clearly. It was a while before he grasped that the mist before his eyes came from the tears streaming down his cheeks. The merciless voice had evidently allowed for this.

Did it really happen? Did I really just witness the last few seconds of my son's short life?

He felt like getting up, ripping the DVD from the player and hurling the television out of the window, but he was too traumatized to lift a finger. The only movement of which his body was still capable took place without his volition: his legs were trembling uncontrollably.

Who is doing this to me? And why?

The scene was changing. His fear intensified.

The neonatal ward had been replaced by the industrial estate where Carina had kept him waiting yesterday. These shots had been taken on a sunny day in spring or summer.

'Yesterday afternoon you discovered some human remains on the site of a former paint factory.'

The voice inserted another pause. Stern blinked as he recognized the tool shed.

'We waited a very long time for this to happen. Fifteen years, to be exact. After such a long interval we'd actually assumed the dead man would be accidentally discovered by some tramp or a dog. Instead of that, you turned up. For a purpose. With two companions. That's why you're now involved, Herr Stern. Whether you like it or not.'

The camera panned round 360 degrees. Apart from derelict buildings, it briefly showed an unmarked delivery van. Then it focused on the charred remains of the building into which Stern had followed Simon Sachs only hours before.

'I want you to tell me who murdered the man you found in that cellar yesterday.'

Stern shook his head in bewilderment.

What is all this? What does it have to do with Felix?

'Who killed the man? To me, the answer to that question is a matter of extreme urgency.'

Stern stared at the DVD player's bluish digital display as if the cause of his mental anguish resided in that silver box.

'I want you to take Simon's case. If you knew who I am, you would understand why I can't do so myself. That's why *you* must represent him. Find out how the boy knew about the body.'

The voice laughed softly.

'However, because I know that lawyers never work for nothing, I'll make you an offer. Whether or not you accept it, Herr Stern, will depend entirely on how you answer my original question: Do you believe in the possibility of reincarnation?'

The screen began to fill with snow like an old black-and-white set with an ill-adjusted indoor aerial. Then the picture quality abruptly improved. The derelict factory had disappeared. The superimposed time and date indicated that these new, colourful images were only a few weeks old. Stern's nausea returned. Discounting the year, the date was that of his dead son's birthday.

9

'Well, do you recognize him?'

The sun-tanned youngster with the shoulder-length, slightly curly hair was bare-chested and wearing a black coral necklace. Aware that he was being filmed, he sat there looking expectantly at the camera. All at once he got up rather awkwardly and walked off. Stern's heart stood still when the boy turned away. There was a dark violet birthmark on his left shoulder. It resembled a miniature boot.

It can't be! It's impossible!

Stern's cheeks burned as if someone had slapped him. The boy, whose face looked at once unfamiliar and agonizingly familiar, came back into shot with a knife in his hand. Someone off screen apparently called something to him. He gave a sheepish smile, drew a deep breath and pursed his lips. The camera panned down to reveal a birthday cake on a table. A Black Forest gateau. It took the boy two attempts to blow out the ten candles embedded in the whipped cream.

'Look closely, Herr Stern. Think of the last pictures of Felix you saw just now. Remember the body in the little coffin you carried into the crematorium yourself. And then answer a very simple question: Do you believe in a life after death?'

Stern raised his hand. For a brief moment he felt tempted to press his fingers against the screen. The blood pounded in his ears. He was overcome by a weird sensation: he was gazing into a mirror – a rejuvenating mirror.

Is it . . . ? It can't be. Felix is dead. He was cold when I took him from Sophie's arms. I buried his ashes myself, and . . .

'Looking at these pictures, you could be forgiven for wondering, couldn't you?'

. . . and I saw him die. Just now!

Stern gave a choking cough. He had been holding his breath in shocked suspense, but now, as the merciless succession of unbelievable images continued to unfold, his lungs cried out for oxygen.

But that can only be . . . must *be a coincidence!*

The ten-year-old boy was left-handed. So was he.

Stern began to tremble all over. He felt he was watching a replica of himself. He had looked just like that as a boy. Absolutely everything fitted. The hair, the rather wide-set eyes, the prominent chin, the dimple that appeared in his right cheek only when he smiled. If he dug out those old photo albums in the packing cases in the cellar downstairs, he felt sure he would find a faded snapshot of himself looking at the camera just like this boy. At the age of ten.

And he's got the birthmark too.

It was bigger now, of course, but its proportions exactly corresponded to those of the one Sophie had spotted the first time she held Felix naked in her arms.

'Here's the deal.'

The voice was once more claiming Stern's attention, and it sounded even more inhuman than before.

'I'll give you an answer for an answer. You tell me who split that man's skull with an axe fifteen years ago, and I'll tell you if there's a life after death.'

So saying, the DVD faded out the birthday boy and transported Stern ten years back in time to the neonatal ward. He was presented with a terrible, rhythmical alternation of two freeze-framed images. Felix in his cot. First alive, then dead.

Alive . . . Dead . . . Alive . . .

He strove to stand up and vent his anguish in a despairing cry, but every ounce of strength had deserted him.

Dead.

'An answer for an answer. You take care of Simon Sachs, we'll deal with the psychologist. You have five days, not an hour longer. Fail to meet that deadline and you'll never hear from me again, never learn the truth. Oh yes, one more thing.'

The voice sounded bored now, like a medicine commercial warning of possible risks and side effects.

'Don't go to the police. If you do, I'll kill the twins.'

The screen went black.

10

'Are you drunk?'

Sophie was standing barefoot in the passage outside the bedroom, where she'd fled with the phone so as not to wake her husband. Patrick was due to leave on a business trip to Japan in a few hours' time and he needed his sleep. Besides, it was just after half past twelve, and she would have found it hard to explain why her ex-husband was calling her in the middle of the night when he hadn't even done so on her birthday in recent years.

'Sorry to disturb you, I know it's late. Are the children all right?'

Even though he hadn't answered her question, she could hear the answer in his voice. He sounded terrible.

'Yes, of course they're all right. They're asleep. Fast asleep, like any normal person at this hour. What on earth do you want?'

'The thing is—' Stern broke off and started again. 'Look, I'm sorry, but there's something I must ask you.'

'Now? Can't it wait till tomorrow?'

'It's already waited too long.'

Sophie paused on the sisal runner that led to the living room.

'What are you talking about?' The hour, his tone of voice,

his vague allusions – everything about this phone call alarmed her. No wonder she was shivering, especially as all she wore in bed was a T-shirt and knickers.

'Back then, were you ever in any doubt . . .'

Sophie shut her eyes as Stern went on talking. Few words summoned up more negative emotions in her than *back then*, especially coming from the man who had taken Felix from her arms.

'I mean, there was absolutely no reason why—'

'What are you driving at?' She was getting really angry.

'You didn't smoke during your pregnancy, Felix wasn't too warmly clad – he was wearing a sleepsuit that prevented him from lying on his tummy, and—'

'I'd better hang up now.'

It defeated Sophie why he should wake her up in order to list the potential causes of cot death, or sudden infant death syndrome. Although some forty per cent of all cases of infant mortality were embraced by this mysterious collective term, its causes were largely unidentified. Which wasn't really surprising, given that every inexplicable death of an apparently healthy child was assigned to this dread category.

'Wait, please! Just answer one question.'

'Well, what is it?' Sophie caught sight of herself in the hall mirror and winced at the expression on her face. She detected a mixture of sorrow, despair and fatigue.

'I know you've hated me ever since it happened.'

'Are you running a temperature?' she asked. It wasn't just his slurred speech. He sounded as if he had a bad cold.

'No, I'm fine. All I need is an answer.'

'Damn you, Robert! Look, I just don't understand what you're getting at.' Having spat out the first words in a fury, she strove to moderate her voice for fear of waking Patrick and the twins.

'He wasn't breathing – in fact he'd stiffened a little by the time you finally opened the bathroom door.'

The phone went silent for a moment or two.

'The question is, why weren't you sure even so? Why, in spite of everything, did you believe that Felix was still alive?'

Sophie lowered the phone and let her arm hang limp at her side. Her tiredness had given way to the sort of torpor that normally overcame her only after taking sleeping pills. At the same time, she felt as if she'd just caught a burglar rifling through her underwear. *And that's just what's happened*, she thought as she made slowly for the children's bedroom. Robert's phone call had broken into her world and wrenched open a drawer in her psyche – one she had laboriously striven to nail shut with the help of her new husband, the wonderful twins and a qualified psychoanalyst.

She opened the door with bated breath. Frieda had kicked her bedclothes to the foot of the bed and was sleeping peacefully with her arm around a cuddly penguin. Natalie's little chest, too, was rising and falling at regular intervals. During the first critical year after the twins' birth, Sophie had set the alarm clock to go off every two hours and looked in on them. Now she did that only when waking them at night for a pee. The paralysing fear she used to feel had been replaced by a loving routine.

Or had been until just now. Until Robert called.

'*Why did you believe Felix was still alive?*'

The soft mattress yielded beneath her as she perched on the edge of Natalie's bed and brushed the dream-damp hair off her brow.

'There are times when I still believe it,' she whispered. Then she kissed her daughter gently on the forehead and started to weep.

The Quest

Just as we have thousands of dreams
in our present life, so our present life
is only one among thousands which we have entered
from another, more real life, and to which,
after death, we shall return.

Leo Tolstoy

Every person brings something new into the world;
something inexistent heretofore, something primal and
unique.

Martin Buber

Birthmarks and birth defects are proof of people's
recurrent lives on earth.

Ian Stevenson

1

Perhaps it was because he was overtired. Perhaps the collision occurred because, instead of looking where he was going, he was watching the DVD unfold once more in his mind's eye.

He wouldn't have dared to watch it again last night. Not all of it, at least. He had no desire for another sight of Felix in his death throes. That was why he had skipped to the shots of the birthday boy. He'd stared at the nameless youngster again and again. In slow motion, freeze-frame and fast-forward. After the tenth time his eyes had smarted so much, he fancied he could detect reddish signs of wear on the DVD.

This morning, after a sleepless night, he felt as helpless and emotionally drained as he had on the day of Felix's funeral. He had lost his grip on reality. His rational lawyer's brain was trained to always see problems from two sides. A client was either guilty or innocent. In this respect, the personal nightmare into which he'd stumbled yesterday was no different from the tragedies he had to deal with professionally. Here, too, only two possibilities existed: Felix was either dead or still alive. The former was the more likely. The boy with the birthmark might have been a chip off the same block as himself, but that was far from being proof.

Proof of what? Stern asked himself as he emerged from the hospital lift. As ever, when he pondered a difficult problem, his mind's eye envisioned a bare white wall on which he stuck Post-it notes recording his main hypotheses. Where important cases were concerned, his brain contained a kind of cell to which he withdrew whenever he wanted to sort out his thoughts. The biggest Post-it of all bore the words **FELIX ALIVE?** in bold capitals.

Later on, long after the burial in the woodland cemetery, he'd naturally wondered whether the boy had been exchanged. But Felix had been the only male child in the ward. The other three mothers had given birth to girls, which completely precluded the risk of a mix-up. Besides, before the post mortem Stern had satisfied himself that he was really mourning the right child. He still recalled how he felt when he lifted the inert little body lying on the autopsy table in order to run his fingers over the birthmark in farewell.

What, then? Rebirth? Reincarnation?

He tore up that mental Post-it before giving it serious consideration. He was a lawyer. He couldn't resolve problems by resorting to parapsychology, much as it pained him to accept the fact. **FELIX = DEAD**, he wrote on a third Post-it. He was just trying to entrench this in his mind when his thoughts performed another somersault.

If he's dead, why is someone casting doubt on his death? And what has it all to do with Simon Sachs? How in the world did the boy know about the body in the cellar?

Stern wondered what it said about his state of mind this Saturday morning that he had set off for the Seehaus Clinic determined to get to the bottom of the last question. He was so engrossed in his sombre thoughts that he failed to hear the male nurse who was pushing an elderly patient to the physiotherapy department in a wheelchair. The two men were humming the ABBA classic 'Money, Money, Money' in unison as Stern rounded the corner and blundered into them.

He crashed into the chrome-plated chariot sideways on, lost his balance, and made a desperate grab for the nurse's sleeve but missed. Having briefly supported himself by planting one hand on the patient's head, he gripped his wrist as he tumbled and eventually fell flat on the mint-green linoleum, but not before pulling out the cannula that connected the old man to his drip.

2

'Jesus! Are you OK, Herr Losensky?' The bearded nurse knelt down beside the wheelchair, looking concerned, but his patient seemed half amused and waved him away.

'It's nothing, nothing. I've got a guardian angel.' The old man reached under his open-necked shirt and pulled out a chain with a cross dangling from it. 'Better look after our friend there.'

Stern massaged his palms, which he'd bruised on the unyielding floor when trying to break his fall. He ignored the throbbing pains in his knees rather than present an even more pathetic picture.

'I'm terribly sorry,' he said apologetically when he had regained his feet. 'Is everything OK?'

'That depends,' the nurse growled. He carefully slid the old man's sleeve up his arm to the elbow. 'That cannula will have to be replaced in due course,' he muttered, looking at the back of the patient's age-freckled hand, and told him to hold a ball of cotton wool over the puncture mark. Then he examined his bony arm for bruises or blood blisters. Although his hands would have graced a prizefighter, his movements were gentle – almost caressing.

'Why in such a hurry? Cops after you, or something?'

Stern was relieved that the nurse hadn't discovered any cause for concern.

'I'm really sorry, Herr . . .' He couldn't decipher the scratched plastic ID card on the nurse's scrubs.

'Franz Marc. Like the painter, but everyone calls me Picasso because I prefer his pictures.'

'I see. I do apologize, I was a million miles away.'

'We'd never have known, would we, Herr Losensky?'

Immediately below Picasso's earlobes, two luxuriant side-burns ran down his cheeks like strips of Velcro and culminated in a chestnut-brown beard. When he smiled, baring two rows of massive teeth, he looked like a carved wooden nutcracker.

'I'll naturally pay for any damage I've caused.'

Stern produced his wallet from the breast pocket of his suit.

'No, no,' Picasso protested, 'we don't do that here.'

'You misunderstand me. I was going to give you my card.'

'You can put it back. Can't he?' The old man in the wheelchair nodded, cocking one of his bushy eyebrows with a look of amusement. Unlike the hair on his head, which was sparse, they presided over his sunken eyes like two big tufts of steel wool.

'I'm afraid I don't understand.'

'You just gave us both a nasty shock, and Herr Losensky can't take too much excitement after his second heart attack. Can you, Frederik?'

The old man shook his head.

'So a few euro notes won't be enough to get you off the hook just like that.'

'What will, then?' Stern wondered if he was up against two lunatics. He grinned nervously.

'We want you to bow down in shame.'

Stern was about to tap his forehead and walk off when

he saw the joke. Smiling, he bent down and retrieved the black baseball cap he must have knocked off the old man's head, then gave it back to him.

'Perfect. Now we're quits,' Picasso said with a laugh. His elderly protégé chuckled like a schoolboy.

'Are you a fan?' Stern asked as the old man carefully adjusted the cap with both hands. It bore the legend ABBA in gold letters.

'Of course. Their music is divine.' Losensky lifted the peak of his cap once more and tucked a strand of snow-white hair beneath it. 'What's your favourite ABBA number?'

Stern was rather at a loss. 'I don't really know,' he replied. He wanted to visit Simon Sachs and talk about yesterday's events with him. He wasn't in the mood for small talk about a 1970s Swedish pop group.

'That makes two of us,' Losensky said with a grin. 'They're all good.'

The wheelchair's brand-new tyres whirred across the shiny floor as Picasso set it in motion again.

'Who did you want to see?' he called over his shoulder.

'I'm looking for Room 217.'

'Simon?'

Stern caught them up again. 'Yes, do you know him?'

'Simon Sachs, our orphan?' said Picasso. He took another few steps, then paused outside a gunmetal-grey door marked 'Physiotherapy'. 'Of course I know him.'

'Who doesn't?' the old man muttered as he was wheeled into a big, light room equipped with wall bars, foam mattresses and sundry keep-fit machines. He sounded almost hurt that the conversation had ceased to revolve around himself.

'Simon is our little ray of sunshine,' Picasso said enthusiastically. He brought the wheelchair to a halt beside a massage table. 'It's a shame about him. First he has to be taken into care because his mother nearly starves him to death, and now they've found a tumour in his skull. A benign one, so the doctors say, because it isn't forming any metastases. Bah!'

For a moment Stern thought the nurse was going to spit on the floor at his feet.

'I don't know what's so benign about the thing if it goes on growing and ends by occluding his brain.'

The door to an adjoining office opened and an Asian girl in judo gear and tiny orthopedic shoes came in. Losensky obviously fancied her because he started whistling 'Money, Money, Money' again, but this time it sounded more reminiscent of a labourer's wolf-whistling at a pneumatic blonde.

Back outside in the passage, which was rather busier now, Picasso pointed to the second door on the left beside the staff room.

'That's it, by the way,' he told Stern.

'What?'

'Room 217. Simon's got it to himself, but you can't just waltz in there.'

'Why not?' Stern feared the worst. Was the boy so ill you couldn't enter his room without sterile clothing?

'You haven't brought him a present.'

'Huh?'

'Visitors always bring flowers or chocolates. Or at a pinch, when the patient's a boy of ten, a pop magazine or something of the kind. You can't turn up empty-handed, not when he could be dead a week from now . . .'

The nurse left his sentence unfinished. Catching sight of something out of the corner of his eye, Stern swung round and located the source of the alarm signal, a flashing red light above a door. Then he hurried after Picasso, who was already on his way to the emergency, and caught him up just outside Room 217.

3

He had woken up the first time just before four and rung for the nurse. Carina hadn't come, which troubled him far more than his unremitting nausea. In the mornings this hovered somewhere between his throat and his stomach and could usually be brought under control with forty drops of MCP solution. Only when he woke up too late and the pains in his head had already welded their iron bands around his temples did they sometimes take several days to return to 4 on the scale.

That was how Carina always gauged his general condition. The first thing she asked him for every morning was a number, 1 meaning pain-free and 10 unendurable.

Simon couldn't remember when he'd last been better than 3. Still, it might happen today if the sad-looking man remained at his bedside a little longer. It was good to see his face again.

'I'm sorry if I gave you a shock. I only meant to turn the television on.'

'That's OK.' Agitation had given way to relief when it transpired that Simon had pressed the alarm bell by mistake. Having satisfied himself that the boy was all right, Picasso had left him alone with the nervous Stern.

'Carina likes you,' said Simon, 'and I like Carina, so I

guess I like you too.' He drew up his knees, forming an inverted V under the bedclothes. 'Is it her day off?'

'Er, no. That's to say, I don't know.' Somewhat awkwardly, Stern pulled a chair up to the only bed in the room and sat down. It struck Simon that he was wearing almost the same clothes as he had when they met at the factory two days ago. His wardrobe evidently contained several copies of the same dark suit.

'Aren't you feeling well?' he asked.

'Why?'

'Carina would say you look like something the cat brought in.'

'I slept badly.'

'But that's no reason to look so grim.'

'It is sometimes.'

'Oh, I know what's bothering you.' Simon reached into the compartment beneath his bedside table and brought out a wig. 'You never spotted it, did you? It's all my own hair. They cut it off before Professor Müller started on me with his ink eradicator.'

'His what?'

The boy deftly clapped his wig over the fluffy down on his head.

'They treat me like a little kid in here sometimes. Of course I know what chemotherapy is, but the medical director explained it to me like I was a baby. He said there was a big, dark patch inside my head, and the tablets I took would dissolve it. Like ink eradicator, in other words.'

He saw Stern run his eyes over the side table next to his bed.

'I've stopped taking interferon. The doctor said I could manage without it now, but Carina told me the truth.'

'Which is?'

'The side effects are too dangerous.' Simon grinned faintly

and raised his wig for a moment. 'They can't eradicate the thing without killing me. A month ago I got pneumonia and had to spend some time in intensive care. There was no more chemo or radiotherapy after that.'

'I'm sorry.'

'I'm not. At least I don't get nosebleeds any more, and I only feel sick in the mornings.' Simon sat up and wedged a bolster behind his back. 'But now it's your turn,' he said, doing his best to sound like one of the grown-ups in the crime series he watched on television. 'Are you going to take my case?'

Stern laughed, looking likeable for the first time.

'I don't know yet.'

'The thing is, I'm afraid I did something bad, and I don't want to . . .'

. . . die not knowing whether I'm really guilty, he'd been going to say, but grown-ups always reacted so strangely when he mentioned death. They looked sad and patted his cheek or quickly changed the subject. Simon left it at that because he felt the lawyer had understood in any case.

'I've come to ask you a few questions,' Stern said.

'Carry on.'

'Well, first I'd like to know exactly what you did on your birthday.'

'My session with Dr Tiefensee, you mean?'

'Precisely.' Stern opened a leather-bound notebook and proceeded to write in it with a little ballpoint. 'I'd like to know all about it. What happened to you there and anything you know about the body.'

'What body?' Simon stopped grinning when he saw the look of dismay on Stern's face.

'Well, the man whose remains we found. The one you—'

'Oh, you mean the man I killed with an axe,' said Simon. He was relieved to have cleared up any misunderstanding.

His lawyer still seemed rather perplexed, however, so he tried to explain with his eyes shut. He found that to be the best way of concentrating on the voices in his head and the terrible scenes that became more and more vivid the more often he lapsed into unconsciousness.

The man suffocating in the garage with a plastic bag over his head.

The child screaming on the hotplate.

The blood on the walls of the camper van.

He could bear to think of those scenes only because they were so remote. Decades away.

In another life.

'But that was only *one* dead body,' he said quietly, opening his eyes again. 'I've killed lots of people.'

4

'Hang on, not so fast. Take it slowly, one thing at a time.'

Stern went to the window and ran his fingers over a drawing stuck to the pane. Using crayons, Simon had drawn a remarkably realistic church with a lush green field in front of it. For some reason he had signed his drawing 'Pluto'.

Stern turned to face the boy.

'These unpleasant, er, memories . . .' he searched for a better word but failed to find one. 'Have you always had them?'

'No, only since my birthday.' The boy took a carton of apple juice from the bedside table and stuck a straw in it. 'I'd never had a regression before.'

'So tell me. How did it go, exactly?'

'I thought it was fun. The only trouble was, I had to take off my new trainers.'

Stern smiled at Simon in the hope of steering his flow of words into channels of greater interest.

'The doctor works in a great building. He said it was near the television tower, but I never saw it while we were there.'

'Did he give you anything to eat or drink during your visit?'

Any medication? Psychiatric drugs?

'Yes, some warm milk and honey. That was great too. Then I had to lie down on a blue mattress on the floor. Carina was there – she wrapped me up in two blankets. I was really warm and cosy. Only my head was sticking out.'

'What did the, er, doctor do then?' Stern hesitated before using the professional title because he felt sure Tiefensee's qualifications must have been forged or purchased.

'Nothing, really. I didn't see him after that.'

'But he was still in the room?'

'Yes, of course. He just talked and talked. He had a nice, soft voice like the doctor in the radio series I listen to.'

'And what did Herr Tiefensee tell you?'

'He said, "I don't normally do this with children of your age."'

What a relief, Stern thought sarcastically. *So the conman only cons adults as a rule*.

'But he made an exception because of my illness and Carina.'

Carina. Stern wrote her name in his notebook and filled in the 'a's with his ballpoint. He resolved to question her about her relationship with this charlatan immediately afterwards. Tiefensee couldn't have been a random choice on her part.

'He asked me a lot of questions. What were the nicest times I've ever had? Where did I like being best? On holiday, with friends, or just mucking around? Then he told me to shut my eyes and imagine myself in the most wonderful place in the world.'

Putting the subject into a somnambulistic state. Stern gave an involuntary nod as he recalled the keyword he'd encountered several times on the Internet last night. After making his ill-considered call to Sophie he'd sat down at the computer. One single search command had brought up innumerable websites belonging to parapsychological crackpots and obscure freaks, but also some respectable sources that addressed the subject of regression seriously. Most of them pointed out the inherent dangers. While not disputing the possibility of reincarnation as such, several warned of potential damage to the psyche, for example if a regression subject relived a severe trauma from his or her past while under hypnosis.

'I imagined a lovely beach,' said Simon. 'I was having a party with some friends, and we were all eating ice-creams.'

'What happened then?'

'I got very tired. At some stage the doctor asked if I could see a big electrical switch.'

Simon's eyelids were fluttering, and Stern was afraid he might pass out again, purely as a result of recounting his memories. But the boy hadn't coughed yet, and he remembered from what Carina had said that, ever since his pneumonia, coughing had always preceded an epileptic fit or a spell of unconsciousness.

'So I looked for a switch in my head. The kind you turn lights on and off with.'

'Did you succeed?'

'Yes, it took a while, but then I saw one. It was kind of spooky, because I had my eyes shut.'

Stern knew what was coming next. To manipulate patients, the therapist had to deactivate their consciousness. Switching off the mind with the aid of an imaginary light switch was a favourite method. After that, parapsychologists could talk a patient into believing things at their leisure. All that puzzled Stern was what motive Tiefensee could have had. Why Simon? Why a terminally ill boy with an inoperable tumour? And why hadn't Carina taken all this in? She might be a little scatty and believe in supernatural phenomena, but she would never have permitted a child to be abused in this way, least of all one that was a patient in her care.

'At first I couldn't do it – I couldn't keep the switch down,' Simon went on quietly. 'It kept clicking up again. It was funny, but Dr Tiefensee gave me some sticky tape.'

'Really?'

'No, not really. Only in my imagination. He told me to imagine taping the switch down, and it really worked. It stayed down and I got into a lift.'

Stern said nothing for fear of distracting the boy, because now came the regression proper: the descent into his subconscious.

5

'Inside the lift was a brass plate with a lot of buttons on it. It was up to me which one I chose, so I pressed the one marked 11. There was a jerk and the lift set off. It went down a very long way. When the doors finally opened I got out and saw . . .'

. . . *the world before I was born*, Stern amplified in his head. It surprised him when Simon completed the sentence quite differently.

'. . . nothing. I couldn't see a thing. Just total darkness.'

The dreamy look in Simon's eyes had disappeared. He had a drink of his apple juice. As he replaced the carton on the tray on his bedside table, his T-shirt rode up. Stern froze inwardly. For an instant he had glimpsed an elongated birthmark just above the boy's hip bone.

The scars of the reincarnated! he thought involuntarily. This skin blemish bore no resemblance to those of Felix or the boy on the DVD, but it reminded him inescapably of the article on Ian Stevenson he had read that very morning. The late professor and senior psychiatrist at the University of Virginia was one of the few reincarnation researchers whose case studies were seriously discussed by reputable scientists. Stevenson had believed that moles and birthmarks were like spiritual maps indicating where people had been injured in previous lives. The Canadian parapsychologist had amassed hundreds of medical records and autopsy reports and found them to contain striking similarities to the skin defects of allegedly reincarnated children.

Stern strove to concentrate on what Simon was saying. 'I don't understand,' he said. 'How did you know about the murdered man's body if you didn't see it while you were with Dr Tiefensee?'

'Well, I did see something, but not until I woke up. Carina said I'd been asleep for two hours. I remember how sad I felt. It was my birthday, and all at once it was nearly over. It was already dark outside.'

'And these unpleasant memories came back to you when you woke up?'

'Not right away. Only when I was sitting in the car and Carina asked me how it had gone. That was when I told her. About the pictures, I mean.'

'What pictures?'

'The ones in my head. I only see them very dimly. In the dark. It's like when I'm dreaming just before I wake up. Know what I mean?'

'Yes, maybe.' Stern did know what the boy meant, but his own daydreams were nowhere near as morbid. Except when he thought of Felix.

Simon turned his head and stared thoughtfully out of the window. Stern thought at first that he had lost interest in their conversation and expected him to fish a computer game out of the bedside cabinet at any minute. But then he saw that the boy's lips were moving silently. He was obviously searching for the right words to describe his impressions.

'Once, back in the children's home,' he began quietly, 'the light bulb in the cellar had to be changed. We were all scared of going down there, so we drew matches and I lost.

It was really spooky. The bare bulb was hanging from the ceiling on a length of flex. It looked like a tennis ball, all yellow and furry with dust and cobwebs. And it made clicking noises like Jonas – that's a friend of mine. He can crack his knuckles really loudly. It sounded just like that. The light went on and off, and each time it sounded the way Jonas does when he cracks his knuckles. Or used to until some grown-up told him he should stop because he'd wind up with gout and rheumatism.'

Stern asked no questions and simply let the boy run on. Looking down at his own hands, he saw that he'd unconsciously clasped them together like a man at prayer.

'The bulb was flickering and clicking away when I got down to the cellar. On, off, on. Sometimes it was light for a little, then dark. But even when the light came on I couldn't see much, the bulb was just too dirty. I knew, of course, that sheets and towels were hung up to dry on one side of the cellar, and on the other side were the baskets with our jeans and T-shirts in them. But the light was flickering even worse than I was trembling, and I was scared someone was hiding behind the sheets, ready to grab me. I was much younger then, and I nearly did it in my pants.'

Stern raised his eyebrows and nodded at the same time. For one thing because he could empathize with Simon's fear; for another because he was beginning to see what the boy was getting at.

'And is it like that now? With the pictures you see?'

'Yes. When I remember myself in my previous life, it's like that day at the children's home. I'm back in the cellar and the dirty bulb is flickering.'

Click. Click.

'That's why I only see outlines, shadows. Everything's blurred . . . But the light seems to be getting brighter every night.'

'You mean you can remember things better when you wake up?'

'Yes. Like yesterday I began to wonder if I'd really killed the man at all. With the axe, I mean. But this morning it was quite clear again. Just like that number.'

Click.

'What number?'

'The 6. It's only painted on it.'

'Painted on what?'

Click. Click.

'A door. A metal door. It's near some water.'

Stern suddenly longed for something to drink. There was an unpleasant taste in his mouth and he wanted to rinse it away. That and the terrible presentiment Simon's words were giving rise to.

'What happened there?' he asked without meaning to.

What happened behind the door numbered 6?

A man started whistling and footsteps went by in the passage outside, but Stern's brain filtered out these acoustic distractions until only Simon's voice remained. The voice that was describing the death throes of a man he claimed to have murdered twelve years ago.

Two years before he was born.

Stern fervently hoped that someone would interrupt them and spare him from having to listen to every last detail. For instance, the serrated knife with which the victim had managed to wound his assailant before he died. Roughly in the same part of his body as Simon's milk-chocolate birthmark.

He looked desperately at the door, but it remained shut. No doctor or nurse interrupted Simon's terrible story, which he recounted in an almost dispassionate tone. His big eyes were closed again.

'Do you remember the address?' Stern asked breathlessly

when the boy had finished at last. He could scarcely hear himself speak, the blood was pounding so loudly in his ears.

'I'm not sure. Yes, perhaps.'

Simon said only one more word, but it was enough to bring Stern's whole body out in goose pimples. He knew the place. He had sometimes gone walking there. With Sophie. During her pregnancy.

6

'No, I don't have a search warrant. I'm not a policeman either.'

Stern wondered whether the yob with the unwashed hair and the ring in his nose had ever been to school. An expanse of pink gum showed beneath his short upper lip. That, combined with a very pronounced overbite, endowed him with the semblance of a permanent grin.

'Then you can't,' Sly mumbled, propping his legs on the desk. He had proudly introduced himself by that ludicrous pseudonym a few minutes ago, when Stern entered the little office on the ground floor of the haulage company's headquarters.

'What do you want with Number 6 anyway? I don't think we rent out the single-figure garages any more.'

Simon had preserved only a fragmentary recollection of the address back at the hospital, but his reference to Spree Garages had been quite enough. Stern knew the dilapidated warehouses beside the canal in the Alt-Moabit district. The headquarters of the long-established Berlin firm was a sandstone-coloured brick building overlooking the water. Just behind it were the garages used by some customers as storage space for furniture, electrical appliances and other junk. Trade wasn't as good now that immigrant labourers were prepared to dispose of old washing machines for two euros fifty an hour, so the owners hadn't bothered to renovate the place.

The grimy office stank of cigarette smoke and public lavatories, probably thanks to the air freshener Sly had suspended from the overhead light to save himself the trouble of airing the place regularly. No wonder the closed blinds were coated with mildew from windowsill to ceiling. Stern couldn't understand why anyone would have wanted to shut out the little light there was on such a dark and rainy autumn day.

He trotted out the story he'd come up with on the drive from the hospital. 'I'm an executor in search of the heirs to what could be a substantial estate. We think Garage Number 6 may contain clues of potential use to us.'

While speaking he had opened his wallet and extracted two fifty-euro notes. Sly took his legs off the desk. His imbecilic grin widened.

'I wouldn't risk my job for a hundred smackers,' he said with feigned self-righteousness.

'You bet you would.'

Stern turned to look at the man who had just come panting into the office. He put his money away.

'Christ, this place stinks like a Turkish brothel.'

The sweating, bald-headed newcomer looked like an ambulant Buddha. A thirty-two-inch widescreen TV would have fitted on Andreas Borchert's back without overlapping his shoulders.

'Who the fuck are you?' Sly demanded, jumping to his feet. The grin had been wiped off his face like chalk off a blackboard.

'Please don't disturb yourself. You're welcome to remain seated.'

Borchert unceremoniously thrust the man back on his

chair and went over to a key board hanging on the wall beside a poster-sized street map of Berlin.

'Which one is it, Robert?'

'Number 6.' Stern wondered if it had been wise to call his former client and enlist his help. He was familiar with Andi Borchert's arbitrary problem-solving methods. Two years ago Borchert had been a producer of cheap 'adult entertainment', dreadful hard-core porn that had made him a small fortune until the day when one of his 'actresses' was brutally raped on set. Everything pointed to Borchert's guilt until Stern managed to convince the court otherwise. After his acquittal, Borchert had got off with a suspended sentence for seeking out the real culprit and beating him into a speechless pulp. Secured once again by Stern's skilful courtroom tactics, this much-reduced penalty had unintentionally gained him Andi Borchert's undying friendship.

'Try calling the cops,' Borchert growled in Sly's direction as he took the relevant key from the board, 'and you and I will go for a little ride together, understand?'

Stern couldn't suppress a smile when his ex-client simply strode out of the office without waiting for a submissive nod from the clerk. He caught him up and trudged across the stretch of open ground that led to the garages.

'OK, once more for the benefit of someone with no school-leaver's certificate.'

Borchert didn't seem to mind treading in a puddle every other step in his white boxing boots. His propensity to sweat at the least physical exertion had earned him several nicknames including 'Mr Sumo'. Borchert knew them all, not that anyone had ever used them in his presence.

'All I gathered on the phone was, you need help because a boy of ten has murdered a man.'

'More than one, actually.' Stern told him the incredible story as they made their way across the haulage company's yard, speaking faster and faster the more sceptical his ex-client's expression became. They paused for a moment beside a rusty skip. A black cat was just climbing into it.

'What? Fifteen years ago in a previous life? You're pulling my leg!'

'You think I'd have asked for your help if I had any choice?' Stern brushed his damp hair back and gestured to Borchert to accompany him to the garages.

'Martin Engler has been on the case since I found that body two days ago. You know, the inspector who was after your blood.'

'I remember the bastard.'

'And he remembers how I wrecked his nice, open-and-shut case.'

When investigating Andi Borchert, Engler had omitted to look at his medical history. The big man had suffered since adolescence from partial erectile dysfunction. To put it in the vernacular, he was almost impotent and could only get it up, if at all, on home territory and after lengthy foreplay. Ergo, he couldn't have raped the girl.

Borchert was eternally grateful to Stern, not only for getting him off but for ensuring that it was a closed trial. A porn film producer who couldn't get it up would have been a public laughing stock. Although none of the salacious details had got out, thanks to Stern, Borchert had turned his back on film-making and now ran several successful nightclubs in Berlin and the surrounding area.

'Engler would love to pin something on me,' said Stern.

Borchert kicked aside an empty beer can. 'Sure I'll help you, but I still don't understand. Why get involved?'

Stern avoided the question. 'I've taken the boy's case, OK?'

He didn't want to tell Borchert about the DVD yet, even though that would immediately explain why he needed some back-up. Andi was the only person Stern knew who was imperturbable enough to wallow in the mire on his behalf without asking too many questions. However, he was afraid his ex-client would think him insane if he revealed the true reason why he was retracing the road Simon claimed to have trodden in a previous life.

Maybe I really have gone insane? There was that two-minute video. On the other hand, there were all the laws of nature that weighed against the possibility his son could still be alive. Then again, they also weighed against the fact that Simon appeared to remember a murder committed well before he was born.

'OK, your honour, no more questions.' Borchert raised his hands like the victim of a stick-up. 'But please don't tell me we're looking for another body.'

'We are. I was with Simon at the hospital earlier on, and he gave me this address.'

The drizzle had eased a little, and Stern could at last look ahead without having to blink away droplets the whole time. They were no more than fifty metres from the metal door of Number 6, which was part of a block of shabby-looking lock-ups a stone's throw from the Spree.

'Simon says the man wouldn't fit into the freezer, so he cut his legs off.'

7

Stern didn't really know what he'd expected to see when they opened the door. A horde of rats dragging a severed leg across the concrete floor perhaps, or a buzzing black cloud of fruit flies and blowflies hovering over a half-open chest freezer. His mind's eye had been prepared for the sight of any harbinger of death, which was why the reality made him feel so unutterably sad.

He ought really to have felt relieved when the garage turned out to be empty. No furniture. No electrical appliances. No books. The dusty light bulb cast a dim glow over two small crates filled with old crockery and a worn-out office chair, nothing more. Stern felt as if all hope were escaping from a valve in his side. He became painfully aware how fiercely and irrationally he had wanted to find something lifeless in the garage. The more inexplicable Simon's memories were, the more reasonable it seemed to believe in a connection between Felix and a ten-year-old boy with a birthmark on his shoulder. He could scarcely grasp that he'd rooted this irrational equation in his subconscious.

'So much for your feng shui shit,' Borchert growled. Stern didn't trouble to explain that the classical Chinese philosophy of building and garden design had nothing to do with reincarnation or the transmigration of souls. To the club owner, anything he couldn't actually touch was psychobabble concocted by people with too much time on their hands. It was precisely this straightforward attitude that Stern had found so appealing only a short time ago.

'What are you up to now?' asked Borchert. Stern had abruptly knelt down and was shuffling along on all fours. He didn't reply, just went on running his fingers over the dusty concrete floor in search of irregularities. He sensed the pointlessness of this long before he gave up.

'No dice,' he said eventually, getting to his feet and patting the dust off his camel-hair coat. 'No double floor. Nothing.'

'That's odd, considering the rest of your story sounded so plausible,' Borchert said sarcastically. For some reason his forehead was once more beaded with sweat although he hadn't budged from the spot for the last couple of minutes.

Stern paused on the way out and glanced thoughtfully over his shoulder. Then he turned off the light and left his companion to shut the heavy door.

'I don't know,' he muttered to himself. 'Something doesn't add up.'

'I've noticed that too, now you come to mention it.' Borchert withdrew the key from the lock and grinned. 'Maybe it's the fact that we're standing here in the drizzle after looking for a corpse in an empty garage.'

'I don't mean that. You'd understand if you'd been with me two days ago. I mean, that boy had been in hospital for the last few months, and before that in a children's home. How could he have known about the body in the factory cellar? He even knew the man's approximate date of death.'

'Has that been confirmed?'

'Yes,' Stern said without mentioning the source. Till now he'd been dependent on the DVD voice.

'Somebody must have told him, then.'

'I guess so, but it doesn't add up all the same.'

Borchert shrugged. 'Children talk to imaginary friends, so I've heard.'

'When they're three or four, maybe. Simon isn't schizophrenic, if that's what you mean. He doesn't suffer from hallucinations. The guy with his skull split open actually existed, I found him myself. And what about this here?' Stern indicated the door. The paint was peeling badly. 'It has a 6 painted on it, just the way Simon said.'

'Then he must have been here and seen it sometime.'

'He was in a children's home in Karlshorst, nearly an hour from here by car. It's highly improbable, but even if you're right it doesn't make sense. Why should the boy believe himself to be a murderer just because someone else says so?'

'What is this, a quiz show? How should I know?' Borchert said irritably, but Stern wasn't listening. His questions were more a way of sorting out his own thoughts than a request for answers.

'OK, let's assume Simon is being used by someone. Why should the murderer enlist the services of a little boy, of all people, to lead us to his victim or victims? Why bother? He could simply pick up a phone and call the police.'

'Hey, you two!' came a yell from the entrance to the main building. A bent-backed little man in blue overalls was waddling towards them across the rainswept yard.

'It's old Giesbach – he owns the business,' Borchert explained. 'Not surprising he walks like that. He slipped a disc after hefting one packing case too many.'

'What are you doing on my premises?' the haulage boss demanded, waving his arms, and Stern mentally prepared himself for another confrontation. Then the old man stopped short and gave a hoarse laugh.

'Oh, it's you, Borchert. Now I know why that useless nephew of mine was shitting himself.'

'You weren't around and we were in a hurry, Giesbach.'

'All right, all right. You might have called me, though.'

The old man took the key from Borchert and looked at Stern.

'Number 6, eh?'

Stern would happily have taken a closer look at Giesbach's weather-beaten face, but he had to avert his head. From the viscous skeins of spittle escaping his lips with every word, the haulage boss might have been chewing a slice of cheese-topped pizza.

'What did you want in there?'

Borchert grinned. 'My pal's looking for a holiday home.'

'Just asking. Number 6, eh? Fancy that.'

'Meaning what?' said Stern.

'It was the only lock-up I ever rented out long-term.'

'Who to?'

'Man, you think I ask for ID when someone pays ten years in advance – in cash?'

'Why should anyone rent an empty garage?'

'Empty?'

The instant the old man cackled derisively, Stern realized what had escaped his attention inside the garage. *Scuff marks in the dust.*

'It was chock-a-block. We cleared it out last week. The lease had expired.'

'What!' the other two exclaimed in unison. 'Where did you dump the stuff?' Stern demanded.

'Where it belonged. In that skip.'

Stern felt his heart miss two beats as he followed the direction of the crippled haulier's gaze. All at once it had returned: hope.

'Should have cleared the place out two years ago. We failed to notice the lease had expired because we don't rent out that range of garages any more. They're due for demolition.'

Stern turned and made his way back, as if in slow motion, to the rusty skip they'd passed on their way to the garages. When he was close enough to peer over the edge, he saw the black cat was still in there, sitting on a stack of old newspapers in front of an overturned chest freezer discoloured with age. It seemed to relish the pale-yellow liquid seeping from under the lid. In any event, it didn't take fright when Stern climbed into the skip, it just went on licking the rubber seal of the freezer, which definitely hadn't seen the inside of a showroom for a dozen years or more.

8

'How do you expect me to manage it?'

Carina slammed the car door with her foot and made for the hospital entrance with the mobile phone to her ear. She'd had to park her car right outside because all the parking spaces were obstructed by vehicles that almost certainly had no right to be there. She herself had no business in a staff parking space either, strictly speaking, because officially she was suspended. Unofficially, she'd been told to look for another job.

'The hospital isn't a high-security jail,' she heard Stern say. His voice sounded jerky and was sporadically drowned by the sound of traffic in the background. 'There must be some way of getting Simon out of there.'

Carina thoroughly disliked the direction this phone call was taking. She had spent two days waiting in vain for a sign of life from Robert Stern, and now this. Instead of quietly discussing the mysterious course of events with her, he was clearly determined to get her into even more trouble.

'What do you want with him?'

'I'm doing what you asked me to do. I'm investigating his allegations.'

Great.

This was all her fault. She had brought them together,

after all. She had asked him to take an interest in the boy.

But not this way!

Not as his lawyer. The fact was, she had been totally naive. Simon had been her prime concern, of course. Thanks to her stupidity in arranging the regression, his fear of death had been overlaid by even worse fears. He believed himself to be a murderer, and she had to put a stop to that idea.

But she hadn't wanted Stern to enter that cellar. Picasso would probably have been more of a help in that respect. No, her aim had been to introduce the lawyer to Simon in the hope that they would establish a rapport – that Stern would allay the boy's fears and be rewarded with a chink in his own psychological armour. Because Simon possessed a truly inexplicable ability: despite his own grave illness, his mere presence was enough to bring a smile to disheartened patients' lips and dispel some of their melancholy and depression.

What a fool I've been, she thought. *One mistake after another*.

Glancing at her watch, she could hardly believe that only forty-two hours had gone by since the lunacy began. It was just before eleven in the morning, and she couldn't remember ever turning up at the hospital at this hour.

'What do you want him to tell you?' Carina whispered hoarsely with the mobile to her ear. She greeted a nurse who was hurrying past by raising the hand with her empty sports bag in it. Her real, original reason for returning was to collect some personal belongings from her locker and say goodbye to her colleagues. Stern's latest request had definitely not been on her agenda.

'I went to see him early this morning and he provided me with a new lead. You'll never believe it, but we've found another.'

'Another *what*?' Carina walked up the wheelchair ramp and into the reception area. A gust of wind sent her hair swirling around her face. She shivered. It felt as if someone had blown moist air at the nape of her neck through a straw.

'A man's dead body. It was in a chest freezer. Suffocated with a plastic bag, just the way Simon described it.'

The forced smile Carina had meant to give the hospital receptionist didn't come off. She hurried to the lifts.

She felt dizzy. Although she'd always suspected that contact with Robert Stern would someday land her in serious trouble, she had spent three years turning a deaf ear to the inner voice warning her. His gloomy cast of mind was like radioactivity: invisible but fraught with dire consequences for all who were exposed to it. She feared an overdose of bad energy if she had too much to do with him, yet she constantly sought his company unprotected. This time it seemed she'd got too close to him. Their joint experiences were threatening more than her state of mind.

'And we found something else.'

We? she wondered, but she asked the far more important question: 'What was it?'

Her fingertip had left an imprint on the lift's call button when she pressed it.

'A piece of paper. It was with the man's remains. In his decomposed fingers, to be more precise.'

'What was on it?' She didn't want to know.

'You've seen it for yourself.'

'What?'

'In Simon's room.'

'You're joking.'

The lift doors seemed to open painfully slowly. Carina drummed her fingertips nervously on the door surround. She couldn't wait to disappear into the aluminium cocoon.

'It was a child's drawing,' said Stern. 'Of a little church in a field.'

It can't be true.

She pressed the button for Neurology and shut her eyes.

The picture on Simon's window. He drew it three days ago, after the regression.

'Now do you understand why I've got to see him?'

'Yes,' she whispered, although she really didn't understand anything any more. She was feeling the way she had three years ago, when their relationship broke up – when Stern had applied the emergency brake because everything was happening too fast for him.

'Please bring him to the zoo,' said Stern. 'Let's meet at the Elephant Gate at half past twelve. A couple with a child won't attract attention.'

'Why so complicated? Why not pay him another visit at the hospital?'

'This makes two dead bodies, and I've been first on the scene each time. Can you imagine where I'll come on Engler's list of suspects after this?'

'I understand,' she whispered. The lift doors opened, and she had to force herself not to return to the ground floor. All she wanted to do right now was make herself scarce.

'That's why I left before the police turned up, but it's only a matter of time before they discover it was me who found the body. I've only a short head start, but I want to make the most of it.'

'To do what?'

Stern drew a deep breath before he replied, and Carina thought she detected a hint of mistrust in his voice as she opened the door to Room 217.

'I've another appointment first. With a friend of yours.'

Carina would normally have asked at once what he meant,

but she couldn't find the words. She knew Simon always watched a repeat of his favourite crime series about now. But the television was burbling away on its own.

His bed was empty.

9

'So you want to interrogate him?'

Professor H. J. Müller scrawled his almost illegible signature on a letter to a fellow neurologist, the medical director of a hospital in Mainz, and closed the folder. Then he picked up a silver paperknife and removed a piece of bluish fluff from under his thumbnail.

'*Interrogate* is definitely the wrong word to use in this context.' The policeman sitting opposite him cleared his throat. 'We merely want to ask him a few questions.'

Pull the other one, thought Müller, eyeing the man who had introduced himself as Inspector Brandmann. What he was proposing would hardly be a normal question and answer session.

'I really don't know if I can sanction such a procedure. Is it legally permissible?'

'Yes, of course.'

Really? Müller could hardly believe it didn't require special authorization by the chief of police or, at the very least, a public prosecutor.

'Where's your colleague got to?' Müller consulted the desk diary in front of him. 'My secretary told me to expect a Herr Dengler.'

'Engler,' Brandmann amended. 'My colleague sends his apologies. He's detained at another crime scene – one that appears to be directly connected to the present case.'

'I see.' The corners of the medical director's mouth turned down as they always did when he was examining someone. For a brief moment the overweight man in the visitor's chair in front of his desk had ceased to be a policeman and become a patient. One whom he would seriously advise to diet and undergo a thyroid examination, to judge by the way his Adam's apple protruded from his throat.

Müller shook his head and replaced the paperknife on his prescription pad.

'No. My answer is no. I don't want to subject the patient to unnecessary stress. I presume you're familiar with his diagnosis?' Müller folded his slender hands. 'Simon Sachs is suffering from an S-PNET, a supratentorial primitive neuroectodermal tumour of the cerebrum. This is gradually spreading from the right-hand to the left-hand hemisphere of the brain. In other words, it has already crossed the corpus callosum. Having carried out the biopsy myself after opening the skull, I found the tumour to be inoperable.'

The medical director did his best to smile amiably.

'Or let me put it in language more intelligible to a layman like yourself: Simon is gravely ill.'

'Quite,' said Brandmann. 'That's why we want to carry out this test as soon as possible. It will spare him a lot of onerous questioning and us a great deal of time. I was told the boy almost died of pneumonia. Is that correct?'

Aha, so that's the way the wind's blowing.

The boy was their most important witness. They were anxious to question him while they still could. After chemo and radiotherapy had exposed Simon to a potentially fatal bout of pneumonia, Müller had gone against his colleagues' advice and decided to discontinue aggressive treatment – a measure that, although it might not have prolonged his life, had certainly mitigated his suffering.

'That's right,' he said. 'At present Simon is only taking cortisone for swelling of the brain and carbamazepine as an anticonvulsant. I've booked him for a further examination that will help me to decide whether we should recommence radiotherapy after all. However, I fear his prospects are extremely poor.'

The neurologist got up from his desk and went over to a massive lectern near the window.

'How far have you got with your enquiries? Do you know the identity of the murdered man you found with Simon's assistance?'

'Let me put it this way . . .' Brandmann twisted his neck like a tortoise as he turned his head in the professor's direction. 'If Simon Sachs really has been reincarnated, he did us a great favour in his former life.'

'The dead man was a criminal, you mean?'

'Yes, a regular villain named Harald Zucker. He disappeared without trace fifteen years ago. Interpol long suspected him of involvement in some barbaric crimes in South America, but it seems he didn't skip the country after all.'

'Zucker, eh?' Müller leafed absently through some handwritten lecture notes on his reading stand.

There was a knock and the door opened before he could say 'Come in'. The first to enter was the male nurse everyone in the hospital called Picasso, although Müller could detect nothing artistic about his uncouth exterior. Picasso's right hand rested on the shoulder of a little boy, and was gently propelling him into the office.

'Hello, Simon.' Brandmann heaved his bulk out of the visitor's chair and greeted the boy with the familiarity of an old acquaintance. Simon just nodded shyly. He was wearing pale-blue jeans with patch pockets, a cord jacket and a pair of brand-new white trainers. The headphones of an MP3 player dangled from his neck.

Müller came out from behind his lectern. 'How are you feeling today?'

The boy looked quite well, but that could have been down to his wig, which tended to distract attention from his pallor.

'Pretty good. A bit tired, that's all.'

'Fine.' While speaking to Simon, Müller drew himself up in an attempt to offset the inspector's obvious height advantage. 'This gentleman is from the police. He would like to ask you some questions about what happened the day before yesterday. To be more precise, he wants to carry out a test on you, and I'm not sure if I should ask you to undergo it.'

'What sort of test?'

Brandmann cleared his throat and took great care to give the boy a disarming smile.

'Simon, do you know what a lie detector is?'

10

The Hackescher Markt district of Berlin seldom had a parking space when you needed one, so Borchert simply double-parked his four-wheel drive when they reached their destination in Rosenthaler Strasse. Stern had spent the drive from Moabit to the city centre making various phone calls, among them one to Information. This had yielded several entries for Dr Johann Tiefensee. To his surprise, Tiefensee proved to be a psychiatrist as well as a psychologist; in other words, a qualified medical man. He was even, it seemed, a lecturer in medical hypnosis at Humboldt University.

'Just a moment, Robert.'

Stern, in the act of undoing his seat belt, felt Borchert's hand close on his wrist like a vice.

'You may be able to kid that girl Carina, but I'm not buying it.'

Stern tried to free his hand but failed. 'I don't know what you mean.'

'Why are you playing the gravedigger? The defence lawyer I know only sets foot outside his house for a fee, he certainly doesn't work for mentally disturbed children. No, let me have my say.'

Stern's arm had gone numb, Borchert was squeezing his

wrist so hard. He seemed quite unaware of the drivers tooting him as they drove past.

'I'm not an idiot. Lawyers like you don't skedaddle from the police for no reason, so tell me why we didn't wait at the haulage depot.'

'I didn't want any aggro with Engler, that's all.'

'Bullshit. You'll get aggro in spades if old Giesbach spills the beans. So what's going on?'

Stern looked through the tinted window on the passenger side. The street was busy, the wide pavement teeming with people. It was only late October, but the window of the Café an der Ecke was already sporting a Santa Claus.

'You're right,' he said with a sigh. Allowed to move his hand at last, he reached inside his jacket. Borchert raised his eyebrows when the DVD was held under his nose. 'This was among my mail yesterday.'

'What's on it?'

In lieu of a reply, Stern inserted the disc in the CD player and the little satnav screen lit up.

'See for yourself.'

He shut his eyes and waited for the sinister voice to ooze from the car's speakers like poison gas. Instead all he heard was a faint hiss.

'Is this your idea of a joke, Robert?'

Mystified, Stern opened his eyes and peered at the screen, which was flecked with red.

'I don't understand.' He pressed a button, hurriedly withdrew the DVD from the player and examined it for scratches from every angle. 'It must have got damaged. It was all there last night.'

Or were those signs of wear not an optical illusion after all?

'What was all there?' Borchert asked.

'Everything. The disguised voice, the neonatal ward . . .'

Stern felt feverish, overwhelmed by a rising tide of panic. 'The shots of Felix's death. And that child who looked as if he could be my son.'

Seeing the incomprehension on Andi Borchert's face, he began at the beginning and told him, as best he could, about the shocking images that had confronted him last night.

'That's why I can't go to the police. He said he'd kill the twins, so I'll have to find out on my own how Simon knows about the murders. I've got four days left,' Stern concluded, feeling thoroughly ridiculous all of a sudden. If anyone had tried to sell him such a fantastic yarn two days ago, he would have laughed them to scorn and sent them off with an earful.

Borchert took the DVD from him without comment and turned on the interior light. Thanks to the perpetual drizzle, it was as misty as a Turkish bath outside.

'I believe you,' he said at length, handing back the silver disc.

'Really?'

'I mean, I believe you when you say there was something on it last night. This thing is an EZ-D.'

'A what?'

'A throw-away DVD. Only a prototype existed when I was in the film business. It's got a special polycarbonate coating that reacts to oxygen. Take it out of the recorder after playing it, and light and oxygen render it useless. It was really developed for DVD libraries, so people didn't have to return a film after renting it.'

'OK, that proves it. But what am I supposed to do with a throw-away DVD? There was information on it I'm not meant to pass on.'

'Robert, don't get me wrong, but . . .' Borchert scratched his hairless head. 'First we find that stiff and now you're being blackmailed by some unknown man who claims your son is still alive. Could this voice exist only in your head?'

Looking at Borchert's flushed cheeks, Stern realized that the question was fully justified.

Perhaps Felix's death really had robbed him of his reason ten years after the event. That must be it. Every objective fact clearly indicated that Felix was dead, yet the cruel voice on the DVD and Simon's memories had, with merciless precision, revealed something deep inside him – something he himself had never dreamed about until now: a definite receptivity to supernatural phenomena. He was shocked to admit that the absence of any rational explanation didn't matter to him as long as some higher power enabled him to see his son again. Borchert was right.

He was genuinely on the verge of cracking up. He put his hand on Borchert's shoulder, his eyes filling with tears.

'Know something? I only held him in my arms three times.' Stern couldn't have explained why he'd said that. 'And the last time he was dead.'

The words came pouring out, beyond his control.

'Sometimes I wake up in the middle of the night, even now, with the smell of him in my nostrils. Felix's body was cold by the time Sophie finally let go of him, but he still smelled the way he did the morning I held him for the first time and rubbed him with baby lotion.'

'And now you seriously want to find out if he . . .'

Stern could tell how hard Borchert found it to get the word out.

'. . . if he's been *reincarnated*?'

'Yes. No.' Stern sniffed. 'I don't know, Andi, but I've got to admit I can't find a rational explanation for the resemblance.'

He told Borchert about the birthmark on the boy blowing out the candles on his birthday cake.

'It's just where Felix had one. On the shoulder, and that's

very rare. They're mostly on the face or neck. It's much bigger now, of course, but the weirdest thing is its shape. It looks like a boot.'

'And Felix . . .' Borchert hesitated. 'I mean, the baby you buried. Did he also have a birthmark like that?'

'Yes, I saw it myself. Before he died and afterwards.'

Stern closed his eyes as if hoping to shut out the memories. What he failed to shut out were the neonatal ward and the metal autopsy table on which his son was lying.

'I'm sorry.' Nervously, he ran a hand over his brow. After a second's hesitation he got out of the car. 'I'll quite understand if you don't believe me and want nothing more to do with this.'

He slammed the passenger door and made for the entrance to the building without waiting for Borchert to reply.

A brief glance at the discreet nameplate on the wrought-iron gate told him that he'd come to the right address. He was about to ring the bell when he noticed the chock that prevented the gate from closing. Uncertain whether he would need a key for the lift, a feature of many Berlin apartment houses, he set off up the stairs. It took him a while to reach the top floor. He leaned against the worn banisters, breathing hard, then froze in alarm. It wasn't his poor condition that concerned him, but the door to Dr Tiefensee's practice.

It was wide open.

11

'Feeling all right, Simon?' Professor Müller asked, keeping the intercom's talk button depressed. He looked through the plate-glass window into the adjoining room, where the snow-white MRI scanner was located. Clad only in a T-shirt and boxer shorts, Simon was lying inside the tube they'd slid him into, like a loaf ready for baking. This was the fifth time in two years he'd had to undergo the half-hour procedure. Unfortunately, the previous magnetic resonance shots of his brain had revealed nothing but a rampant growth of cells inside the skull. Today, for a change, his tumour would not be the object of investigation.

'Yes, everything's OK.'

Simon's voice issued from the speaker loud and clear.

'And it really works?' Müller had released the talk button to prevent the boy next door from hearing what they were saying. His sole reason for consenting to such a test was curiosity. Having so far only read of this neuroradiological experiment, he was eager to witness it at first hand. In addition to himself and the police inspector, the computer room was occupied by an androgynous blonde technician. Introduced to Müller as a medically trained interrogation expert attached to the Federal CID, she was currently fiddling with something beneath the monitor table.

'Yes. In fact, this method is far more accurate than testing with traditional polygraphs. Besides, you wouldn't have allowed Simon to leave here in his state of health, so we're falling back on the Seehaus Clinic's very own in-house lie detector.' Brandmann laughed. 'You didn't realize your hospital had such a thing, did you?'

'Professor Müller?' Simon asked over the intercom.

'Yes?'

'I've got an itch.'

'No problem. You can still move.'

'What does he mean?' asked Brandmann.

'It's his ears. They always itch after a while, when the foam earplugs warm up.'

'OK, I'm all set.' The gum-chewing blonde crawled out from under the table, having evidently succeeded in hooking up her computer to that of the hospital. She pulled up an office chair, sat down in front of a small grey monitor and pressed the intercom button.

'Hello, Simon, I'm Laura.' Her voice sounded unexpectedly friendly.

'Hello.'

'In a minute I'm going to ask you some questions. Most of them you must answer by simply saying yes or no, is that clear?'

'Was that the first question?'

The three adults couldn't help smiling.

'Good, that's settled. Then we can begin. Just one more thing: whatever happens, you mustn't open your eyes under any circumstances.'

'All right.'

'Gentlemen?' Laura made a gesture of invitation.

With practised movements, Müller activated the MRI scanner's electronics and the test began, accompanied by the typical, monotonous crashes that sounded like a pile-driver in action. In spite of the soundproof door, they could not only hear the thuds but feel them. After a few minutes these sounds gave way to deep bass notes that seemed to tug at the stomach lining.

'For a start,' said Laura, 'please tell me your first name and surname.'

'Simon Sachs.'

'How old are you?'

'Ten.'

'What is your mother's name?'

'Sandra.'

'And your father's?'

'I don't know.'

Laura looked round at Müller, who shrugged his shoulders. 'He's in care. His mother gave him up. He never knew his father.'

'OK, Simon, now it gets serious. I want you to lie to me.'

'Why?'

'You've seen the computer pictures they've taken of your brain?'

'Yes, they look like walnuts cut in half.'

The policewoman laughed. 'Exactly. At this moment we're taking some more of those walnut pictures. You'll be able to watch them later on video. When you lie to me, you'll notice something really weird.'

'OK.'

Laura glanced at Brandmann and the professor in turn, then proceeded with her questioning.

'Do you have a driving licence?'

'Er, yes.'

Müller stared in fascination at the high-definition 3D images. None of the previous questions had elicited a reaction, but now a red rash had suddenly appeared at the front of the neocortex.

'What sort of car do you drive?'

'A Ferrari.'

'And where do you live?'

'In Africa.'

Laura took her finger off the talk button. 'You see?' she said to Müller. 'Heightened cerebral activity in the thalamus and amygdala. Note also the readings in all other areas responsible for Simon's emotions, conflict resolution and thought control.'

She tapped another pulsating red spot on the screen with the tip of a much-chewed ballpoint pen.

'That's quite typical. If someone tells the truth it remains cold, but when subjects are lying they have to exercise their imagination and concentrate harder. Our software colours this intense cerebration red and makes the lies visible.'

'Amazing,' Müller blurted out. No wonder this new system was far superior to traditional lie detectors. A conventional polygraph only measured changes in pulse rate, blood pressure, breathing and perspiration. Well-trained and psychologically prepared subjects could suppress some of those reflexes when lying, but no one could control biochemical changes in the brain – or not, at least, without years of practice.

Laura swallowed her chewing gum and pressed the talk button again.

'Very good, Simon, you're doing fine. Just a few more questions and then we're through. But from now on you must tell the truth straight away, OK?'

'No problem.'

'What did you get for your birthday?'

'Some trainers.'

'Anything else?'

'A regression.'

'With Dr Tiefensee?'

'Yes.'

'From Carina?'

'Yes.'

'Were you hypnotized?'

'I don't know. I think I fell asleep first.'

'How do you know?'

'Carina and the doctor told me. But you can check that yourself.'

'How?' Laura was now looking as mystified as Inspector Brandmann. She hadn't been expecting this answer.

'Easy. Dr Tiefensee recorded the whole session on video. You could watch it.'

'OK, thanks for the tip. What happened when you woke up?'

'I had that memory in my head.'

'Which one?'

'About the dead body. The one in the cellar.'

'Had you ever had that memory before?'

'No.'

'Has anyone ever mentioned the name "Harald Zucker" to you?'

'No.'

'Who told you to go to the factory?'

'No one. I asked Carina if she could find me a lawyer.'

Müller glanced at Brandmann, who could hardly tear his eyes away from the screen. There hadn't been the smallest discolouration so far.

'Why did you need a lawyer?'

'I wanted to go to the police. I've done something wrong and I've got to tell someone, but in films the first thing they always ask for is a lawyer.'

'Good, we're almost through. Now comes my most important question, Simon: Have you ever murdered anyone?'

'Yes.'

'When was that?'

'I killed one man fifteen years ago and the other three years later.'

Müller took a step towards the screen as if he'd become short-sighted.

'Simon, I'm now going to ask you to think of all the people who've talked to you in the last few weeks and months, whether in the hospital or outside. Think of Robert Stern, Carina Freitag, Dr Tiefensee, your doctors – no matter who. Did any of them tell you to tell us this story?'

'No. I know you think I'm fibbing.' Simon sounded very tired now, but more sad than indignant. 'You think I'm trying to make myself look important – just repeating what someone else told me to say.'

Laura and Brandmann caught each other nodding.

'But it isn't true,' Simon went on, growing steadily more heated. 'It was *me*. *I* murdered those men. The first one I killed with an axe fifteen years ago, the other I suffocated. There were some more as well, but I'm not sure how many.'

Laura turned to Brandmann and Müller and shook her head in bewilderment.

The absence of any change on the screen was simply incomprehensible.

12

That a front door in Berlin should be open was not so unusual when it belonged to a medical practice. That the reception desk should be unoccupied and the waiting room deserted was another matter. Stern had to control his instinct for self-preservation as he made his way inside and called the psychiatrist's name.

'Dr Tiefensee? Hello? Are you there?'

The softly illuminated glass sign in the lobby was out of keeping with the way in which professional medics usually advertised their services. The interior decoration, too, differed appreciably from that of any medical practice Stern had ever been to in the past. This was immediately apparent from the waiting room itself, in which patients could take their ease in wing chairs that wouldn't have looked out of place in an English country house.

Stern took out his mobile and dialled the number given him by directory enquiries. Moments later a ringtone could be heard issuing from a room along the passage. He let it ring ten times until the answerphone cut in. He now heard the psychiatrist's sonorous voice not only in his ear but, with a slight time lapse, coming from some twenty metres away.

The passage made a left turn halfway along. Stern rounded the corner and Tiefensee's recorded message grew louder. It was stating his hours of business. Today was Saturday. Consultations by special appointment only.

Could he be with a patient right now? Is that why he isn't answering?

Stern knocked on the door of the first room he came to – the one in which he thought the answerphone, now silent, had been broadcasting its message. There was no response, so he went in and recognized it as the room Simon had described that morning: blue gym mat on the floor, everything scrupulously neat and clean. Although the gloomy light of the autumn afternoon barely penetrated its windows, the room made a friendly, welcoming impression.

'Anyone there?' Stern called again, then swung round abruptly. A muffled crash had come from the room next door.

What was that?

Another crash. It had a wooden, almost bony quality. Stern dashed out into the passage and along to the door of the adjoining room. He depressed the curved brass handle. No use, the door was locked.

'Dr Tiefensee?' He knelt down and squinted through the keyhole. His eyes took a moment to get used to the different lighting conditions because the psychiatrist's desk lamp was dazzling him. He blinked a couple of times, and then he saw it: a chair overturned on the parquet floor. At first he couldn't decide what was casting that wavering shadow on the floor, but the sound of choking dispelled all doubt. He wrenched at the handle again with all his might. Still no use, so he threw his weight against the door. He tried again, shoulder-charging it this time. The varnished pinewood panels trembled and the hinges groaned, but it only gave way at the fourth attempt.

There was a deafening crash, and Stern tore the shoulder of his suit on a long sliver of wood as he toppled forwards into the stylish consulting room, along with the splintered door.

13

Not again, please!

Stern froze with his hand to his mouth, staring transfixed at Tiefensee's legs. Encased in well-pressed, pale-grey flannels, they were jerking convulsively a metre from the floor. Much as Stern wanted to avert his gaze, it travelled higher. He could hardly bear the sight of the bulging eyes that stared so desperately into his own, but it was the psychiatrist's hands that were to haunt his direst dreams in time to come. Tiefensee's fingers were clawing in vain at the wire noose that had bitten deep into his throat.

The hook in the old moulded ceiling had been designed to support a heavy chandelier, which was why it bore the tall man's weight with ease.

Stern wasted precious seconds setting the chair on its legs. For some mysterious reason the psychiatrist was hanging too high. His feet wouldn't reach the seat from which he'd jumped.

Or been pushed?

Stern tried to grab hold of his legs, but they were thrashing around too violently. He simply couldn't raise the man enough to relieve the pressure on his neck.

Damn, damn, damn . . .

'Hang on!' he called as he strove to haul the heavy

Biedermeier desk into position beneath the dying man, whose laboured breathing was growing steadily fainter. More precious seconds went by, and it wasn't until Tiefensee's convulsive movements slowed that Stern abandoned the desk and climbed on the chair himself. He caught hold of him around the knees and lifted him.

'Too late.'

The phone-distorted voice startled him so much, he almost let go.

'Who's that?' he gasped, unable to turn round.

'Don't you know?'

Of course I do. I could never forget that voice even if I wanted to.

'Where are you?'

'Here. Right behind you.'

Stern looked down at the desk, which he'd scarcely managed to budge. The flashing red light of the computer monitor's webcam was directed straight at him. The bastard was talking to him over the Internet!

'What the hell have you done?' Stern demanded breathlessly. Tiefensee seemed to get heavier with every word he uttered, and he wondered how much longer he could support him.

'I think you can let go now,' the voice advised.

Stern looked up. Tiefensee's head was lolling forwards, his mouth open in a last, soundless cry. Although his eyes were completely lifeless, Stern refused to release his grip. To give up now would seem a betrayal.

'What's going on?' he cried desperately.

'The question is, what are you doing here? We had an agreement. You were to take care of the boy and we would deal with the psychologist.'

'Why did you kill him?'

'I didn't. He had a fair chance. If he'd told me the murderer's name he'd still be alive.'

'You bastard!'

'Let's not get emotional, please. We had a friendly chat with the man, that's all.'

Stern's arms felt as if they were clasping a red-hot stove. Unable to hold on any longer, he let go. The ceiling hook creaked under its renewed burden.

'Tiefensee could have ended his martyrdom quite easily, but he refused, so my associates perched him on the back of the chair. I was able to watch him from here. I timed how long he managed to stand on tiptoe: twelve minutes forty-four seconds. Pretty good for a man of his age.'

'You're perverted. Completely insane.' Stern walked unsteadily towards the computer.

'Why? You really ought to be pleased. Believe me, if Tiefensee knew how Simon was able to find the bodies, he would have told me before he lost his balance.'

Stern's mobile started vibrating in his pocket, but he ignored it.

'That means you've got one less suspect to worry about. From now on, though, you should make better use of your time.'

'Who are you?'

Stern took hold of the mouse and the screensaver on the monitor disappeared, but he could see nothing apart from a normal user's screen. He was about to check the Internet browser when the LED on the monitor went out. The voice had severed the connection. At the same time, an external program deleted all the browser entries and the computer shut down automatically. The voice was obliterating its digital footsteps.

Damnation!

Bathed in sweat, Stern flopped down on the chair behind the desk and stared at the psychiatrist's lifeless body, which was suspended from the ceiling like a horrific pendulum. It was several seconds before he noticed that one of the lights on the office telephone in front of him was flashing.

'Is that you again?' he demanded.

'Of course,' the voice replied. 'But *you* had better hang up.'

'Why should I?'

'Can't you hear?'

Stern got up and stepped away from the desk. He stared in the direction of the open doorway. Sure enough, it sounded as if a metal cable in the stairwell had drawn taut.

The lift.

'You've got a visitor. Take a look at the desk diary.'

Stern's eyes widened when he saw the entry underlined in red: Pol. interview – Insp. Martin Engler.

He checked his watch. The voice laughed.

'I reckon he'll be with you in about thirty seconds.'

Goddammit, why didn't Andi warn me? Stern pulled out his mobile. He felt sick when he saw all the unanswered calls. He must have muted his phone by mistake.

At that instant his phone flashed and started ringing – much louder than ever before. The shrill note filled not only the consulting room but the entire practice, passage and reception area included. It was a moment before he realized that the source of the noise wasn't his mobile. It was the doorbell. Engler was already on the threshold.

14

'Hello? Dr Tiefensee? Are you there?'

The inspector's cold had definitely worsened in the last two days and gone to his chest. Stern could hear what an effort it cost him to raise his hoarse voice sufficiently to carry as far as Tiefensee's consulting room.

'What now?' Stern whispered. He had turned off the hands-free system and picked up the portable handset so as not to attract the policeman's attention. Engler was still in the reception area, but it wouldn't be long before he came down the passage, turned the corner and saw the splintered door. *And then . . .*

'Anyone there?' Engler called again. The words ended on a cough. Somewhere, an unoiled door handle squeaked. Stern pressed the phone even tighter to his ear. Panic was propelling the blood through his auditory canals at such a rate, he found it hard to understand the distorted voice.

'You want me to help you?' it said softly. 'Me, of all people?'

'You'd better get me out of here if you don't want me talking to the police,' Stern hissed angrily. 'Is there a rear entrance?'

'No, and don't try climbing out of a window. You'd break your neck.'

'In that case, what?'

From the sound they made on the creaking parquet floor, Engler was wearing hobnailed boots. He had evidently left the reception and set off along the passage. There was the muffled sound of a door closing.

'Go over to the doorway and stand beside the medicine cabinet.'

All right.

Stern tiptoed across the room, trying not to make a noise. He nearly tripped over a file that had fallen to the floor but recovered his balance just in time. In so doing he collided with Tiefensee's body and set it swinging again. The ceiling hook creaked alarmingly.

'Well, what now?' He had reached the doorway and flattened himself against the wall between the door frame and a white medical cabinet with faceted glass insets.

'Open it.'

He did so.

Three rooms along the passage another door handle was depressed. So Engler was proceeding systematically, looking into each treatment room in turn. Disappointed, he shut that door too.

'See those surgical scissors in the second compartment from the bottom?'

'Yes.'

Stern took hold of the gleaming instrument. It was cold to the touch.

'Good. Take them and wait for Engler to get to you.' The voice was also whispering now. 'Wait till he sees the body. That'll give you the advantage of surprise.'

'What then?'

'You stab him in the heart.'

'Are you crazy?'

The metal instrument in Stern's hand suddenly burned

like fire. Was this a dream or was it real? Was he really standing in a room with a corpse dangling from the ceiling, armed with a pair of scissors and talking to a psychopath?

'Do you have a better idea?'

'No, but I'm not killing anyone!'

'Sometimes it's the best solution.'

More creaking footsteps in the passage. Engler was checking another room.

The distorted voice chuckled mirthlessly.

'Oh well, I guess I'll have to give you a helping hand.'

Stern felt a current of air fan his perspiring face, as if a window had been opened somewhere. It couldn't be Engler, who was walking down the passage again. Another two steps, three at most, and he would turn the corner and see the splintered door lying on the floor. Stern expected to see the policeman's toecaps peeping around the door frame at any moment.

'Hello?' someone called suddenly. His heart almost choked on the blood that was trying to flow ever faster through his veins.

It can't be true.

The 'voice' had been there all the time, only one room further along. Unlike Engler's boots, his rubber soles scarcely made a sound.

'Are you looking for me?'

Stern held his breath. His ears popped, he was tensing up so much. Everything around him suddenly sounded far louder, but he couldn't put a face to the voice.

'Please excuse my get-up,' the man said. 'I was in the middle of an experiment.' Although his voice was now undistorted by a telephone it sounded muffled, as if he were speaking through a handkerchief.

'Are you Dr Tiefensee?' Engler asked warily.

'No, the doctor just slipped out for something to eat.

Hang on, what am I saying? You're in luck – here he is.'

The last thing Stern heard Engler say was 'Where?' Then came a short, strangled cry followed by an electrostatic report. It sounded as if a light bulb had popped, but very much louder.

A stun gun, thought Stern. Everything inside him itched to dash outside and see what was going on in the passage, but he was too afraid. Not of Engler or of being arrested, but of the madman whose undisguised voice he had just heard for the first time.

Unaware that he'd been clutching his mouth in suspense, he lowered his hand. Then he heard the receding footsteps of someone wearing rubber-soled shoes. They sounded like a child's ball bouncing up and down.

Gingerly, Stern detached himself from the wall he'd been leaning against and stole out into the passage on trembling legs. Just in time to see a long-haired figure slam the heavy front door. He gave a start, then looked down at Engler. The detective was lying motionless on the floor, as he'd expected. His arms and legs were unnaturally splayed as if he'd been thrown from a car travelling at high speed.

Stern bent over the inspector and felt for his pulse. Reassured to find that he was still alive, he made his way cautiously to the front door. He speeded up a bit once he'd emerged on to the landing and descended the first flight of stairs, and when he reached the third floor he started running, holding on to the banisters as he raced down the remaining flights. But, when he dashed out of the building and into the busy street, he realized he was too late. Far too late. The long-haired figure in the doctor's white coat – the man who had murdered Tiefensee and put Engler out of action – had vanished into a throng of tourists, businesspeople and passers-by. And, with him, the truth about Felix.

15

The nocturnally active animals were housed in the basement of the predators' compound. The gloom that had greeted them inside reminded Stern of the times he'd got to the cinema late and been compelled to find his seat in the near-dark. On the other hand, the warm, steamy atmosphere smelled like an overheated pet shop.

'This is great,' said Simon, towing him over to a plate-glass window behind which several balls of fur with big, wide eyes were scurrying around. For some reason, people tended to lower their voices as soon as they entered a darkened room, and Simon was no exception. 'They look strong,' he whispered.

'Dwarf Plumploris.' Stern read out the name on the dimly illuminated noticeboard without even glancing at the tiny semi-monkeys; he was still far too shocked. After his hurried exit from Tiefensee's practice, Andi Borchert had driven him to his meeting with Carina. Now he was standing in the nocturnal house, his brain still unable to take in any new impressions. The same inexplicable questions kept going round in his head like an endless loop tape:

Who is the 'voice'? How did Simon know about the bodies? Who killed those men in the past? Why should someone commit murder now *to find out what happened* then*?*

Stern was surprised to have to admit that those questions

interested him for one reason only: because the answers might reunite him with his son. He shut his eyes.

Insane of me.

He was seriously hoping that Simon's memories would provide evidence of his reincarnation and, thus, of Felix's continued existence. Despite all objective facts to the contrary.

'I'm sorry. What did you say?'

Simon was tugging at his sleeve. He bent down. The boy had said something, but it had gone astray somewhere in the darkness. He repeated the question.

'Will Carina be back soon?'

Stern nodded. Carina had gone to the visitors' toilet to weep in private.

She had seldom been as angry with him as she was when they met at the Elephant Gate. Having narrowly succeeded in smuggling Simon out of the hospital with Picasso's help, she asked him straight out why she'd had to take such a risk. So Stern told her the whole story, whispering so as not to be overheard by Simon as they strolled through the largely deserted zoo: the DVD, the boy with the birthmark, and the sinister task the voice had set him. Unlike Borchert, Carina believed him at once. Stern could sense how genuinely receptive she was to the possibility of Felix's reincarnation – much more so than he himself had been.

But, when he told her about Tiefensee's horrific end, she had grasped the danger that threatened them all. Although she'd managed to keep her composure when wriggling out of his embrace, he knew what was going on inside her. He also realized that it would have been a mistake to run after her if she wanted to be alone.

'Yes, she won't be long,' he said in a low voice, and they moved on to the next enclosure.

'Good,' said Simon. 'The thing is, Picasso said we've got to be back by four or he'll have to tell on us.'

Picasso? It was a moment before the bearded nurse's image surfaced in his mind's eye. Although Stern's collision with him and the elderly ABBA fan had occurred only that morning, he remembered their encounter as if it were a scene from another life altogether. From that point of view, he and Simon could be said to have something in common.

'Don't worry,' he said, patting the boy's wig. 'And don't worry about that lie-detector test either.'

'I passed,' had been Simon's first rueful words to him. Stern knew how it must look to the boy. Although the result cleared him of lying, it had simultaneously branded him a murderer. Simon was telling the truth. Stern felt almost ashamed of himself for welcoming this news, but the more impenetrable Simon's secret became, the higher his own hopes rose where Felix was concerned.

'You really mustn't worry,' he said again as they paused outside a terrarium containing some rat-like degus.

'Why should I? They can't get out.'

'I don't mean that. I'm talking about your bad memories. Don't they scare you?'

'Yes, they do, but . . .'

'But what?'

'Perhaps it's my punishment.'

'What for?'

'Maybe that's why I'm ill, because I did such bad things before.'

'You mustn't think that, you hear?' Stern caught hold of the boy by the shoulder of his jacket. 'Whoever killed those people, the Simon Sachs standing here in front of me wasn't responsible.'

'Who was, then?'

'That's what I'm trying to find out. And for that I need your help.'

The nocturnal house was even more sparsely frequented

than the rest of the zoo. Stern welcomed the fact that nobody could overhear their absurd conversation. He decided to delve a little deeper into Simon's reincarnation fantasy as they walked on.

'Did you have a different name fifteen years ago?'

'Dunno.'

'Or look different?'

'No idea.'

He let go of Simon's shoulder. The boy crooked his forefinger and tapped a pane of glass with his knuckle. The small terrarium inside contained a small mound of earth and various desert plants, but no animal could be seen.

Carina, who had rejoined them, was hovering in the background as though reluctant to interrupt their conversation. Stern was momentarily struck by the thought that talking about inexplicable sensory phenomena outside the vampire bat enclosure might be more than merely coincidental. The aerial bloodsuckers that lived here 'saw' their environment in the form of ultrasound echoes.

'Do you know *why* you killed those men?' he asked, reflecting that any passer-by who chanced to overhear that question would instantly call security.

'No, I don't. I guess they were bad men.'

Click. Click.

Stern was reminded of the flickering cellar light Simon had described to him that morning.

On. Off.

Before he could ask if he remembered anything else, Simon emitted a dry cough. Stern shot a worried glance at Carina, who had also heard it and came hurrying over.

'Everything OK?' she asked anxiously, feeling Simon's forehead. She shepherded him over to the middle of the spacious underground room, where visitors could consult a noticeboard listing the animals housed there. It was the lightest spot in the entire chamber, so more could be seen of people than their dim silhouettes. Stern was reassured to note the look of relief on Carina's face. Simon was smiling. He had merely swallowed the wrong way.

Stern took advantage of this interlude to produce a rather fragile piece of paper from his coat pocket. It was remarkably well preserved, given that it had spent a decade in a dead man's hand.

'Simon, take a look at this. Do you recognize it?'

Carina's shadow was obscuring the drawing. She stepped aside.

'I didn't draw that,' Simon said.

Click.

'I know, but the one at the hospital looks very like it.'

'A bit like it.'

'When did you do that drawing?'

Click.

'When I woke up. The day after the regression. I dreamed about it.'

'But why?' Stern looked at Carina, but she only shrugged. 'Why this field?'

'It isn't a field,' said Simon. He gave another cough and shut his eyes.

Stern felt sure of it now: the dusty light bulb in the cellar had started to flicker, casting a fitful light over Simon's memories.

'So what is it?'

'A graveyard.'

Click.

'Who's buried there?'

Click. *Click*.

Stern felt a hand on his shoulder, the fingers digging into his flesh as if he were a shoplifter trying to escape. He was grateful to Carina for that minor discomfort. It distracted him a little from the horror of Simon's answer:

'I think his name was Lucas. I could take you to him if you like, but . . .'

'But what?'

'There's nothing in the grave but his head.'

16

He was so tired. First all those questions, then the soporific noises inside the scanner, then the fresh air, and finally the dim lighting in that underground room at the zoo. He wanted to stay awake and listen but was finding it harder and harder, especially as the car smelled so nice and was purring along so smoothly.

Simon rested his head against Carina's soft shoulder and closed his eyes. Her stomach was rumbling and he sensed that she wasn't feeling well. She hadn't felt well ever since his mention of the grave made her tremble and the lawyer put his arms around her. Or perhaps she simply didn't like the fat man who was driving. Stern addressed him as 'Borchert'. He had a strange, breathy way of speaking, and although the day was very chilly he only wore a thin T-shirt with semicircular stains under the arms.

'Anyone been to Ferch before?' Stern asked from the passenger seat. Simon blinked at the sound of the name, which he'd told them before they left the zoo. Actually, he wasn't sure the graveyard was really there, not any more. It was only a vague hunch. *Ferch*. The five letters appeared like glittering exclamation marks as soon as he shut his eyes.

'Yes,' said the driver, 'it's just past Caputh beside the lake.'

‘How do you know?’ Stern asked suspiciously.

‘Because the Titanic’s near there. Used to be my biggest club.’

Simon felt Carina adjust her position beside him.

‘Will we make it back by four o’clock?’ she said.

‘My satnav says we’ll be there in forty-five minutes,’ said Borchert. ‘It’ll be tight. We won’t have much time to look around.’

Stern sighed. ‘Is the boy asleep?’ His voice sounded louder, as if he’d turned round to speak to Carina.

Simon felt her bend over him. He hardly dared breathe.

‘Yes, I think so.’

‘Good, then I want to ask you something. But please be honest, because I think I’m beginning to lose my mind. Do you really believe in that sort of thing?’

‘What?’

‘The transmigration of souls. Reincarnation. Previous existences.’

‘Well, I . . .’ Carina spoke hesitantly, as if she wanted to see his reaction before definitely committing herself. ‘Yes, I think so. People who have had near-death experiences appear to confirm it. They nearly all felt the soul leave the body before they were resuscitated. What’s more, some of them say they already knew, while dying, which body their soul would migrate to after death.’

‘That’s apocryphal. There’s no solid evidence.’

‘There is, you know.’

‘Like what?’ Simon heard the lawyer ask.

‘Haven’t you ever heard of Taranjit Singh?’

There was no response, so Simon surmised that Stern had shaken his head.

‘A six-year-old boy living in the Jalandhar district of India. This really happened – there was an in-depth article on it not that long ago. Reincarnation is a staple component of Hinduism. The Hindus believe we all possess an immortal soul that enters another body after we die, sometimes even that of an animal or a plant.'

'I don't see why that should interest me now,' Stern muttered to himself, so softly that Simon could hardly hear him.

'Taranjit's is only one of numerous well-documented cases of rebirth in India. Over three thousand children were questioned there by a reputable researcher named Ian Stevenson.'

'Him I've heard of,' Stern grunted.

'What about this Tanjit?' asked Borchert.

'Taranjit,' Carina amended. 'The boy claimed to be the reincarnation of a youth from a neighbouring village who had lost his life in a road accident in 1992. He could recall the most incredible details even though he'd never left his native village.'

'Then he must have overheard his parents discussing the accident. Or read about it in a newspaper.'

'Yes, that's how most people try to explain it away. But listen to this.'

Simon could feel Carina's heart beating faster.

'A very well-known Indian criminologist, Raj Singh Chauhan, wanted some objective proof, so what did he do?'

'Submit the boy to a lie-detector test like Simon?'

'Better than that. Chauhan is an expert in the field of forensic graphology. He compared Taranjit's handwriting with that of the dead boy.'

'Oh, come on . . .'

'No, it's true. Their handwriting was identical. Explain that!'

Simon didn't hear Stern's answer. Although he had firmly resolved to remain awake for another minute at least, he couldn't fight off sleep any longer. He caught the name Felix and some reference to a voice on a DVD, and then he finally drifted off. His disturbing dream began as usual, but today the door opened rather more easily.

Nor did he find it as difficult as he had the first time to descend the steps that led down into the gloomy cellar.

17

Simon woke up, thrown forward in his seat when the car came to a sudden stop.

'Be more careful, can't you?' Carina said angrily. Her voice sounded rather husky, as if she'd been crying again.

'Sorry,' Borchert growled, 'I thought there was a filter light.' A moment later Simon felt his head pressed into Carina's bosom as the car rounded a corner. The tyres began to make a drumming sound, which indicated that they were driving over cobblestones.

'Do you know why you were sent that DVD, Robert?'

Simon stifled a yawn. He had no idea what they were talking about.

'The bastard wants me to do his dirty work – find the murderer.'

'Nonsense,' said Carina. 'No one capable of putting together a video like that, which incorporates material over ten years old, needs to enlist the help of some stray lawyer.'

'The lady has a point,' said Borchert.

'So what's *your* explanation?'

'When someone goes to such lengths after so many years, only two things spring to mind: money and money.'

'Very funny, Andi. Can't you come up with something a bit more concrete?'

'Yes, try this for size. Simon said they were bad men – criminals, in other words. Maybe they were all in the same outfit, or something. Maybe they'd made a fat profit on a drugs deal and one of them wouldn't split the proceeds. He wasted all the others bar one.'

'The owner of the voice on the DVD,' said Stern.

'Exactly. And now he's after the murderer because he wants his cut.'

'Maybe,' said Carina. 'It sounds plausible, actually, but how can Simon know all this if you deny the possibility of his rebirth? And who's the boy with the birthmark? We don't have any answers. Only one thing's for sure, Robert: you're being used. The question is, why?'

'OK, people.' Borchert applied the brakes. 'We're nearly there.'

Simon blinked. His sleepy eyes focused first on two swollen raindrops trickling like tears down the tinted window. Then he looked out. A neatly trimmed hedge was gliding past. Rising beyond it was a grassy hill strewn with dead, sodden leaves.

Visibility improved as Borchert reduced speed once more. Simon extricated himself from Carina's embrace and pressed his sweaty palm against the cold glass. Although the hill ahead didn't ring a bell, he had seen the sandstone church before. It looked just like the one in his drawing on the hospital window.

18

'I don't believe this!'

Borchert's laughter drew some black looks from the members of the funeral procession. He put out his tongue at the lady with the knife-edge parting in her short black hair and grinned when she faced the front again, indignant.

'No, honestly, this day will really go down in the annals.'

Even Stern had to admit that the situation wasn't without an element of comedy.

They had found it hard to believe their eyes and ears on entering the sandstone church ten minutes earlier. Standing at the unadorned Protestant altar was a man with a crewcut and bright, friendly eyes. He was not wearing clerical vestments, just a dark-blue three-piece suit. In lieu of a tie he had draped a green scarf round his shoulders, and the fact that this was rather clumsily knotted together on his chest seemed somehow endearing. The same went for his obituary address. Having just mentioned the deceased's habit of rolling in wild boar dung during his many walks in the forest, he held up an over-life-size photo of the dear departed, and the predominantly female members of the congregation cast a sorrowful eye over the tawny Basset Hound, which must have weighed at least thirty kilos.

Ecumenical Animal Funerals. Officiating priest: Rev. Thomas

Ahrendt. Last Saturday in the month. Such was the wording of a notice in the porch, but they hadn't spotted it until they followed the rest of the mourners outside. Now they were trudging through the drizzle along a rough gravel path beyond the church. Not for the first time, Stern cursed himself for not bringing an umbrella. His shirt was clinging to his chest as if he'd taken it straight from the wash. Much more of this and he would catch pneumonia like Simon. Fortunately, the boy had stayed behind in the warm car with Carina.

'I don't believe this,' Borchert said again with a laugh that sounded like someone trying to cough up a fishbone. 'They're actually toting the fat brute along in a coffin.'

'That's OK. I did the same with the first dog I owned.'

'You're joking.'

'Why not? I was Simon's age at the time, and I was grateful to my father for organizing his send-off. Mind you, we buried him in the garden, not in a regular graveyard like this.'

They were nearing the fence that separated the church's official precincts from the animal home's private plot.

Stern lengthened his stride and caught up with the unconventional parson, who was holding open a waist-high gate for the mourners to pass through. He greeted Stern with a handshake and a broad smile that bared his gummy dentures. Stern would almost have preferred him not to look so friendly.

'Please forgive me for intruding, but is this also the way to the official graveyard?'

Ahrendt raised his eyebrows. 'Oh, so you aren't one of Hannibal's nearest and dearest?'

'Afraid not. I'm looking for a last resting place for a, er, human friend.'

'In that case I must disappoint you. The animal home rents this site from us. Our parish is too poor to maintain a graveyard for people. You'll have to go to our local town.'

'I see.'

The parson excused himself, and Stern watched him waddle over to the mourners, who were waiting beside a big rhododendron bush at the far end of the field.

Borchert was still shaking his head at the parson's last words, which he'd been just in time to catch. 'It's crazy,' he muttered. 'They can't afford a proper graveyard, but they reserve a whole football pitch for animals.'

This was something of an exaggeration. The animal graveyard, which was divided into plots, could not have measured more than fifty metres by fifty. It did, however, seem remarkably spacious for its purpose. Stern could hardly believe there was any great demand for animal burials in the district, but the scattered tombstones appeared to refute this. Somewhat untidily arranged and interspersed with coniferous trees, they jutted from the ground like crooked teeth. He decided to take a closer look before returning to the car.

'I'll wait here,' Borchert called after him. Having found a dry spot beneath a massive oak tree, he was clearly reluctant to abandon it.

Lili, Micky, Molly, Bella, Dandy, Hunk . . . The names on the animal graves he passed were as varied as their tombstones. Most of the latter consisted of a white cross or a small slab of granite with a plain inscription. A few owners had dug a bit deeper into their pockets and invested in some form of grave maintenance. Lying in front of 'Alfons', for example, were two white orchids and a freshly woven wreath. As for 'Cleopatra', she must have been a true queen among cats before she was 'murdered by a motorist' six months earlier. At least, so said the inscription on a brass plate screwed to the miniature Pyramid of Khufu that served as her tombstone.

'This is pointless,' Borchert called. 'There's no Lucas here.'

'How do you know?' Stern turned round. Borchert had found a green display case near his oak tree and was tapping the glass with his thumbnail.

'This is a list of all the animals buried here – from Attila to Zoe.'

Raindrops the size of raisins were spattering the nape of Stern's neck at irregular intervals. He felt as if he were standing under a sodden tree and someone was shaking it violently.

'There's no Lucas, though. Let's go. We can't dig up the whole graveyard – those old girls would have a fit.'

Stern looked over at the parson, who was delivering a final address with his back to them. The freshening breeze from the lake was carrying his words away in the opposite direction.

'OK,' Stern said at length. *Anyway, I've had enough dead bodies for one day.* He was just bending down to scrape a brownish wad of wet leaves from the toe of his shoe when he stopped short.

There's no Lucas . . . Borchert's words were floating around in his head. He shielded his eyes from the rain with his hand and tried to make some sense of the scene in front of him. It was like viewing his surroundings through a dirty windscreen equipped with worn wipers. The more he blinked, the more blurred the overall picture became.

That little group of people with the parson. The Pyramid of Khufu. Those orchids.

Something was wrong here.

He had seen something significant but failed to classify it correctly. Like entering an important appointment in the wrong space in a desk diary.

'What is it?' asked Borchert, who had spotted his sudden tension.

Stern raised the forefinger of his left hand and used the other hand to fish out his mobile. At the same time he made his way back to the row of graves he had just been examining.

'Is Simon asleep?' he asked.

Carina picked up at the first ringtone. 'No, but I'm glad you called.'

He ignored the note of concern in her voice because he himself felt scared of the question he was about to ask Simon.

'Let me speak to him.'

'No, not right now.'

'Why not?'

'He can't talk now.'

Stern bent over one of the less elaborate tombstones. A nagging pain in his forehead was spreading to his eyes. He tilted his head back.

'Is he all right?'

'Yes. What did you want to say to him?'

'Please ask him what name he wrote on the picture he drew at the hospital. Please, this is very important. Ask him how he signed it.'

The phone was laid aside. Stern wasn't sure, but he thought he heard a car door creak open. The rustling and hissing in the background sounded like poor radio reception. At least half a minute went by before he heard a beep – Carina had inadvertently pressed a key when picking up the phone again.

'Are you there?'

'Yes.' Stern's fingers trembled as he ran them over the letters carved into the granite. He mouthed the name to himself as Carina said it.

'"Pluto". Simon signed his drawing "Pluto". But you'd better come here right away.'

Stern had stopped listening. His replies were purely automatic.

'Why?' he asked softly, still staring at the tombstone bearing the name of the cartoon character. The rain made it look as if it were steeped in oil.

An animal? A human? A head?

He couldn't think why Simon had brought them to this place, which corresponded to a drawing made by more than one person. By a boy and by someone dead. At this moment he could only try to work out why Carina was close to yelling at him in panic.

'What's happened, for God's sake?'

'It's Simon,' she replied in a clipped voice. 'He says he's going to do it again.'

'Do what?' Stern straightened up and looked over at Borchert. 'What's he going to do?'

And what does 'again' mean?

'Hurry. I think he'd better tell you that himself.'

19

There was no one else there. The church was deserted, and he found it hard to believe that anyone could derive spiritual consolation from these bare surroundings. Stern took off his wet overcoat and draped it over his arm. He regretted this at once. It was cold and draughty inside. The air smelled of dust and old hymn books. It was lucky the sun wasn't shining through the stained-glass windows or the peeling plaster might have seemed even more obvious. Stern wouldn't have been surprised if the verger had hung the crucifix on the wall purely to conceal some structural defect. The church certainly didn't generate an intimate atmosphere.

'. . . I don't know what to do. Is it right? Is it wrong? Should I do it, or should I . . .'

Stern listened with bated breath to the low murmur coming from the second pew from the front. He had, of course, spotted Simon as soon as he came in. At this range he looked like a miniature adult, an introspective little old man communing with his Maker. Stern tiptoed towards the source of the whispers but couldn't prevent his leather soles from crunching on the dusty flagstones.

'Please give me a sign . . .'

Simon gave a start and looked up. He quickly unclasped his hands as if embarrassed to be seen at prayer.

'I'm sorry,' said Stern, 'I didn't mean to interrupt you.'

'It's all right.' The boy shuffled sideways to make room for him.

No wonder church attendances are falling if the pews are so hard, flashed through Stern's mind as he sat down.

'I won't be a moment,' Simon whispered, looking back at the altar. Stern wanted to grab the boy and hurry him outside. Carina, nervously smoking a cigarette, was waiting in the porch with Borchert.

'Are you praying to God?' he asked in a low voice. Alone or not, they were whispering as they had in that cellar at the zoo.

'Yes.'

'For something in particular?'

'That depends.'

'Never mind, it's none of my business.'

'No, it isn't that. All I mean is . . .'

'What?'

'You wouldn't understand. *You* don't believe in God.'

'Who says so?'

'Carina. She says something bad happened to you once, and since then you've never loved anyone. Not even yourself.'

Stern looked at the boy. In the semi-darkness of the church he suddenly realized what aid workers meant when they spoke of the blank expressions on the faces of boy soldiers. Smooth-skinned youngsters with death in their eyes. He cleared his throat.

'Just now you said something about a sign. What do you want God to tell you?'

'Whether I should carry on doing it.'

Stern remembered Carina's words: *He says he's going to do it again . . .*

'Doing what?'

'Well, *it*.'

'I don't follow you.'

'I fell asleep in the car. Earlier on.'

'You mean you had another dream?'

Click. The candle on the altar seemed to mutate into the flickering light bulb that illuminated Simon's nightmare memories.

'Yes.'

'About the murders?'

'Yes, exactly.' Simon cast a surreptitious glance at his upturned hands like a schoolboy with a crib written on the skin in ballpoint. Apart from the delicate tracery of lines on his fingers and palms, Stern could see nothing that was helping him to find the right words.

'I've remembered why I wrote "Pluto" on the picture.'

Click.

'Why?'

'It was his favourite soft toy.'

'Whose?'

'Lucas Schneider. He was exactly the same age as me. Back then, I mean. Twelve years ago.'

'You think you killed him?'

Back then. In your other life?

Stern's headache grew worse the closer he got to the heart of this crazy enigma.

'No!' Simon glared at him indignantly. The life had come back into his eyes, albeit mingled with anger. 'I didn't murder any children!'

'I know. But the others, the criminals?'

'Yes.'

'You were a sort of avenger?'

'Maybe.'

Simon's shoulders began to shake.

Stern was about to call Carina. If Simon was going to

have a fit, he hoped she'd brought the right medication with her. Then he noticed tears on the boy's cheeks.

'It's all right. Come on.' He put out his hand – gingerly, as if the boy's shoulder might scorch it. 'Let's go.'

'No, not yet.' Simon sniffed. 'I haven't finished yet. I must ask him if I really ought to do it.'

Click. Click. Click.

Having steadied for a brief moment, the cellar light seemed to be flickering more violently than before.

'Do what?'

'I didn't finish the job.'

'I don't understand, Simon. What do you mean? What didn't you finish?'

'Those men. I killed a lot of them earlier on, I know that for a fact. Not just the two you've already found. There were more – lots more, but I didn't deal with them all. There's still one to go.'

Now it was Stern who found it hard to hold back his tears. The boy was in urgent need of a psychologist, not a lawyer.

'I think that's why I came back again, to finish the job.'

Please don't. Please stop talking.

'To kill him. The last one. Two days from now. In Berlin. On a bridge.'

Simon turned away and looked at the figure of Jesus above the altar. He clasped his hands together, shut his eyes and began to pray.

The Realization

Death is not a phase of existence
but only an intermediate occurrence, a transition
from one form of endless being to another.

Wilhelm von Humboldt

If the soul migrates, that can only work with
a constant number of people. Today, however, there are
six billion of them. Do souls now splinter and divide?
Are ninety-nine per cent of them empty vessels?

From an Internet forum on the
possibility of reincarnation

Science has ascertained that nothing can disappear
without trace. Nature does not know extinction; all it
knows is transformation. Everything science has taught me,
and continues to teach me, strengthens my belief in
the continuity of our spiritual existence after death.

Wernher von Braun

If all who claim that they witnessed
Christ's crucifixion in an earlier life had really
been present, the Roman soldiers would probably not
have found any standing room on that occasion.

Ian Stevenson

1

Engler could scarcely find words to describe how pissed off he was with the whole situation as he ducked beneath the crime-scene tape and, with a curt gesture, relinquished the site to the forensic pathologist. He had planned to spend the afternoon watching television in his warm bed, armed with a jumbo box of tissues, four aspirins and a six-pack of beer, while other people did the work for him. Instead, he was having to search for a dead body in a downpour. Or, more precisely, for the rest of it. The head that had been found in the Rottweiler's grave was so small, it could be taken away in a ladies' shoebox once forensics were through.

Fuming, Engler splashed through a puddle and plodded over to the temporary shelter just behind the fence. The downpour had grown heavier by the minute since their arrival, and Brandmann had to poke the plastic tarpaulin roof with a stick at regular intervals, sending torrents of rainwater cascading over the sides.

'Shit!' Some of the latest flood had found its way down the special investigator's neck. Not for the first time, Engler wondered how such a clumsy oaf could have made it into the Federal CID. He couldn't wait for the overgrown schoolboy to leave. Then they would at last be able to revert to the tried and tested operational procedures they normally used.

‘How’s your head?’ Brandmann asked when Engler squeezed into the shelter beside him, shivering.

‘What do you mean, head? The bugger rammed a stun gun into my back.’

‘And you’re sure it wasn’t Stern?’

‘How many more times?’ Engler suppressed an urge to send a mouthful of phlegm onto Brandmann’s shoes. ‘I could only see the man’s eyes. He was wearing a surgical mask, a white coat and probably a wig. No, I’m not sure, but his voice sounded different and he looked a bit shorter.’

‘Funny. I bet we’ll find Stern’s prints at the scene.’

‘And I bet we—’

Engler broke off in mid-sentence, fished out his vibrating mobile and looked at the scratched display, which was signalling a call from an unknown number. He put a finger to his lips – although Brandmann wasn’t trying to say anything for once – and opened the phone.

‘Hello?’

‘Was I right?’ he heard Robert Stern’s familiar voice ask.

2

Engler sniffed. He nodded gratefully to the uniformed policewoman who had just handed him a cardboard cup of steaming coffee.

'Afraid so, yes. The coffin contained a skull.'

'Human?'

'Yes, but why did the information come from you? How did you know about the grave?'

Stern paused as if the answer had slipped his mind.

'From Simon,' he said eventually.

Engler thought for a moment, then put the call on speaker. The hands-free facility of his police-issue mobile was so poor that Brandmann had to crowd him so as not to miss the conversation.

'That's crap, Stern. Come on, what's your personal involvement in this?'

'I can't tell you that.'

Two loudly arguing policemen approached the shelter. Silenced by Engler's furious gestures, they promptly veered off out of earshot.

'How come you're calling me again?'

'I need some time. Take my tip-off about the graveyard as proof that I've nothing to hide. Simon is as much of a riddle to me as he is to you. I'll crack it, but only if you leave me alone.'

'Afraid it's too late for that now.'

'Why? I haven't committed any crime.'

'I take a different view. We found your car. It happened to be parked near the premises of a haulage firm in Moabit.'

'So give me a ticket if it was in a no-parking zone.'

'We got a description of the man who opened the freezer with the body in it. It fits you, curiously enough. Funny, no? Talking about parking restrictions, there was a black four-wheel drive double-parked outside Tiefensee's practice in the Hackescher Markt. Were you there too?'

'No.'

'But a certain Andreas Borchert was – we checked the licence number. It seems you and the rapist are all buddy-buddies again.'

'Andi was acquitted.'

'So was O.J. Simpson. But enough of that. What's more important is, I've had to cordon off another crime scene thanks to you.'

'Would I have informed you about these murders if they were down to me?'

'No. I don't believe you're a killer, Stern.'

They were the only words that tripped off Engler's tongue.

The sun had gone down and the light had steadily faded the longer the conversation lasted. Engler was grateful for the inspection lamp that was dispelling a little of the gloom inside the shelter. He hesitated and cast an enquiring glance at Brandmann.

Should he really do it? He was very reluctant to, but Brandmann gave him an encouraging nod, so he stuck to the strategy they'd previously agreed in consultation with Chief Superintendent Hertzlich.

'All right, I'm going to give you some info, but only

because it'll be in all the papers tomorrow morning. The name of the guy with the axe in his skull was Harald Zucker. The one in the freezer was Samuel Probtyeszki. We hadn't heard anything of them for fifteen and twelve years respectively. Would you like to know why we couldn't have given a shit about them till now?'

'They were criminals.'

'Correct. Villains of the first order. Murder, rape, prostitution, torture. They worked their way through all the capital crimes in the penal code and left a bloodstained trail the length and breadth of the country. We still haven't managed to clear up the mess they left behind.'

Engler heard Brandmann light a cigarette.

'Zucker and Probtyeszki belonged to a gang of psychopaths. They weren't the only ones to disappear over the years. We failed to trace a total of seven of them.'

In the distance, forensics officers were combing the rain-sodden field with halogen spotlights. Two of the team were down in the mud in their white overalls, digging up another grave. Pluto might not be the only resident here. Engler couldn't help thinking of Charlie. Fortunately, a girlfriend of his was looking after the poor beast today and taking him for his walkies, though he doubted if the Labrador would enjoy it in this rain.

'What about this latest find?' Stern asked. He sounded rather absent, as though still digesting the information he'd just been given. 'How does it fit into the series? A child, wasn't it?'

'Yes. We think he was a ten-year-old boy named Lucas Schneider. He's down to Probtyeszki – the victim of an unsuccessful ransom attempt on the gang's part. His body was discovered on a rubbish dump, but we never managed to find the head. Until today.'

Engler groped in his trousers for a handkerchief. He failed

to find it in time, so he sneezed through his mouth and pinched his nose at the same time. Someone had warned him that this built up pressure in the head and laid him open to the risk of a stroke, but he could hardly imagine the sword of Damocles would descend on him in an animal cemetery, of all places.

'Why are you telling me all this?' he heard Stern ask. He looked indignantly at Brandmann. That was just the question he himself had asked earlier on, during their conference with Hertzlich. It was such a cheap trick, any fool was bound to see through it. Stern certainly would.

'Because I know what your game is,' Engler replied reluctantly, as agreed.

'Really? I can't wait to hear.'

'You're no pro, Stern, you make too many mistakes. The only smart thing you've done so far is to exchange your mobile for the satellite phone you're calling me on right now, but you probably got that tip from Borchert.'

'I'm not on the run. I haven't murdered anyone.'

'I'm not saying you have.'

'Well?'

'OK, I'll summarize the facts for you. Number one, seven psychopaths have disappeared from the scene in recent years. Number two, you've delivered two of them to us – as stiffs. And number three, you're a defence lawyer by trade.'

Engler heard Stern groan at the other end of the line.

'What are you getting at?'

'It's your profession, associating with scum. This has nothing to do with Simon Sachs. He's just window dressing. I suspect that one of your perverted clients has been tipping you off about the location of the bodies.'

'Why should anyone do that? For what purpose?'

'Maybe this client has hidden something with the victims – something you're supposed to get for him. No idea what, but you'll tell me in due course. As soon as I've arrested you.'

'That's a ridiculous idea. Totally absurd.'

Engler waved away a cloud of Brandmann's cigarette smoke, which was wafting into his eyes.

'You think so? The judge considered it very believable half an hour ago, when he signed a warrant for your arrest. We're killing three birds with one stone, by the way. Carina Freitag and Andreas Borchert are being charged with aiding and abetting the abduction of a minor.'

Engler hung up, still fuming. He couldn't understand why Brandmann was holding out his fleshy paw.

'What is it?' he demanded, incensed at the way the conversation had gone. In his view, it had taken a wholly mistaken direction.

'Your mobile,' said Brandmann.

'What for?'

'To give to the technical boys. They may be able to pinpoint the call. Even when a number is withheld—'

'There's a possibility of tracing the caller. I'm aware of that.' Engler tossed him the mobile and took a step closer. 'That was the last time. I'm never doing that again, OK?'

'What?'

'That charade. I may be wrong – Stern may have something to do with the murders after all – but we're shooting ourselves in the foot if we let him in on our investigations.'

'I disagree. Didn't you hear his voice? It steadily rose in pitch. That means you scared him. Stern is a beginner at this. He's an inexperienced, nervous civilian on the run with a cancer-ridden youngster in tow. If he gets any more nervous he'll make a mistake. He'll trip up and come a cropper, and then, to borrow the chief's expression, we can squash him like a bug.'

Brandmann dropped his cigarette butt on the muddy

grass and ground it out with his right heel, exerting his full weight like someone trying to drive a nail into a thick plank. He left the shelter without another word and, avoiding a number of small puddles, plodded down the hillside towards his car.

Engler watched him go. As the bizarre special investigator gradually disappeared from view, he tried to remember if he knew anyone at Federal CID headquarters who could get him a copy of his personal file.

3

Stern pressed his burning cheek against the one-way mirror.

Seven psychopaths have disappeared from the scene in recent years.

The detective's words reverberated in his head as he looked down at the gleaming dancefloor twenty metres below him.

The office presided like a glass crow's nest over the heart of the complex, which could only have been designed by a would-be ship's captain. Even from the outside the giant club resembled a ship. Its emblem, a floodlit pink funnel, loomed over the main building's snow-white bow. Visible for kilometres after nightfall, it attracted the disco-dancing teenagers of Brandenburg like a magnet. Borchert still had a key, which was why the Titanic was providing them with a hideaway for the next three hours. At least until the club opened to the public.

Stern moved to join his three companions on the dancefloor. As he rode down in a glass-sided lift worthy of a five-star hotel, he wondered how to break it to them. From here on they were fugitives from the law. Andi Borchert was familiar with that situation, but for Carina it would definitely be a first. He didn't hear the music until the lift door opened.

'Hey, the boy's got good taste,' Borchert sang out. He

was standing at the other end of the floor with Simon, wiggling his hips. The boy was laughing delightedly and clapping in time to the rock song blaring from the speakers.

'He's hooked up Simon's MP3 to the in-house sound system,' Carina explained. Stern, who hadn't seen her coming up behind him, gave a start.

Fifteen metres away Borchert was singing with his head back and trailing an invisible mike lead behind him like a dog leash.

Stern came straight to the point without trying to sweeten the pill. 'We'll have to turn ourselves in,' he said, and went on to summarize his conversation with Engler. 'I'm sorry,' he concluded, searching Carina's face in vain for any signs of alarm.

'You needn't be,' she replied. 'I brought the two of you together. You wouldn't be in this mess if it wasn't for me.'

'Why are you taking it all so calmly?' Stern was suddenly reminded of a scene two years ago. In the McDonald's car park, where he had terminated their relationship and Carina had smiled anyway.

'Because it's been worth it.'

'I don't understand.'

'Just look over there. I've known Simon for eighteen months, and I've seldom seen him so happy.'

Stern saw Borchert beckoning to him. He wondered if he would ever see the world through Carina's eyes. They had actually spent a mere ten days together when he ended their affair to avoid falling genuinely in love with her. When she'd smiled and gently stroked his cheek in farewell, he discovered something important about himself. He realized that he lacked the existential filter that enabled Carina to fade out the negative in any given set of circumstances, however unpleasant. She was the kind of person who would discover a rose on the edge of a battlefield.

Now, once again, he saw that same light in her eyes and those tiny laughter lines around her mouth. To Carina at that moment, no criminals, no cerebral tumour or arrest warrant mattered. She was simply happy to see a child disco-dancing for the first time. Stern, by contrast, was becoming more and more depressed – consumed with pity for a boy who would never get into hot water for coming home too late on a Saturday night after a prolonged necking session with his first love.

As if in tune with Stern's negative thoughts, another track began. The hall was filled with the melancholy strains of a ballad with string backing.

'Hey, they're playing your song!' said Borchert. Grinning, he disappeared behind an ornamental Ionic column. Moments later there was a hiss and the dancefloor was enveloped in a cloud of dry ice.

'Cool!' Simon cried delightedly, sitting down on the floor. Only his curly brown head protruded from the artificial fog.

Stern felt Carina take his hand. 'We must get him back to the hospital,' he protested.

'Come on. Only for a minute.'

She led him on to the dancefloor just as she had led him into her bedroom that first night. As before, he didn't know why he let it happen.

'We can't—'

'Ssh . . .' She put her finger on his lips and stroked his hair. Then she drew him towards her just as the refrain began.

Stern hesitated, still reluctant to return her cautious embrace. He felt like a parcel bearing a 'Fragile' sticker. Afraid of damaging something inside him if he held her close, he eventually overcame his foolish fear and put out his arms to her.

He couldn't help thinking as he did so of the fleeting

moment in Borchert's car when he'd seen Simon asleep in her arms in the rear-view mirror. He had been unable to identify his emotion at first, but he knew now that what had filled him once more was a mixture of yearning and remorse. Yearning for Felix as well as for a similarly loving embrace. Remorse that he had denied Carina two things by rejecting her so abruptly: a child of her own and someone for whom she still, quite clearly, had feelings. Even though he couldn't have been less deserving of them.

Carina, who sensed the contradictory emotions warring within him, demolished the last remaining physical barrier between them by nestling against him. Intoxicated by the feel of her warm, clinging body, Stern closed his eyes. His regrets evaporated, but not, alas, for long. The magic moment when he seemed to feel their hearts beating in time to the music was rudely interrupted by a high-pitched beep. He froze in Carina's arms.

Impossible!

Borchert had told him that nobody knew the number. Despite this, the satellite phone in his trouser pocket had just received a text message.

4

'Dammit, what's going on?'

'I've no idea.'

Borchert keyed an Internet address into the text field and clicked on 'Change to'.

'You said you'd never given anyone the number.'

'Yes, yes, yes, give it a rest. I only use the thing in an emergency, and then *I* do the calling, OK?'

Like a number of Berlin entrepreneurs, Borchert didn't put everything through his official books. When he was holding illegal conversations with his accountant, corrupt drinks suppliers or moonlighters, he called them by satellite phone. Now that the others had followed his advice and removed the batteries from their mobiles, the bulky satphone was their only link with the outside world.

'So what *is* going on?'

'We'll soon know, *mes enfants*.'

Borchert got up from the desk and made room for Stern, who took his place in front of the flat screen. They had all gone up to the boss's office after the text message came in. It consisted of only one line:

http://gmtp.sorbjana.org/net.fmx/eu.html

Nothing happened at first. The browser continued to display the Titanic club's homepage. Carina read out the message in the bottom left corner: 'Searching for proxy settings.'

Then the screen went black. A bright load bar appeared in the centre, and ten seconds later a postcard-sized video field opened up. Stern could see nothing of any significance, just a few erratic specks of light flashing across the dark field at irregular intervals, like shooting stars.

Borchert turned the loudspeaker boxes up to maximum volume, but it made no difference.

'No picture, no sound,' he muttered. 'What the—'

He was just saying 'Balls!' when the satphone rang. This time the square display signalled 'Caller unknown'.

Stern's stomach rumbled as he picked up.

5

'You haven't kept to our agreement.'

The distortion was slightly modified. The voice sounded rather more human, and, for that very reason, far more menacing than it had on the DVD.

Stern wondered why the speaker didn't dispense with a voice changer altogether. He had recognized the voice from those few undistorted words he'd heard at Tiefensee's practice.

'What gives you that idea?' he asked evasively. And pointlessly.

'Don't lie to me – don't even think of it. You can do that with the police. They're stupid, I'm not.'

'All right, I did call Engler, but only because I wanted to gain time. I didn't say anything about the DVD and our agreement.'

'I know. If you had, the twins would be dead.'

The image on the screen jumped violently and changed colour. To Stern it looked as if someone had inserted a tinted filter over the lens. The video shots took on a greenish hue, and Stern could at last recognize what they were being shown. His stomach muscles tensed.

'I think my night-vision camera gives an excellent picture of the graveyard, don't you?' said the voice. 'You see our friend Engler over there? And his obese colleague Brandmann blithely smoking a filterless cigarette. I'm sitting in the dry, fortunately, while those poor devils are doing overtime in the rain because of you.'

'How did you get this number?' To Stern, that was the burning question right now.

'My dear lawyer, your naivety really surprises me sometimes. Surely you must have gathered by now how I earn my living. My favourite stamping ground is the Internet. That's where I offer my wares for sale and where I obtain my information. Ask Borchert how he pays his satphone bill.'

'Online,' Borchert whispered.

'You see? I'm not only good at covering my tracks on the Net, I'm an expert information-gatherer.'

'Why are you calling?'

'I want to show you something.'

It was as if a blood vessel had burst behind Stern's eardrum. He heard a whistling sound that gave way to a roar then an unpleasant sensation of deafness.

'Do you recognize them?'

Carina clapped a hand over her mouth. The night-vision images on the screen disappeared, and the trio watching now became witnesses to an agonizingly slow camera sequence. It began with a shot of a nursery door being opened by a ghostly hand and ended with a close-up of two little girls asleep. Frieda and Natalie.

Although Stern hadn't seen Sophie's children very often, he was in no doubt that these were her four-year-old twins.

'Why are you doing this?'

'To show you that I can.'

The message was all too clear: the voice was omnipresent. It was watching his every step and would not shrink from murdering two little children to get what it wanted. Carina was right: no one this evil and this well equipped with technological gadgets would need to rely on his services as an informant, so what did the voice really want from him?

As Stern was asking himself this question the screen displayed a different picture. All he saw at first were some unsteady shots of drab expanses of concrete and asphalt that might have been filmed by someone out jogging. Their quality was very poor and grainy, and Stern couldn't make out anything much until the camera zoomed in and panned upwards.

'That's a door over there,' said Carina. Stern and Borchert spotted it a moment later.

'What is this?' Stern asked with the satphone to his ear.

The voice chuckled. 'Look familiar?'

'No.' The point of these amateurish shots escaped him.

Blurred pictures taken by someone running towards a closed door? He hadn't the least idea of their purpose until Borchert gave a sudden exclamation and thumped his bald head.

'Shit, I don't believe this!'

Carina looked alarmed. 'Why, what is it?'

'Well, Andi?' Stern demanded.

Borchert ignored them both. He opened the top drawer of the desk, then the next one down. The bottom drawer yielded what he was looking for: a 9mm automatic.

'What door is it?' Stern shouted the words so loudly that Simon, who was sitting on the sofa, put his hands over his ears.

Borchert didn't answer, just pointed to an illuminated red button on the desk beside the computer. It was flashing. *On. Off. On. Off.*

'The staff entrance,' he said hoarsely and pointed to the screen. 'Someone just rang the bell.'

6

Love is . . .

Just a greetings card. Nothing else.

When Borchert wrenched the door open, gun in hand, and dashed outside with the safety catch off, Stern had fully expected to be the helpless witness to an execution.

'He won't be on his own, Andi. They'll kill you. You'll die if you go out there!'

Borchert had ignored all Stern's warnings with an expression that made the lawyer doubt his former client's sanity. It looked as if his basest instincts had taken over.

Once outside, however, Borchert found no one to do battle with. Nothing but a laminated, salmon-coloured greetings card.

Stern fished the envelope off the doormat while Borchert vented his pent-up aggression.

'Come back, you yellow bastard!' he yelled. 'Come back and I'll fill you full of holes!'

His voice rang out across the rainswept backyard and carried as far as the woods into which the voice's errand boy had obviously high-tailed it.

Love is . . . – Stern opened the card – *. . . when you can tell each other everything*. Beneath this vapid preprinted message, in handwritten capitals, were the words ANY NEWS?

'Well, do you like my little token of affection?'

Anxious not to miss a word the voice uttered, Stern had kept the satphone glued to his ear while they were running downstairs to the staff entrance. Now it had resumed their conversation.

'What's the point of these theatricals?'

Disgustedly, Stern spat the words into the phone. He noticed only now how much Borchert's outburst had pumped him up too. Maybe it wasn't a good idea to yell at his potential murderer, but maybe he had nothing to lose anyway.

'You're sick.'

'That's a matter of opinion.'

Despite its artificial distortion, the deep voice was as penetrating as the bass notes at a rock concert.

'The first day of your ultimatum is already over. It would interest me to know what you've found out.'

The voice was accompanied through the ether by the distant blare of an HGV sounding its horn.

'Why ask me when you already know everything anyway? The man in the freezer. The child's head in the dog's grave. Good God, you're actually there. What more can *I* tell you?'

'Something that leads me to the killer of Harald Zucker and Samuel Probtyeszki. Think. What did the boy tell you today?'

'Nothing much.' Stern cleared his throat. He was already hoarse from talking so much, but he could also have caught a cold in this lousy weather. 'I don't know what to make of it myself,' he went on reluctantly. 'Simon says he isn't finished yet. He says he's going to kill someone else.'

'Give him to me.'

'The boy, you mean?'

'Yes, I want a word with him.'

Stern looked round. He had followed Carina and Borchert while talking, blind to his surroundings. They were back at the edge of the dancefloor. Simon's MP3 player had fallen silent, but the sweetish smell of dry ice still lingered in the air, which would soon be thick with the emanations of hundreds of dancers.

'No, that's not on.' Stern looked over at Simon, who had seated himself at the champagne bar and was spinning around on a leather-topped bar stool.

'It wasn't a request.' The voice became more peremptory with every word it uttered. 'Call the boy to the phone, I want to speak to him. At once. Or shall I show you the twins again? You wouldn't want them to wind up like Tiefensee, surely?'

Stern shut his eyes, squeezing the eyelids together so tightly that the darkness behind them filled with bright flashes. He felt sick at the thought of what he was about to do to Simon.

7

'Yes, hello?'

'Hello there, Simon.'

The boy was puzzled by the curious quality of the stranger's voice.

'Your voice sounds funny. And how do you know my name?'

'Robert told me.'

'Oh, I see. What's your name?'

'I don't have one.'

'What do you mean? Everyone's got a name.'

'No, not everyone. Take God, for instance. He doesn't have one.'

'But you aren't God.'

'Maybe not, but I'm quite like him.'

'How?'

'Because I make people die sometimes. Just like that, understand? People like Carina and Robert. You're fond of them, aren't you?'

Simon opened and closed his left hand. His arm was tingling, and he knew what that meant. The doctors, who always looked worried when he told them about it, carried out tests and passed electric currents through his fingers. He still couldn't understand, even now, why the nerves on the left-hand side of his body should act up if the tumour was on the right-hand side of his brain.

'You're scaring me,' he whispered, clinging to the chromium-plated rail that ran along the edge of the champagne bar's stainless steel counter.

'I'll stop it if you answer me one question.'

'And you won't do anything to them?'

'Word of honour. But you must tell me something in return.'

'What?'

'Robert Stern said you want to kill someone else. Is that true?'

'No. I don't *want* to but I know I'm going to.'

'OK, so you know it. Who is this man? Who are you going to kill?'

'I don't know his name.'

'What does he look like?'

'I don't know that either.'

'Think of Robert and Carina. Take another close look at them, please. You don't want them to die, do you?'

Simon followed orders and turned to look. Carina and Stern were flanking him at the counter. The satphone had no loudspeaker, so they had moved as close to him as possible in order to catch at least some snatches of the horrific dialogue.

'No, I don't want them to die.'

'Good, because there's something you should know. Whether they live or die depends on you. You alone.'

The tingling in Simon's arm ebbed and flowed. At the moment it was flowing fast.

'But what am I supposed to tell you? I only know the day it will happen.'

'Which is?'

'The day after tomorrow.'

'November 1st?'

'Yes. At six o'clock in the morning.'

'Where?'

'I'll meet a man on a bridge, that's all I know.'

Simon removed the phone from his ear as the ugly laughter on the line grew louder and louder.

8

'All right, that's enough.'

Stern had retrieved the phone. To him, the voice at the other end sounded as if its owner was having an asthma attack. Then he realized the laughter was directed at him.

'What's so funny?'

'Nothing whatsoever. Goodbye.'

Bang.

It was like a door slamming inside Stern. He felt cold.

'What do you mean? What am I to do now?'

'Nothing at all.'

'But when . . .' He started stammering in his bewilderment. 'I mean, when will you call me again?'

'Never.'

Bang.

The door was bolted, cutting him off for good from all that was happening here.

'But . . . I don't understand. I haven't given you a name yet.' Out of the corner of his eye, Stern saw Simon sink down on a sofa and lie back.

'No, that's why our deal just fell through.'

'You won't tell me what you know about Felix?'

'No.'

'But why not? What have I done wrong?'

'Nothing at all.'

'Then please reinstate the deadline we agreed on. You said I had five days. It's only Saturday. I'll get you the name of the murderer and you tell me who the boy with the birthmark is.'

Stern registered Carina's look of surprise. He was surprised at the unprecedented note of entreaty in his own voice.

'Oh, I can tell you that now. He's your son Felix, and he lives in a nice place with his adoptive parents.'

'What! Where?'

'Why should I tell you?'

'Because I'm sticking to our agreement. I'll take you to the murderer, I promise.'

'I'm afraid that won't be necessary now.'

'Why not?'

'Think it over very carefully. The man on the bridge the day after tomorrow will be me.'

'I don't understand.'

'Yes, you do. *I'm* the one with the appointment in two days' time. Simon intends to kill *me*. You've just found that out, and that's enough of a warning for me. I don't need any more information from you. Goodbye, Mr Lawyer.'

Stern thought he heard a faint, derisive mwah-mwah before the line went dead.

9

The car's broad-gauge tyres were speeding over the wet asphalt of the dual carriageway. Seated in the back beside Simon, who was asleep, Stern tried to catch a glimpse of what was going on inside the grey blocks of flats gliding past. He longed to see something real and ordinary. Not people opening coffins or cutting dead men down from ceilings, but normal families preparing supper with the TV flickering or friends visiting for the weekend. Sadly, the lights of everyday life were flying past him far too quickly.

Almost as fast as his own tangled thoughts.

Criminals. Villains of the first order. Murder, rape, prostitution, torture. They worked their way through all the capital crimes in the penal code . . .

'What did you say?' asked Carina, who was sitting up front.

She was just gathering her abundant hair into a ponytail. Stern hadn't realized he was thinking aloud.

'If Engler's telling the truth, the murdered men were renowned for their brutality.'

They left a bloodstained trail the length and breadth of the country. We still haven't managed to clear up the mess they left.

'Until someone appeared on the scene who murdered the

murderers,' said Borchert, smacking his lips. Already on his third piece of gum since driving away from the Titanic, he'd revealed an unpleasant habit: he stuck the discarded wads to the dashboard.

'Yes, an avenger, if Simon is to be believed. He has eliminated them all in turn. All except the last one. The voice may even have been the boss of the outfit.'

Stern leaned forward, gripping the nape of his neck. The muscles were bone-hard with tension.

'At least that would explain why he's so obsessed with hunting for the killer of his pals.' Borchert looked in the rear-view mirror. 'The lengths he goes to, it has to be something personal.'

It would also mean that the biggest psychopath of all is the only person who knows where Felix is – who may even have him in his power.

Stern kept these thoughts to himself although he guessed that Carina was perceptive enough to share them.

'I have to go on,' he said quietly, more to himself than the others. 'I can't stop now.'

He knew that his decision was based on two irrational hypotheses. On the one hand, he assumed that Simon's vision of a murder in the future would prove as accurate as his memories of the past. On the other, he believed the voice's assertion that his son was still alive. Both were impossibilities even though he already had objective proof of them: the voice *knew* about the bridge and *knew* the exact date of the confrontation.

'Do you believe Simon will prove to be right again?' Borchert asked as if he'd read Stern's thoughts. Until now, Stern had thought that only Carina possessed that ability.

'I don't know.'

Perhaps someone really would appear on that bridge the day after tomorrow. Intent on killing.

But who?

Despite everything, Stern was unwilling to believe that Simon was a reincarnated serial murderer who had returned to earth to carry out his final execution. There had to be someone else, a real-life avenger, and he had to find him if he wanted to get to the bottom of the mystery surrounding Felix.

The bridge is the key. I must find it.

He was about to share that thought with Borchert and Carina when Simon's foot began to twitch uncontrollably.

10

'Stop!' Stern shouted to Borchert. 'Pull over!'

Still on the motorway, they were just passing the broad expanse of Tempelhof Airport.

'Why, what . . . Oh, shit!' Borchert had only glanced over his shoulder, but he realized immediately why he was getting nudged in the back through the seat. Simon was having a fit. Although Stern was bearing down on his leg as hard as he could, it kept lashing out. At the same time, the boy was rolling his eyes like a madman.

'I'll pull on to the hard shoulder,' said Borchert, signalling right.

'No, don't do that!'

Carina unbuckled her seat belt and climbed over the passenger seat into the back. Stern was concentrating so hard on Simon, he scarcely noticed at first. The boy's convulsions were steadily intensifying. His lips were blowing frothy bubbles and his head was shaking so violently to and fro that his wig had slipped sideways. 'Move over,' said Carina, not waiting for Stern to react, just squeezing in between him and Simon. She ended up half on his lap.

'My bag,' she hissed. 'I need my goddamned . . . thanks.'

Borchert passed it back to her. She unzipped it, took out

another bag about the size of a sponge bag, and rummaged around inside it.

Stern looked surprised. 'Why don't we pull over?'

'Park on the hard shoulder in a stolen car? What do you think?'

Carina had found a disposable syringe in the medicine bag. She removed the protective cap with her teeth and spat it into the footwell. Then she took out a little glass bottle, shook it and turned it upside down. Finally, she inserted the needle through the seal.

'Let's keep going, it's less conspicuous.'

Borchert nodded. He had 'borrowed' the Mercedes estate from the Titanic's underground car park, and it was not beyond the bounds of possibility that its owner had already notified the police.

'Less conspicuous?' Stern said excitedly. 'You mean you're prepared to let the boy die rather than risk arrest?'

'Robert?' Carina removed the syringe, now full, and held it up in front of his nose.

'Yes?'

'Shut up.'

She pinned Simon's head back against the head rest with the flat of her hand and deftly squirted the contents of the syringe into the right-hand side of his mouth. He quietened within seconds, as if she had pulled out an invisible electric plug. His foot stopped twitching, his eyes closed, his breathing steadied. Another minute, and the exhausted boy fell asleep in Carina's arms.

'This is crazy. It's got to stop.' Borchert was still making no attempt to pull over, so Stern had climbed up front, hoping to get to grips with the situation from the passenger seat. 'Take the next exit. The boy's in urgent need of medical assistance. He belongs in a hospital, not in this nightmare.'

'Oh yes? Why?'

'Why? Are you blind? You saw him yourself—'

'Know what I hate about you smart-arse lawyers?' Carina broke in. 'You're always shooting your mouth off about things you don't understand. This was a straightforward epileptic fit. Not nice, but it doesn't call for intensive care. Simon should have been given his carbamazepine a bit sooner, then he wouldn't have needed this emergency treatment.'

'What are you talking about? The question isn't *what* he had but *why* he had it. There's a tumour growing inside his skull. You don't go running around zoos with that, let alone digging up dead bodies.'

'You're talking bullshit again. You don't know the first thing about Simon's condition. Simon has a frontal lobe tumour, but that doesn't mean he needs medical supervision 24/7. He gets that only when he's undergoing chemo or radiotherapy. He spends only two weeks out of six at the hospital. If Professor Müller wasn't currently re-reassessing him with a view to the possibility of resuming radiotherapy, he'd be living in a normal children's home.'

'Even that would be better than racing around from one place to the next.'

Borchert had suggested spending the night at a club belonging to another acquaintance of his, which, he claimed, had a secret back room that would elude the most rigorous police raid.

'Know what Simon would say to us if he were awake?' Stern said angrily. 'He'd tell us to leave him alone.'

Carina shook her head vigorously. 'On the contrary, he'd say *don't* leave me alone. He doesn't like the nights, I know because he told me. He gets scared, not only at the children's home but at the hospital as well. You saw how happy he was earlier on. At the zoo, in the car, dancing, and so on.'

'He has also wept, seen dead bodies and had convulsions.'

'He suffers from those anyway. We can alleviate them by

being with him when he wakes up. Besides, Robert, you seem to have forgotten something. This is about Simon first and foremost, not about you and Felix. The boy is going to die, and I don't want him dying in the belief that he's a murderer, understand? That's why I got in touch with you. We can't stop him dying, but we can relieve him of his feelings of guilt. You've no idea how sensitive he is. It genuinely torments him to think that he has harmed someone. After all the shit he's had to take in the course of his brief life, he simply doesn't deserve that.'

Stern stared through the windscreen, at a loss as to how to reply. Fundamentally, Carina had come to the same conclusion as he had. Futile though it seemed to run from the police with a cancer-ridden child in the hope of getting to the bottom of his reincarnation fantasies, turning themselves in seemed equally pointless. Engler would question them all for hours and remand them in custody. He certainly wouldn't believe their story or try to prevent a possible confrontation between two murderers on some bridge or other. Besides, Berlin had more bridges than Venice.

Whatever crime was committed at 6 a.m. in two days' time, it would happen unobserved. If they were separated from Simon and his mysterious knowledge, Stern would neither be able to prevent that crime nor ever learn what had happened to Felix in the neonatal ward.

'Can you really look after the boy all right on your own?' Borchert unexpectedly butted into the conversation, glancing at Carina in the rear-view mirror as he did so.

'There are no cast-iron guarantees, but I've got everything with me. Cortisone, his anticonvulsives and, if absolutely necessary, some diazepam suppositories.'

Stern was watching a motorcyclist ahead of them change lanes every ten seconds. He looked as if he was practising for a slalom race.

'That's not enough, though,' he said after a while. He raised his arms and clasped them behind his head.

'Why not?' Carina demanded from the back seat. 'He's got a nurse, a lawyer and a bodyguard at his side 24/7. What more does he need?'

'You'll soon see.'

Stern lowered his right arm and signalled to Borchert to leave the motorway at the Köpenick turn-off. Ten minutes later they parked outside a house that he had never, ever meant to visit again.

11

When she slapped his face he knew she wouldn't turn them away. Sophie's first blow, a half-hearted push in the chest, had been laughably ineffective. This had only infuriated her more, so she prepared to deliver another. He could have turned away and blocked or at least parried it with his arm. Instead, he merely shut his eyes in expectation of the full-blooded slap that stung the left-hand side of his face from his ear to his lower jaw.

'How *could* you?' his ex-wife demanded in a muffled voice. He knew she was asking him three questions at once. *Why did you take Felix from me when I didn't want to give him up? Why turn up with this bimbo ten years later? And how could you reopen old wounds by coming here with a dying child?*

He went over to the sink, held a clean tea towel under the cold tap and dabbed his crimson, smarting cheek. The kitchen of this detached house in relatively rural Köpenick, with its homely pinewood furniture, made a totally unsuitable venue for an altercation. The carefree, tranquil atmosphere that Sophie and her family had created for themselves was as obvious there as elsewhere.

No wonder she hadn't wanted to let him in twenty minutes earlier, when he climbed the brick steps to her porch. Borchert had dropped them off and driven on to find a bolt-hole of his own. Sophie had hesitated only because of the sleeping boy in Stern's arms and only for a moment, but that was enough. Stern had seized his chance and simply walked in with Carina at his heels.

'The police were here.' Sophie leaned wearily against the island unit in the middle of the kitchen, which had an array of antique-looking copper saucepans hanging above it. Stern wondered if they were just there for decorative purposes, but the smiling husband in the photo on the fridge looked like an amateur cook who might know how to use them. The couple probably stood at the stove together after a hard day's work, sampling the gravy and laughingly chasing the twins into the living room when they tried to snaffle a titbit.

If for that reason alone, leaving him had been the right decision on Sophie's part. The only time he'd ever tried to give her a culinary treat, even the deep-frozen pizza had been a flop.

'What did you tell them?' he asked.

'The truth. An Inspector Brandmann questioned me. I really didn't have a clue where you were or what you'd done. And to be quite honest, Robert, I don't want to know.'

'Mummy?'

Sophie turned to see Frieda standing barefoot in the doorway with a doll in her hand. Her faded Snoopy T-shirt hung well below her knees.

'What is it, sweetheart? You should have been in bed ages ago.'

'I was, but I wanted to show Cinderella to Simon.'

'All right, but be quick.'

'She doesn't have any stockings on!'

Pouting, the fair-haired little girl held out her favourite doll, bare plastic legs foremost. Sophie opened a drawer and unearthed two woollen socks the size of finger stalls.

'Are these what you're looking for?'

'Yes!' Frieda beamed. She took the miniature socks from Sophie and padded out of the kitchen.

'I'll come and turn the light out in a minute,' Sophie called after her. The maternal smile promptly vanished and Stern found himself confronted once more by a face as angry as it had been before the interruption. Neither of them spoke for a minute. Then he pointed to the phone on the wall.

'Call the police if you like. I can well understand your not wanting to get involved in my problems, especially if your husband left on a business trip this morning.'

Sophie put her head on one side and her eyes darkened. 'You haven't changed, have you? You still think I can't cope without male protection.'

'I wouldn't know. I don't know you any more.'

'So why did you come to me, of all people?'

'Because I'm being blackmailed.'

'Who by?'

'Someone who sent me a video of Felix dying.'

Sophie's face seemed to go transparent all of a sudden, the blood left it so abruptly.

'Was that it? Was that why you called me in the middle of the night?'

Stern nodded. He tried to tell her the story as gently as possible: the DVD, the final shots of their baby, and the anonymous voice's demand. He deliberately omitted the boy with the birthmark, nor did he mention the threat to kill her twins. Unlike him, Sophie had almost succeeded in crossing the threshold into a new life. Renewed doubts about Felix's death would send her crashing back into a slough of melancholia and self-pity, and the fear that her little daughters might meet a violent end would have the same result. So he lied to her – told her that the voice had sent him the DVD as proof of his own omnipotence and had threatened to murder Simon if he didn't cooperate.

'Are you really sure . . .' she began haltingly. She was about to try again but stopped short when Stern nodded.

'Yes, I saw it with my own eyes.'

'And how? I mean, how did he . . .'

'The way the doctors said. He simply stopped breathing.'

A dark, expanding patch appeared on Sophie's cream silk blouse. It was a moment before he recognized its source as her silent tears.

'Why?' she sobbed gently. 'Why didn't I look in on him more often?'

Stern went over and took her hand, half expecting a fierce rebuff. She didn't pull away, but neither did she return the pressure of his fingers.

'You were tired. It was a difficult birth.'

Sophie ran her free hand through her hair, staring down at the flagstones. Her voice was thick with tears.

'I can hardly remember his smile or his gummy little eyes or anything else. It's all faded, like the sound of him crying. Even his smell is gradually fading too. Remember that expensive French baby oil we bought? Perhaps that's why I refused to believe it. He smelled so alive the last time I held him. And now . . .'

Stern suddenly grasped what his revelations had done to her. She had evidently cherished an irrational hope all these years, and now it had been dashed.

Leaning forward and looking into her eyes, he saw that her tears had ceased to flow. He released her hand at once. Had he held it any longer, he would have felt like a murderer. Their brief moment of intimacy was over.

Neither of them spoke for a while. Then Stern turned and left the mother of his son alone in the kitchen. In search of Simon, Carina and a place to sleep, he made his way quietly downstairs. He could hear cold, rain-laden gusts of wind spattering the windows. They seemed to herald a stormy night to come.

12

The guest room was on the lower ground floor. Stern took off his shoes and lay down fully dressed between Simon and Carina, who were already sleeping so soundly that they hadn't heard him come in. They were lying beneath a thin bedspread on opposite sides of the big double bed, like an old married couple who had quarrelled and given each other a wide berth before going to sleep.

Stern was grateful for this, which enabled him to squeeze in between them. Carina tended to roam around a bed while sleeping. Another five minutes, and she would have been bound to entwine herself with Simon and take up the whole of the mattress.

Although the heating was on, Stern shivered as his mind's eye recalled the day's horrific images.

The body in the freezer. Tiefensee. The graveyard. And, again and again, the sight of Felix dying.

He turned over on his side and looked at Carina, whose bare shoulder was peeping out from under the covers. He felt tempted to reach out and touch it. Slight though it was, he felt that even the most fleeting contact would give him a sense of security. Her abundant curly hair was spread out on the pillow like a fan. She was also lying on her side.

He smiled. This was just how he had seen her for the

first time: one arm extended, knees drawn up and eyes closed. It was three years since he had yielded to a sudden impulse on the way home to his empty house and turned into the car park of a furniture store. While walking round the bed department he thought he'd caught sight of a remarkably pretty, lifelike mannequin lying on one of the beds. Then Carina opened her eyes and smiled at him. 'Should I buy it?' she asked. An hour later he had helped her to carry the new mattress up to her top-floor flat in Prenzlauer Berg.

Another memory surfaced in his mind: his reason for dumping Carina three years ago. Lying awake beside her after sex, he had experienced how it would feel to forget – how a passionate embrace could expel those tormenting images from his mind and leave him living in the present alone. Just as he had a moment ago, he had withdrawn his outstretched hand because he felt guilty. He had no right to embark on a new life in which his memories of Felix would sooner or later fade like old photographs on a mantelpiece.

The next day he had taken advantage of some trivial disagreement to terminate their affair before it was too late. Before he lost himself in her.

Those and a thousand other thoughts kept Stern awake for another half-hour. Then exhaustion finally, irresistibly, drew him down into the darkness of a dreamless sleep. He was as oblivious to Carina tossing and turning beside him as he was to the earnest gaze focused on the nape of his neck.

Simon waited a little longer. Then, reassured by the lawyer's regular breathing, he cautiously folded back the bedspread and, retrieving his wig from the floor, tiptoed out of the room.

13

Something went smash. The sound had to get through two doors, a staircase and some twenty metres of air before, much diminished in volume, it reached the guest room. Stern groaned and stirred. He had only perceived it subconsciously. What really woke him was a constricted sensation. In the depths of some dream or other, Carina had draped her arm over him.

Still dazed after his far too brief respite, Stern extricated himself from her unintentional embrace. He stretched, his stiff back digging into the mattress, and suddenly froze. Something was wrong. It didn't take him long to discover what had changed in the darkened room.

He swung round, jumped out of bed and hurried into the adjoining bathroom. Simon wasn't there – he'd gone.

Stern wrenched the door open and ran upstairs in his stockinged feet. He had no idea how long he'd slept for. It was dark outside. No light was coming in through the lattice windows, but that could mean anything so late in the year: early evening, midnight, half past four in the morning . . . His eyes were becoming accustomed to the prevailing gloom. Simultaneously, signs of life typical of a sleeping household were infiltrating his consciousness: radiators creaking, the ticking of the grandfather clock in the living room, the hum of the fridge.

The fridge.

Spinning round, he saw light at the end of the passage. It was coming from under the kitchen door.

'Simon?' he called. Soft enough not to wake anyone upstairs, loud enough to be heard by whoever was lying in wait behind the door. He stole along the passage, trying to identify the sounds coming from the room.

Stern wished Borchert was with him. Andi would probably have dashed in without a second thought. It was only with considerable hesitation that he cautiously turned the handle and went in. His heart raced – with relief.

'I'm sorry.' Simon was crouching down, swabbing the milk-splashed flagstones with a tea towel. He looked up at Stern with an apprehensive expression and got to his feet. 'I was thirsty. The mug slipped through my fingers.'

'Not to worry.' Stern gave a wry smile, trying to banish the tension from his face. 'Come here.' He put his arm round the boy and hugged him gently. 'Did something startle you?'

'Yes.'

'A gust of wind?'

'No.'

'What, then?'

'The photo.'

Stern came closer and looked into Simon's eyes. 'What photo?'

'This one.'

Carefully avoiding the milk on the floor, Simon shut the fridge's stainless steel door. The kitchen abruptly went as dark as the passage outside. Stern turned on the ceiling light above the island.

'It reminded me of something,' said Simon.

The snapshot he removed from the door of the freezer compartment must have been taken at least four years earlier.

It showed Sophie's husband smiling rather nervously at the camera as he strove to keep his baby daughters' heads above the surface of the soapy water in a plastic bathtub.

'What about it?' asked Stern.

'Tomorrow morning, on the bridge. It's about a baby.' The photo in his hand started to tremble.

'Did you dream this, Simon?'

'Mm.' The boy nodded.

Click. Click.

Stern looked up at the ceiling light, red specks dappling his retinas, as Simon continued.

'But I didn't remember it until I saw the photo. It gave me such a start, I dropped the mug.'

Stern looked down again. The shape of the milky puddle reminded him of a map of Iceland. Very appropriate, given the sudden chill that had come over him.

'Do you know what they are going to do with the baby?' he asked. 'On this bridge, I mean?'

Simon nodded wearily. The sodden tea towel slipped from his grasp.

'Sell it,' he said. 'They plan to sell it.'

The Deal

The soul never perishes; rather, it exchanges its former abode for a new residence in which it lives and operates. Everything changes but nothing is destroyed.

Pythagoras

The doctrine of reincarnation is the threat of thousandfold death and millionfold suffering.

Official statement on the subject of 'Rebirth'
from the homepage of a Christian radio station

Jesus answered and said unto him, Verily, verily,
I say unto thee, Except a man be born again,
he cannot see the kingdom of God.

St John, 3:3

1

'You can't be serious.'

Stern took his eyes off the road long enough to glance sideways at Borchert, who was just pulling on a Bayern Munich football shirt.

'Why not? I look good in it.'

His passenger, who was already sweating, grunted and wound his window down. Stern was also grateful for the cool morning air now streaming into the car at sixty kph. He estimated his net sleep intake in the last twenty-four hours at less than forty minutes. This morning he had only just managed to shower and beg a getaway car from his ex-wife in time to pick up Borchert at the Victory Column roundabout. Contrary to expectations, Sophie had surrendered her car keys without demur. She had even permitted Carina and Simon to remain at her Köpenick home until Stern discovered if his plan was working.

'Listen.' He raised his voice to make himself heard above the whistle of the headwind. 'We're sitting in one of the world's most ubiquitous small cars. What's more, it's metallic silver, the most popular bodywork colour on the planet. In other words, we couldn't find a less conspicuous mode of transport. Must you really ruin our camouflage by wearing *that*?'

'Take it easy.' Borchert's window was sticking. He wound it up again. 'Look over there on the left.'

They were just driving past the Philharmonie concert hall. On the opposite pavement, in front of the Berlin State Library, a bunch of young men were trooping in the direction of Potsdamer Platz. All were in full football gear.

'There's a big Bundesliga match this afternoon,' Borchert explained. 'Hertha versus Bayern. Now turn your head to the left again.'

Stern complied. He felt something moist imprint itself on his right cheek.

'What the hell's that?'

'You need some protective colouring too. It looks great.' Chuckling, Borchert angled the rear-view mirror so that Stern could see the Bayern Munich logo.

'The Olympic Stadium is a total sell-out – at least thirty-five thousand fans are expected from outside the city. Some of them have already got here and are rampaging around the streets, as you can see. A lawyer's three-piece suit may be OK when you're sitting in this car, but out there . . .' Borchert pointed through the windscreen at Potsdamer Strasse. 'Out there on a day like this, there's no better camouflage.'

Nuts. Totally nuts, thought Stern. He snatched a glance at the back seat. Andi must have cleaned out a fan shop. Everything was there from scarves to tracksuit bottoms and goalkeepers' gloves. No one would expect to see them in that get-up, far less recognize them, least of all with several thousand lookalikes roaming the capital.

'But I don't know if they'll let us in looking like that.' Stern turned into Kurfürstenstrasse and slowed down.

'In where?'

He brought Borchert up to date. According to Simon, the meeting would take place tomorrow morning on some bridge in Berlin – a meeting at which a baby was to be sold. Stern surmised that the voice was the dealer who had now been warned that he was to be murdered in the course of that transaction, like his accomplices in previous years.

'We have to find someone able to tell us who trafficks in babies. Through them we'll find the bridge and the voice. But for that we'll have to go into certain establishments . . .'

He felt sick when he realized what he was admitting to himself. If the boy with the birthmark had some connection with Felix – if that boy actually existed – his fate was linked with the boss of a criminal operation that trafficked in children: a sadist being hunted by an avenger with whom Simon identified himself in his dreams.

Stern wondered yet again whether this crazy scenario could have a logical explanation – whether Felix had been exchanged or possibly even resuscitated. And, yet again, he was compelled to rule out all rational attempts to explain it. Felix had been the only male infant in the neonatal ward, had lain dead in Sophie's arms for half an hour before she gave him up, had had a birthmark resembling a map of Italy on his left shoulder. Stern himself had caught a last glimpse of Felix in his coffin before it was entrusted to the flames for cremation. No matter which way you looked at it, the idea that his son was still alive was about as plausible as a young boy's knowledge of murders committed long before his birth.

'Hello, anyone at home?'

Borchert had evidently asked a question, not that he'd heard it.

'I asked how long Sophie was alone in that bathroom.'

Stern stared at him in perplexity. 'At the hospital, you mean?'

When she fled into the bathroom with Felix?

'Yes. I could hear your brain grinding away like the engine

of this old banger, so I wondered if you'd thought of that too.'

Of what? That Sophie may have something to do with it?

'You're off your trolley. That's crazy.'

'No crazier than looking for a baby that may only exist in a little boy's imagination.'

'What do you think happened in the bathroom?' Barely able to control his anger, Stern wondered why he was reacting to this theory so aggressively. 'The bathroom door – the *only* door – was locked. You think she had a second, stillborn baby in there and quickly tattooed a map of Italy on its shoulder?'

'OK, OK, forget it.' Borchert raised his hands in surrender. 'Let's just look for this baby.' He peered out of the window. 'Hey, how come we're cruising?'

He turned to look at a prostitute teetering apathetically along the pavement on legs like toothpicks. The stretch between Kurfürsten-, Lützow- and Potsdamer Strasse had long been one of Berlin's most notorious red light districts. Most of the girls had caught hepatitis by the age of twelve or thirteen and were busy passing it on to their clients. Unprotected sex was more cheaply obtainable here than anywhere else.

It was only just after half past eight, but on a day like this, when out-of-towners were thronging the capital, their under-age quarry patrolled the pavements from early morning onwards. Most of the punters weren't bums or anti-social elements eager to buy themselves a whore with their last few euros. They were prosperous business- or family men who relished the sense of power it gave them to be able to demand the most unspeakable services from juveniles too hung up by withdrawal pains to think straight.

'I was once asked to represent a paedophile,' Stern said as he looked for a place to park. 'He wanted to found a political party dedicated to legalizing sex between adults and children of twelve and over. The youngsters were even to be allowed to take part in porn films.'

'You're joking.'

'Afraid not.'

Stern indicated right and pulled into a gap beside the kerb. A girl in ripped jeans and a bomber jacket slid off a junction box and sauntered over to them.

'Before I refused the brief and told him to go to hell, I discovered where he liked to spend his weekends.'

'Let me guess.'

'Exactly. You can get anything here. Drugs, guns, contract killers, under-age whores . . .'

'And babies.'

Stern and Borchert got out. He hissed something to the prostitute in the bomber jacket, who jabbed her middle finger at him and returned to her perch.

'Drug-addicted prostitutes have even been known to thrust their newborn babies through the window of a punter's car,' said Stern, who had also got out. 'Not here, admittedly, but on a stretch of road near the Czech border. Still, that may make our job a bit easier.'

'Why?'

'Selling babies is still something of a rarity, even in Berlin. If Simon has heard about it, so must the people round here. All we have to do is knock on the right door. Someone behind it may be able to give us some information.'

'Which door do you plan to try first?'

'That one.' Stern indicated an entrance across the street. The grimy illuminated sign above it, which looked as if none of its bulbs had worked for ages, read 'JACKO'S PIZZA' in carelessly applied self-adhesive black capitals.

'It's supposed to be in the inner courtyard. A private bell, first floor right.'

'An unlicensed brothel, I know.' Borchert slapped his fleshy neck as if a mosquito had just bitten him. In fact, the beads of sweat trickling down it were making him itch. 'Don't look like that, you know the kind of movies that used to keep me in groceries. A man gets to know more about this scene than he cares to.'

'Good, then you'll realize why I need you with me. I hope you've come armed with something apart from your fists.'

'Sure.' Borchert eased the butt of the 9mm automatic out of the pocket of his Bayern Munich tracksuit bottoms. 'But we aren't going in there all the same.'

'Why not?'

'Because I've got a much better idea.'

'Like what?'

'Over there.' Borchert had already set off for the supermarket on the next corner.

'Oh, sure,' Stern called after him sarcastically. 'I'd completely forgotten. Around here they even sell babies in supermarkets.'

Borchert paused on the traffic island and looked back.

'You better believe it.'

His expression, body language and tone of voice made something crystal clear: he wasn't joking.

2

It was a question of fourth time lucky. The first supermarket proved to be shut, although recent changes in the law permitted shops to trade on Sundays, especially when a major sporting event was in the offing. The second was open for business, but its small ads were unremarkable: piano and Spanish lessons, a lift to Paris in return for a share of the cost of petrol, a rabbit hutch, buyer to collect, et cetera. The blackboard outside the drugstore across the street was dominated by furnished flats, two fridges, and offers of private tuition. Borchert's eye was caught by a photo of a second-hand baby buggy on sale for thirty-nine euros. He tore off one of ten perforated slips bearing the vendor's phone number but uttered a dissatisfied grunt when he saw the area code, and they moved on.

On the way to their last port of call, the biggest and most modern supermarket in the district, they attracted jeers from a Hertha fan driving past.

Stern, who was also in costume, had exchanged his suit for a long-sleeved goalie's shirt. Like Borchert's, his face was hidden beneath a ridiculous football cap that made him feel like a fairground attraction.

A plastic penis on my head would look less conspicuous, he thought, conscious of being stared at by an old woman who was stowing her purchases in a linen shopping bag.

'I'd never heard of this method, Andi.'

'That's why it works.'

They were standing beside the containers in which shoppers could dump unwanted packaging and old batteries. Immediately above these was another typical noticeboard adorned with a forest of small ads.

'I always thought people used the Internet for things like this.'

'They do, but mainly when they're trying to sell pictures, videos or used panties.'

Stern grimaced. As an experienced defence lawyer he knew that the authorities always lagged far behind the professional computer experts of the child pornography industry. There was no special unit with nationwide coverage, no team of computer freaks permanently employed to monitor websites, news groups or forums. Some police forces counted themselves lucky if they possessed a DSL connection at all, and even when they did pull off a coup the laws were insufficient to put the perverts behind bars.

Only a week earlier several child abusers had been caught after detectives had traced thousands of credit card transactions on the Internet. Unfortunately, the tracing of those payments had infringed data protection laws, so the evidence obtained was worthless. The 'bestseller' on the confiscated hard drives was a shot of a newborn baby being abused by a man of pensionable age. Those who took pleasure in its unimaginable sufferings were doubtless exercising their sick minds right now in some Internet café.

'The Net has become too dangerous for actual meetings,' said Borchert, lifting a picture of a motorcycle with an index card hidden beneath it.

'Why?'

'There's a field trial currently in progress. Detectives enter a suspect chatroom posing as an under-age girl. When some perv takes the bait, they make a date with him. The bastard turns up expecting to see a twelve-year-old with braces and winds up in handcuffs.'

'Good idea.'

'Yes, so good that paedophiles are now trying something new. Like this.' Borchert detached a sheet of sky-blue A5 paper from the noticeboard.

'Wanted: bed as illustrated,' Stern read out. The accompanying picture, which had been cut out of a mail order catalogue, showed a child's wooden-framed bed occupied by a little boy grinning at the camera. Laser-printed beneath it in 12-point Univers were the words:

To suit child aged betw. 6 & 12.
Must be clean and comfortable. COD.

Stern felt a cold wave of nausea steal over him.

'I can't believe it.'

Borchert raised his eyebrows. 'Be honest, when was the last time you stuck a small ad on a supermarket's noticeboard?'

'I never did.'

'And how many people do you know who've answered one?'

'None.'

'But the noticeboards are full of them, right?'

'You don't mean . . .'

'Sure I do. Some of them function as a marketplace for this city's sick and perverted individuals.'

'I can't believe it,' Stern said again.

'Then take a closer look. Ever seen such a long phone number?'

'Hm. Unusual.'

'Yes, isn't it? I bet it belongs to some Lebanese prepaid

card owner or something. A throw-away mobile – not a hope of getting at the name behind it. And look . . .' Borchert pointed to the caption. 'That's definite paedo jargon. "*Comfortable*" means "cooperative parents" and "*clean*" means "A virgin or Aids-tested". As for "*COD*", that's obvious. Cheques not accepted.'

'Are you sure?' Stern wondered if it would blow his football-fan cover if he threw up into the nearby wastepaper bin.

'No, but we'll soon find out.'

Borchert groped in his pocket and produced a mobile phone Stern had never seen before, then dialled the eighteen-digit number.

3

'Yes, hello?'

Stern was completely thrown by those first two words. He'd been expecting an oldish man whose degeneracy could be detected from his voice alone – a man who combed his greasy hair forward over his balding scalp and stared at his fungal toenails while answering the phone in a string vest. Instead, Stern heard the melodious, friendly voice of a woman.

'Erm, I, er . . .' he burbled. Borchert had simply handed him the phone as soon as it began to ring. Now he didn't know what to say.

'Sorry, I think I've got the wrong number.'

'Are you calling about the advertisement?' asked the nameless woman. She sounded polite and well educated. Not a trace of a Berlin accent.

'Er, yes.'

'I'm sorry, my husband isn't here at present.'

'I see.'

They had left the supermarket and were on their way back to the car. Stern had to concentrate hard, or her words would have been drowned by the traffic in Potsdamer Strasse and the noises on the line. The connection was poor.

'But you have what we're looking for?' she asked.

'Possibly.'

'How old?'

'Ten,' said Stern, thinking of Simon.

'That would suit. You do know we're looking for a child's bed?'

'Yes, so I read.'

'Good. When can you deliver?'

'Any time. Today, even.'

They passed the grey junction box on which the prostitute had sat waiting for customers. The scrawny creature had disappeared. She was probably on the passenger seat of some car in a side street.

'Fine. Then I suggest we meet to discuss terms at four this afternoon. You know the Madison on Mexikoplatz?'

'Yes,' Stern said mechanically, although he'd never heard of the place. 'Hello, are you still there?' Receiving no answer, he handed the phone back.

'Well?' Borchert asked eagerly, but it was a moment before Stern could compose himself enough to reply. He drew several deep breaths.

'I don't know,' he said eventually, in a kind of daze. 'It sounded like a normal phone conversation. All we really talked about was a bed.'

'But?'

'I sensed all the time that something else was at stake.' Stern repeated the conversation almost word for word.

'You see?' said Borchert.

'No, I don't see at all,' Stern lied. The fact was, his view of the world in which he lived had just undergone a radical change. At the supermarket Borchert had raised a curtain and enabled him to see the dark side of life behind the stage. That was where people removed their carefully cultivated masks of morality and conscience to reveal the true faces beneath.

Stern wasn't naive. He was a lawyer. Of course he was acquainted with evil, but until now it had hidden itself behind writs, judgements and statutes. He could no longer view an abomination of this kind, which threatened to swallow him like a black hole, through the neutralizing filter of a professional brief. He would have to make out the bill for this case himself, and he felt sure the hourly rate would break his emotional budget.

Borchert opened the driver's door and was about to get in, but Stern stopped him in his tracks.

'Where did you get your information?'

The big man scratched his head without removing his cap, then took it off. 'I already told you.'

'Come off it! Shooting adult porn is far from the same as knowing all about the latest trends in child abuse.'

Borchert's face darkened. He got into the car.

'I'll ask you again: How come you're so well up on the subject?' Stern got in beside him.

'Believe me, you don't want to know.' Borchert turned on the ignition and glanced in the rear-view mirror. His neck was mottled with red patches. Then he looked at Stern with his lips pursed in resignation. 'All right. We'd better pay a visit to Harry.'

'Who's Harry?'

'One of my sources. He'll give us a reference.'

Borchert pulled out of the parking space. He kept to the speed limit rather than get pulled up for a minor violation.

'A reference? What the hell do you mean?'

Borchert looked genuinely surprised. 'You don't think you can breeze into that café this afternoon without some form of proof that you're one of them?'

Stern swallowed hard. *One of them . . .* Nervously, he took hold of one end of his Bayern Munich scarf and tugged, heedless of its increasing pressure on his throat. The thought of having to demonstrate membership of a community of perverts had taken his breath away as it was.

4

Hundreds of tourists drove daily through the district where Harry led a miserable existence. They passed within a few metres of his abode, tired after their journey but filled with nervous anticipation at the prospect of what Berlin had to offer them in the next few days. Eager to plunge into the city's night life, visit the Reichstag building or simply luxuriate at their hotel, they certainly had no plans to make an excursion to the eleven grimy square metres where Harry was waiting for death.

His camper van was situated immediately beneath the flyover, a kilometre at most from Schönefeld Airport. Stern was afraid the suspension of Sophie's Corolla wouldn't withstand the potholes when they turned on to the track that led to it.

Borchert eventually saw sense. They parked just short of a sagging wire-mesh fence and covered the last stretch on foot. For the first time, Stern was grateful for the boots Borchert had compelled him to wear. The rain, which had started again, was turning the ground into a quagmire.

'Where is it?' All Stern could see was a chaotic rubbish dump flanked by two massive ferroconcrete columns. The sound of cars thundering past overhead was almost as intolerable as the smell. A throat-catching amalgam of dog shit, rotting food and stagnant water, it grew stronger the further they went.

'Keep going, it's straight ahead.' Borchert hunched his shoulders. He had left his scarf and cap in the car, like Stern, and the rain was spattering the back of his neck.

Stern still hadn't spotted the nicotine-yellow camper van when a man in a scruffy bathrobe suddenly emerged from behind a mound of old tyres. Somewhat taller but considerably thinner than Borchert, he had clearly failed to notice his uninvited visitors, because he fumbled with his crotch, belched loudly, and urinated over a broken-down armchair with his head tilted back. The rain blew into his face as he stared up at the underside of the flyover.

'You're up early, Harry.'

The man swung round. Although they were still three or four car lengths from him, there was no mistaking the look of terror inspired by Borchert's sudden appearance.

'Shit!' Harry promptly forgot about his morning toilette. He fled around the corner in his worn-out slippers and made it to the open door of his mobile home, but even if he'd managed to shut it and lock himself in, Borchert would have found that flimsy obstacle child's play. He could have pushed the whole vehicle back to the main road single-handed. Harry knew this, so he looked suitably intimidated when the two men joined him inside.

'Phew, who's died in here?'

Like Borchert, Stern was holding his nose and breathing through his mouth. The carpet must have been yellow when the van was new. Now, the floor and the plastic walls were green with mould. The kitchenette was piled high with chipped plates, dirty plastic mugs and something that might once have been a salami but now resembled an open wound.

'What do you want?' Harry demanded. He had shrunk

back into the furthest corner of the laminated bench seat. Upholstered with old pizza boxes, it obviously served him as a bed.

'Why ask when you know?' said Borchert, adept at injecting more menace into a single sentence than many a thriller into ninety minutes of screen time.

'What do you mean? I've done nothing.' Harry was breathing fast and trying to make himself as small as possible, whereas Borchert was flexing his shoulders like a boxer.

Stern longed to get out of there, if only to spare himself the sight of the man's face. Harry looked as if he'd spent the night face down in a patch of stinging nettles. His forehead, cheeks and neck were covered with what looked like burn blisters. Some of them were scabby, others open and suppurating.

'We'll go as soon as you give us what we want.'

'Meaning what?'

'Which of your pals trafficks in children?'

'Look, Andi, you know I don't do that sort of thing any more. I'm out of it.'

'Shut up and listen. What do you know about a baby?'

'What baby?'

'A baby that's due to be sold tomorrow morning – to some sick fuck like you. Heard anything about it on the grapevine?'

'No, I swear. I don't have anything more to do with that stuff. I've got no contacts, no information. Nada, nix. Sorry, I'd tell you if I knew anything, but I don't. Nobody talks to me since I did time. Paid the price, didn't I?'

'Don't talk balls.'

'Honestly, Andi. I'd never lie to you, not *you*.' He refocused his cringing gaze on Stern, whose hopes of a quick departure faded accordingly.

'I screwed up. I thought she was sixteen, cross my heart.

It's a long time ago, but nobody believes me. Sometimes they come at night and beat me up. See this?'

He opened his bathrobe and displayed his chest, which was covered with purple bruises. Stern couldn't be sure without an X-ray, but he thought he detected at least one fractured rib.

'That was the local yobs. It's a different bunch each time. Someone told them what I did. They dragged me outside and jumped up and down on me in their boots. Once, they sprayed battery acid in my face.'

Stern shrank back, overcome with a mixture of disgust and pity, as Harry stuck out his raw, blistered face. Borchert remained unmoved. The man's tale of woe seemed to have made little impression on him. On the contrary, he smiled at Harry and punched him in the mouth as hard as he could.

The force of the blow was such that Harry's head cannoned into the plastic wall and left a dent in it.

'Bloody hell,' Harry whimpered, spitting out a blood-stained tooth.

'Andi, stop it!' Stern shouted. 'Are you mad?'

'Go outside, please.'

'No, I won't. You're out of your mind!'

'You don't understand,' said Borchert, drawing his gun. A metallic click told Stern that he'd released the safety catch.

'Get lost. Now.'

'No, I won't. No matter what he's done, violence is no solution.'

'Says who?'

Borchert raised the automatic and levelled it at Stern's head.

'I won't tell you again.'

'No! Please don't go!' Harry's eyes flickered to and fro between Borchert and Stern. He looked like someone who realizes, seconds before his execution, that he's doomed to die.

Borchert, on the other hand, had flipped again. He had crossed the threshold of his inhibitions just as he had at the Titanic the day before, when charging out of the door. He would obey his instincts despite everything and anyone, Stern included.

'Oh my God, please don't leave him alone with me!'

Stern knew that Harry's imploring, panic-stricken voice would continue to ring in his ears long after Borchert thrust him out of the camper van and locked the door.

5

When creatures of the wild display wholly illogical behaviour in a conflict situation, scientists refer to it as a displacement activity. A tern, for example, will start to preen when too stressed to decide whether to defend its brood or fly away. Right then, Robert Stern would have provided a behaviourist with an equally instructive subject for research.

With his back to the swaying camper van, uncertain whether to intervene, summon help or drive off, he was rummaging in the refuse heap like a man possessed. In search of a defensive weapon, or, so he told himself, a pointed object or metal bar that would enable him to lever open the door behind which Harry had stopped screaming a couple of minutes ago. He'd been able to make out what the man was saying at first. Then the agonized cries had died away to liquid gurgles punctuated by thuds that shook the decrepit mobile home at irregular intervals.

Stern redoubled his search. He thrust aside an old car battery and wrenched the hose off an ancient washing machine, only to exchange it for a length of wire as useless as the rest of the stinking rubbish. He wouldn't be able to put a stop to the mayhem in any case – not unless he unearthed a loaded shotgun.

Despite this, he continued to dig in the refuse until the

silence behind him became unbearable. All of a sudden there were no more screams, whimpers or splintering crashes. The roar of passing cars, amplified by the concrete sound box beneath the expressway, had regained its acoustic supremacy.

Stern turned to see if the mayhem was really over or only temporarily so. While trudging across the muddy ground to the camper van he trod in a pile of unidentifiable filth but pressed on regardless. Although dreading the spectacle that might be awaiting him behind the van's scratched Plexiglas window, he went right up to it and stood on tiptoe. He almost fell over backwards when the door on his right burst open and Borchert emerged. His carmine red football strip had changed colour and was clinging to his chest, black with sweat. Stern shuddered at the sight of his face. His forehead and pugilist's nose were sprinkled with tiny droplets that might have been applied by a paint sprayer. He looked as if he'd just redecorated Harry's unfit-for-human habitation in red.

'He really didn't know anything,' he said tersely when he saw Stern. 'Let's go.' He winced with pain and shook his right hand like he had just caught his fingers in a door. From the look of his raw knuckles he might have been punching barbed wire, not Harry.

'That's it,' said Stern. 'Things can't go on like this. I give up.' He turned on his heel and walked off as fast as he could.

'Give up on what?' he heard Borchert call after him.

'This lunacy. It's got to end. I'm going to turn myself in. What's more, I'll tell the police what you just did.'

'Oh? What did I just do?'

Stern swung round.

'You brutalized a weak, totally defenceless man. I don't even dare to check if he's still alive.'

'He is. More's the pity.'

'You're crazy, Andi. Even if my son's life or death is at stake, you can't go around beating up innocent people.'

Borchert spat on the muddy ground.

'You're wrong twice over. For one thing, this isn't just about your reincarnation palaver. Someone's selling a baby tomorrow, remember? And secondly, innocence doesn't come into it. That bastard raped an eleven-year-old girl. He's the lowest of the low. Flushing him down the toilet would be a waste of good water.'

'He paid for it, he says.'

'Yes, he did four years. But since then?'

'He's finished. I mean, look at the man. He's literally rotting away. You didn't have to beat him up, he's dying anyway.'

'Not soon enough.'

Some of the photographs Borchert tossed into the mud at Stern's feet landed face up. Stern bent over them, only to recoil as if he'd been bitten by a poisonous snake.

'Go on, take a good look. I found them under your friend Harry's pizza-box mattress.'

Stern hardly dared breathe for fear of inhaling the evil that seemed to fill the air around him.

'Well?' Borchert himself bent down and retrieved one of the polaroids from the mud. The little girl's staring eyes were protruding from their sockets almost as far as the black rubber bit ball in her mouth.

'Good old Harry, eh? I bet she never made her sixth birthday. And these are just the photos. Shall I go back and get the videos?'

Stern knew it didn't matter when the pictures were taken. The very fact that Harry had them in his possession was evidence enough of his continuing activity.

'All the same,' he wanted to say, but the words refused to cross his lips. He was caught between two worlds: the sick and morbid world of a child abuser and that of Andi Borchert, in which objectives could be attained by violence alone. The third world, his own, had disappeared.

'What now?' he asked as they made their way back to the car in silence. He could scarcely see the path for the rain in his eyes, but the downpour seemed to have no cleansing or clarifying effect. Instead of washing away the dirt, it drove it ever deeper into his pores.

'Now we calm down and make a plan.'

Borchert opened the driver's door and squeezed in behind the Corolla's wheel once more. The weight distribution was so unequal, the car listed dangerously until Stern sat down beside him.

'We've still got three hours before your date in Mexikoplatz.'

Borchert turned on the ignition. The engine gave a couple of violent hiccups and died. 'Please don't do this to me.' He tried again, but without success.

'What about that reference you mentioned?' To Stern the flooded engine was secondary. Of all the problems that had arisen in the last few hours, it was the only one they could get to grips with. Neither Simon's visions nor the 'voice' could be dealt with simply by opening a bonnet and doing something practical.

Borchert laughed. 'We've got it.'

His satisfaction was mainly down to the little car, the engine of which had eventually caught when he tried the starter again and floored the accelerator.

'These are our reference.' He patted the photos in his breast pocket, which he had retrieved before following Stern back to the car. 'You don't get hold of pictures like these without contacts. Anyone in possession of them has to know someone in the fraternity. Put them in front of the lady you're meeting. You couldn't produce a better calling card.'

Stern buckled his seat belt, then buried his face in his

cold hands and tried to feel something other than the nausea raging in his guts.

'I asked you this once before,' he said when the car had lurched into motion. 'How come you know these scum so well? How come you're so well informed?'

The noticeboard at the supermarket. Harry. The pictures.

'You don't give up, do you? OK, I'll tell you. It's because I'm personally involved.'

Stern stiffened.

'Yes, intimately involved. Want to know what Harry's surname is?'

He came out with it before Stern could decide whether he did, in fact, want to know.

'It's Borchert. Like mine. Harry's my dear little step-brother.'

6

The café looked the way Stern felt. Empty, deserted, dead. For a while he stood irresolutely outside the door, on which some high school pop group had stuck a crooked poster advertising its next gig. The window on the right bore a sign saying 'TO LET' in red and white capitals, and beneath it in smaller letters the email address of an estate agent. Stern peered into the dusty interior. There was little to be seen apart from some long, bare tables with rows of upturned wooden chairs on them.

Good, he thought. *If that woman really is waiting for me in there, she obviously isn't interested in buying a bed.*

He turned and treated himself to a sight of the imposing domed roof of Mexikoplatz's Art Nouveau S-Bahn station. He could well imagine what the residents of this elegant square in the heart of Zehlendorf thought of such an eyesore as the abandoned restaurant, but he also wondered how its owner could have gone bust in so prosperous a district.

A train went rattling across the bridge, so he almost failed to hear the sound behind him. Then he registered it and turned round. Sure enough, the door he had vainly tried to open a moment ago was ajar. He glanced over his shoulder. When no passers-by appeared to be looking, he slipped inside. What greeted him first was the smell typical of an empty, disused building. Then he caught a whiff of something quite unexpected: expensive perfume.

The closer he drew to the woman sitting smoking at a table in the far left corner, the more he amended his estimate of her age. Seen from the doorway she had looked forty, whereas now, as he sat down across the table from her, he guessed her to be at least twenty years older. Botox and the scalpel had clearly been her periodic response to the ageing process, a fact that became readily apparent only at close range. The unnatural smoothness and rigidity of her face were in stark contrast to the mottled patches on the backs of her hands, and her flaccid neck cried out for similar treatment. In spite of those attributes, Stern felt sure he would fail to recognize her in a police line-up. She obviously had a good reason for wearing a silver page-boy wig and hiding her eyes behind a pair of dark glasses that made her look like Puck the Housefly.

'May I see your ID, please?'

Unsurprised by her opening question, Stern took out his wallet.

Borchert had warned him that certain paedophile circles regarded the surrender of a person's anonymity as their best protection. Everyone knew everyone else. Like the mafia, members of a paedophile ring took great care to render someone potentially punishable by law before they accepted him into their community. A newcomer would be photographed with his ID in one hand and a piece of illegal pornography in the other. The photo would then be placed on file.

Stern cleared his throat. Uninvited, he deposited Harry's polaroids on the brown-and-white-checked tablecloth.

'I'm not a beginner.'

The woman's sole response was an almost imperceptible twitch of her drumskin-taut cheek. Even if it hadn't been so before, the situation was now as clear as daylight. Any normal person would have taken one look at those photos and called the police, especially if they'd been expecting some innocent sales talk. In the event, the bony woman drew on her cigarette, which was as thin as the fingers that held it. She didn't even trouble to turn the disgusting pictures over.

'For all that, I must ask you to stand up.'

Stern did as he was told.

'Now get undressed.'

He was expecting that too. After all, he could have been an agent provocateur who didn't mind committing a criminal offence, or someone with perfectly forged papers. He and Borchert had discussed at length what would happen if she found out who he really was, a lawyer on the run with a child abducted from a hospital. Borchert thought it could only be all to the good. As a criminal, he would be one of them. In the end, however, the whole discussion had been pointless. If they were to proceed according to plan, they simply didn't have time to fabricate a new ID.

'And your underpants.'

The woman pointed to his nether regions. He slipped off his pants and turned on the spot in front of her, stark naked. She nodded, then opened the faux leather handbag on her lap and brought out a small black rod.

'OK,' she muttered after running the metal detector over him like an airport security guard. She repeated the procedure with his clothes, which were lying in a heap on the table in front of her. Stern had quickly bought an off-the-peg suit, shirt and underpants in a crowded shopping centre half an hour before. He had probably been caught on a dozen CCTV cameras, but that was a risk they'd had to take. He could hardly turn up in a football strip if he wanted to pass for a father eager to sell his own son to sexual perverts.

'All right,' she said without returning his clothes, 'you can sit down again.'

He shrugged. The chair's wooden seat felt cold against his bare bottom.

'Where's the bed?' she asked, her eyes on his hairy chest. He felt disgusted with himself when the cold made his nipples harden. The thought that she might construe it as a sign of sexual arousal made him feel sick.

'It's outside.'

She followed the direction of his gaze. The lower half of the brownish window pane was covered by a lace curtain. It had stopped raining in the last few hours, and the setting sun was bathing the square in pleasant, autumnal shades of red. A man and a woman were walking across it, each with a dog on a lead. They were clearly enjoying their evening stroll. Although the wind had dropped, it still sent dead leaves dancing around their feet.

But Stern was blind to the beauty of the scene. The square seemed to darken before his eyes as he looked across at the parked car in which Simon was awaiting his signal.

7

Two years ago, on the eve of his first MRI scan, Simon had discovered a two-volume encyclopedia at the children's home. He took the first volume from the rickety bookcase in the communal dining room and carried it up to his dormitory.

Fascinated by the information it contained about the Arctic and astronomy, he resolved before going to sleep that he would learn the meaning of one new word every day from then on, proceeding alphabetically from A to Z.

So he wasn't sad, angry or depressed the next morning, when Professor Müller summoned him to his office at the Seehaus Clinic, having previously spoken to the matron of the children's home. He was mainly disappointed to be told the meaning of words like 'cerebral' and 'tumour' before he could learn them for himself.

Today he had learned a new word: *paedophile*. Robert hadn't wanted to repeat it at first. It had slipped out when he was explaining what was going to happen.

Always stay close to me. Don't budge from my side. And no matter what happens, take your instructions from me, nobody else, understand?

Stern's admonitions were still ringing in Simon's ears as he opened the car door.

Do everything I tell you, and don't speak to the people

we're going to meet, you hear? They're paedophiles – bad people. They may smile – they may try to shake hands or touch you, but you mustn't let them.

Stern gave him another wave from the window and he promptly got out. The lawyer was looking sad, his expression like that of those who heard of Simon's illness for the first time. Simon would have liked to tell him not to worry. Today was a good day, actually – only a 3 on his wellness scale. No pain, only slight nausea, and the numbness in his left hand had also diminished. But as usual after a fit, he was feeling very, very tired. He'd dozed off several times on the way here.

Carina, who didn't want to let him go at first, had protested fiercely when Borchert turned up at Sophie's house to collect them both. They and the twins had been watching a cartoon when he knocked on the back door. Then he and Carina had gone into the next room. Simon had only been able to hear snatches of what was said, thanks to the little girls' giggles and the film music.

'. . . *our only chance . . . No, he'll only have to put in an appearance . . . Don't worry . . . there's no danger, I give you my word . . .*'

Carina eventually hurried back into the room, scowling, and helped him on with his cord jacket. On the way, Borchert had dropped her at the spot where she'd parked her VW Golf and they'd driven here in two cars. They had now pulled up in this handsome square, where Stern, whom Simon was pleased to see again, had given him the prearranged signal.

'Bye, Carina,' he wanted to say before setting off, but Stern had expressly forbidden this.

Don't look back or say goodbye.

Looking straight ahead, Simon walked to the door of the Madison and pushed it open with his shoulder, then made his way into the gloomy interior.

The only light in the place was over a table in the far corner. Stern, who had left the window and was standing there, looked rather odd. His hair was tousled, the jacket of his new suit unbuttoned, and his shirt was hanging out of his trousers. He looked as if he'd been in a fight, but it couldn't have been with the weird woman in sunglasses, who had also turned to face Simon. Her costume was uncreased and every hair on her head gleamed as if it had been individually brushed and combed.

Simon stumbled just before he got to the table. Looking down, he saw that the laces of one of his trainers had come untied. He felt a bit dizzy when he bent down to retie them, but he could hear the strange woman's voice loud and clear.

'All right, young man, let's have a look at you.'

He had to push himself up off the floor with both hands in order to regain his feet, but he forgot his tiredness when the woman came and stood right in front of him – in fact he almost burst out laughing. Not only was she wearing dark-brown lipstick, but she reminded him of a skydiver he'd seen on television. The skin over her prominent cheekbones looked as if it was being forced backwards by the wind.

'How old are you?' she asked. Her breath smelled of stale cigarette smoke.

'Ten. Just had my birthday.' Simon bit his tongue and glanced apprehensively at Stern.

He told me not to say anything.

To Simon's relief, Stern didn't look annoyed.

'Good. Excellent.'

The woman had suddenly produced a black metal rod. Quick as lightning, Stern gripped her arm.

'He won't have to—'

'No, no.' The woman gave a sly smile. 'He won't have to take his clothes off. Not until my husband joins us. We'll reserve that treat for later.'

Simon couldn't understand why she was running the metal rod over him, or why he had to put on a funny blindfold that prevented him from seeing a thing, but he did so when Robert showed him how. He wasn't afraid. Not as long as he was with his lawyer. Strangely enough, Stern seemed far more scared than he was.

But what of? Nothing bad can happen as long as we stay together.

So he squeezed Stern's hand really hard, more to reassure the lawyer than himself as the woman led them out of the back entrance and into a yard. The car they got into smelled nice and new. The hand in Simon's began to tremble when they drove off, but he put that down to the engine's faint vibrations.

8

'Are you on their tail?'

'Yes, I'm right behind them.' Borchert heard Carina sink back in her seat with a sigh of relief. He'd been expecting her to call him sooner, having given her this number for emergencies. The prepaid card wasn't in his name and the police would find it hard to trace. Unlike Carina's mobile, so he kept the call as brief as possible.

'Where are you?'

'Just passing the petrol station on Potsdamer Chaussee.'

'Shall I follow you?' she asked.

'No.' That was quite out of the question. Splitting up into two cars had purely been a safety measure. As expected, the 'goods' had left by way of the rear entrance, which Borchert had been covering in the Corolla. Carina had kept watch on the front of the building in her own car. The risk of being spotted would dramatically increase if she didn't leave her Golf where it was.

'We should have nabbed her inside the café and—'

'No,' Borchert cut in sharply. They'd already been talking too long for his liking. He didn't want to intervene until the husband showed his face. The wife might only be a messenger – she mightn't be in possession of any information at all.

He hung up and concentrated on not losing sight of the American saloon with the grey curtain over the rear window. Like him, the woman was strictly adhering to the speed limit.

Borchert felt for the gun in his trousers. The very touch of the automatic galvanized him. He heard the blood pounding in his ears and relished his sense of anticipation. *Going the whole hog, no holds barred* . . . Most people used such expressions without grasping their true significance – without ever experiencing what *he* did. Borchert grinned and depressed the accelerator a little to make the lights at Wannsee S-Bahn station. More and more adrenalin flooded his body as the car accelerated. He would show those sick bastards. He might not be able to say, afterwards, how the blood and splintered bone had got on to his sweatshirt – that often happened when he blew a fuse – but he wouldn't care. Just as long as those perverts got what they—

Huh?

Borchert's mental combat preparations were abruptly cut short. He floored the gas pedal, but to no avail. The pounding in his ears died away and the engine's silence became more apparent. The drivers behind him pulled out, horns blaring angrily, when they noticed he wasn't accelerating.

Sweating, Borchert turned the ignition key. Once, twice. At Harry's place the damned thing had caught at the third attempt, but now it wouldn't even hiccup. As the car ahead of him pulled away, the Corolla coasted slowly to a stop in the middle of the junction.

He reached for his mobile, meaning to call Carina and ask if there was some secret knack of getting the old crock going again. Then it occurred to him that she couldn't help. The car belonged to Stern's ex-wife and he didn't have Sophie's number.

What now? Borchert started to sweat even more profusely.

He could just see the other car's tail lights as he jumped out and went to open the bonnet. Another four seconds, and the car disappeared from his field of vision somewhere on the road between Wannsee and Potsdam.

Borchert still hadn't identified the problem five minutes later, but that was beside the point. He didn't care about the traffic jam he was inflicting on Sunday motorists, nor did he take any notice of his mobile, which had already registered three calls from Carina.

He was wholly and exclusively preoccupied with working out what to say to the traffic cop who had just asked to see his papers.

9

The ambient sounds changed before the car finally came to rest. The engine noise grew louder, suggesting that they had entered a confined space. At the same time, Stern felt as if his eyes had been swathed in another blindfold.

He had tried to count the bends, but the car's numerous changes of lane had rendered that impossible. His built-in clock had failed too. By the time the blindfold was removed and he saw the garage in which they were standing, he couldn't have said whether they'd been driving for ten minutes or an hour.

'Everything OK?' he asked Simon, careful not to sound too friendly. He had an act to keep up, after all. The boy nodded and rubbed his eyes, which were only slowly accustoming themselves to the light of the halogen spots above their heads.

'This way, please.'

The woman had gone on ahead and opened a grey fire door. Beyond it was a flight of stairs. The veining of the shiny marble treads resembled caramelized vanilla ice cream.

'Where are we going?' Stern asked. He coughed. They hadn't exchanged a word throughout the drive and his throat was dry with excitement. Fear, too.

'The main house is directly accessible from the garage,' said the woman, climbing the stairs ahead of them. Sure enough, they came out in a parquet-floored entrance hall bathed in artificial light. It reminded Stern of his own hall, except that his was bare of furniture and certainly had no amaryllis plants standing around in pots. He only hoped Borchert would manage to force an entry somehow. He would need his gun or the crowbar from the boot – probably both, if he was going to penetrate the heavy, brass-bound front door. The windows were secured on the outside with burglar-proof aluminium roller shutters – all the windows, as far as Stern could tell, even those in the living room, into which he and Simon were now ushered.

'Please sit down. My husband won't be long.'

Stern shepherded Simon over to a white leather sofa. Meanwhile, the woman made her way to a small bureau with some drinks and nibbles on it, tittuping rather awkwardly on the soles of her high-heeled shoes.

Puzzled by her peculiar way of walking, Stern thought at first that she was trying not to make a noise. It was only when she was fixing herself a gin and tonic that the penny dropped: she didn't want her stilettos to mark the freshly waxed parquet. This house was unoccupied. They were in a luxuriously renovated but still unlet show house, nicely furnished but devoid of any personal touches. Surveying the room, Stern could recognize the signs quite clearly: the portable telephone on the desk; the leather-bound volumes neatly arrayed in a half-empty bookcase; the brand-new leather sofa on which only a handful of potential purchasers had hitherto sat while being shown the ground plan of the property by the estate agent. Stern would have bet a fortune on the woman's husband being the same estate agent who had the Mexikoplatz café on his books.

'May I offer you something?'

He shook his head. All that he possessed in the way of grey matter was churning around in his skull. It was a perfect set-up. The couple's method was pathologically brilliant. There was nothing here that a victim could remember later. Nothing of value that couldn't be replaced if soiled with blood or body fluids. And no one would be surprised if the whole house underwent thorough cleaning before being handed over to its new owners, who would naturally have no inkling of what had gone on in the rooms in which they looked forward to spending a happy future.

It sickened Stern to realize how well the bogus backdrop of this house symbolized the whole situation in which he'd been embroiled for the last few days. Everything seemed so theatrical: Simon's inexplicable knowledge of murders in the past and his absurd intention of committing one in the future; the voice on the DVD that hinted his son might still be alive; and the obscure paedophile connection between the two dramatic incidents in which he had involuntarily played a leading role.

He gulped a couple of times, assailed by violent heartburn. Watching the boy beside him out of the corner of his eye, he saw that Simon was quite calm, almost relaxed. Unlike Stern himself, Simon didn't give a start when the living-room door opened and a man came in, his bland face wreathed in smiles. At least sixty years old, he was no longer handsome in the classical sense. Age had thinned his once luxuriant hair at the temples and inscribed a network of fine wrinkles around his mouth, but this only added to his air of almost stately elegance. Despite his unconventional mode of dress.

'There you are. How nice.'

His voice sounded warm and friendly – thoroughly in keeping with the sympathetic aura he had about him. Eyes fixed on Simon alone, he clapped his hands in appreciation as he slowly drew nearer. The rustle of his dressing gown covered the sound of this subdued applause, which was almost inaudible in any case. His hands were encased in thick latex gloves.

10

Carina undid her ponytail and pulled off her raspberry-red headband. Borchert had advised her to dress as a jogger. In his opinion there was no better form of camouflage for someone running away from potential pursuers without attracting attention, but the elasticated headband had felt like a steel clamp around her throbbing head.

What's happened? Why isn't Borchert answering his phone? Where's Robert?

Her fears for Simon redoubled with every heartbeat. She waited another minute, then made up her mind. She couldn't sit there idly any longer.

She turned the key in the ignition.

But where should I drive to?

She put the car into reverse. Her rear tyres hit the kerb with a bump. *No matter*. She was about to pull out of the parking bay when an orange delivery van double-parked just ahead, hemming her in.

What the—

A man got out of the van carrying two pizza cartons the size of wagon wheels. She wound her window down.

'You! Move it!' she yelled.

The driver, a young student, gave her an impish grin,

clearly amused by the red blotches on her angry face. He blew her a kiss.

'I'll only be a minute, darling.'

Carina felt her throat tighten with panic. She remembered Borchert's instructions before they split up. *Anything goes*, he'd said, *but we mustn't attract attention*.

So what to do now? The back of the van was obstructing her by a tyre's width, but that was enough. To the rear her escape route was blocked by a tree with railings round it.

This is impossible . . .

Carina sounded her horn, but the student merely gave a casual wave without even looking round.

OK. Don't attract attention.

She threw the car into reverse, crunching the gears, and it mounted the pavement with both rear wheels. Then she engaged first, removed her foot from the brake, and floored the accelerator.

'Hey, hey, hey!'

The Golf crashed into the van's rear door sideways on.

'Are you *crazy*?' she heard the driver yell. He dropped the pizza boxes and stared in horror at his van, which was now jutting into the road. The force of the collision had shattered its rear window.

Yes, I am, thought Carina, and did it again. The second impact not only reduced her near-side wing to scrap metal but bulldozed the van far enough for her to exit the bay.

'Hey! Stop!'

She roared off down Argentinische Allee heedless of the yelling delivery man, who was spinning like a top as he looked around for witnesses to this outrageous incident.

Carina knew that her own car had sustained some damage, judging by the sound of the tyre scuffing the wheel arch, but it didn't stop her from driving even faster.

What had Borchert said?

She sped towards a red light, wondering feverishly which direction to take after the crossing.

Borchert's words came back to her: *Just passing the petrol station on Potsdamer Chaussee . . .*

Damn it, Andi, there's a petrol station on every other corner.

She ignored the red light and turned sharp right. Somehow, heading out of town seemed more logical to her than driving back to the city centre. It was utter nonsense, of course, but she had to make a decision. She only hoped that fate had dealt her a decent hand of cards. For once.

11

Where's he got to?

Stern's anger was focused on Borchert. For some unknown reason he was taking much too long. Five minutes at most, he'd said. Then he would break into the house and overpower the couple. After the intermezzo in Harry's camper van, Stern felt confident that Borchert would manage to extract the information they needed – provided there was anything of value in the couple's sick heads. He realized they were clutching at straws, of course. Stern had made up his mind that this operation must be their last, desperate attempt to get at the truth of Simon's predictions.

And find Felix.

Afterwards, no matter how things turned out, he would call Engler and turn himself in. He was a lawyer, not a criminal, far less an undercover investigator of the paedophile world, one of whose fully paid-up members was sitting on the sofa beside him, fondling Simon's knee.

'How much?' the man asked blithely, without taking his eyes off the boy. Stern tried to detect something diabolical in his profile, but he still looked like a nice old gentleman whom Stern would unhesitatingly have helped if his car had broken down.

'We haven't discussed that yet, my dear.'

The woman was still standing beside the bureau. She gestured to Simon with her glass. 'But take a good look at the boy. He looks ill to me.'

'Really?' The man lifted Simon's chin. His latex gloves were even paler than the boy's cheeks.

'We advertised for clean goods. What's wrong with him?'

Stern felt like grabbing the man's hand and breaking his fingers. He wouldn't be able to control himself for much longer in the couple's presence. If Borchert didn't come in soon he would settle matters himself. The old man weighed twenty pounds less than him and would be easy to overpower, and the snake in shades shouldn't present any problem as long as he retained the element of surprise. He would have to use the standard lamp's extension lead to tie them up with. The only thing was . . .

Stern was puzzled when the estate agent removed his latex-sheathed hand from Simon's knee before he could intervene. Then he heard a faint hum. The vibration became more audible when the paedophile took a wafer-thin mobile phone from the pocket of his dressing gown.

'I see, thanks,' he said after some innocent preliminaries. Stern's heartbeat accelerated. Although he couldn't hear what was said on the other end of the line, the two parties appeared to be on good terms. The estate agent laughed and expressed his thanks twice more. Then his smile abruptly vanished and he stared at Stern.

'All clear, I understand,' he said, and hung up.

The sofa emitted a sigh of relief as he rose and took Simon's hand.

'He's a lawyer,' he said, turning to his wife. 'He's wanted by the police for abducting this child from a hospital.'

'What is all this nonsense?' asked Stern, doing his best to sound calm and composed. In reality, his pulse was racing with fear. His heart beat all the faster when the woman pointed a gun at him.

'Take that thing out of my face,' he demanded. 'What's going on?'

'I could ask you the same thing, Herr Stern. What game are you playing?'

'No game. I came here to—' Stern broke off. The man was still holding Simon's hand.

'While you're talking business, my dear,' he purred, 'we'll go upstairs, shall we?' He blew his wife a kiss.

'Robert?' Simon said timidly as the man pulled him to his feet.

Stern started to rise, but the woman jerked the gun at him. He blinked and shut his eyes for a moment, trying to collect the thoughts whirling so ineffectually around in his head.

What shall I do? Where's Borchert? What the hell shall I do?

The handsome old monster holding the boy's hand was a few steps from the door, and he had no idea how to stop them leaving the room.

'Robert?' Simon said again softly. He might have been asking permission to spend the night at a schoolfriend's. He was still totally confident that his 'lawyer' would not put him in jeopardy. After all, Stern had promised to clear things up and protect him from any kind of danger. Whatever happened.

Besides, the boy still firmly believed he was destined to kill someone on a bridge tomorrow morning. That being so, nothing could happen to him here and now.

Stern sensed Simon's train of thought, so he knew what would happen if he didn't intervene at once.

He had perhaps five seconds left before the brute to whose

mercies he'd consigned the boy walked out and took him to his darkroom on another floor.

Stern was wrong. They disappeared after only four seconds.

12

A speed camera caught her doing ninety kph past the cemetery. She didn't even notice, but she took her foot off the gas even so. The traffic was suddenly slowing.

What's happening up ahead?

All at once, on a level with Dreilinden, the cars ahead of her were pulling over into the right-hand lane.

A tailback? At this hour?

If anywhere, it should have been on the opposite carriageway, where Berliners who had been out for a day's drive in the country were now heading home.

She pulled over too and slowed down. Then she spotted the trouble. A police car was occupying the fast lane in front of the lights before the junction.

Oh no, please no.

Why did there have to be a police roadblock now of all times?

She neared the flashing blue light and looked for a traffic cop flagging cars down at the side of the road. But there was no one and the traffic was flowing surprisingly smoothly. Most of it turned off right towards the station so as not to—

Oh no . . .

Tears sprang to Carina's eyes. She took both hands off

the wheel and clasped her mouth. Stationary beyond the patrol car was a small silver saloon the hazard lights of which were working on one side only. Borchert was nowhere to be seen, but there was no doubt who owned the Corolla.

Andi must have broken down. Oh my God . . .

Carina was slow to grasp the full implications. For a few seconds her mind refused to accept the truth. This was no police checkpoint. She wasn't being flagged down or arrested. Something far worse was happening. Now. At this very moment. To Simon. At a place known only to Robert Stern, who was relying on help that would never arrive.

And now? What now?

Carina could only think in fragmentary sentences. She drove slowly past the Corolla and across the junction in a stream of traffic, searching for a clue as to where Stern and Simon had been taken. Looking in her rear-view mirror, she saw two sturdy traffic cops start pushing Sophie's car off the road.

All at once a thought struck her. She turned and looked back.

The direction of travel.

The car was pointing straight on. Towards Potsdam. It wasn't much to go on, but still. Once past the junction Carina speeded up, spurred on by the thought that so far she hadn't made a mistake. She was driving along the right road in the right direction. That irrational hope buoyed her, but only for some two hundred metres.

And now?

She shot past the turning to Grosser Wannsee without knowing whether she'd lost the trail.

13

'Abducted from a hospital? What's the matter with the poor little mite?'

The cynical creature sounded like a worried aunt as she continued to hold Stern in check with the gun. 'I trust it's nothing infectious?'

Stern was still staring at the doorway through which Simon and the old pervert had just disappeared. He was incapable of replying and reluctant even to breathe. The thought of inhaling the same air as this woman – of sharing what had previously issued from her mouth and nose – was utterly repugnant to him.

'You realize we won't pay for damaged goods, don't you?' The face obscured by the sunglasses gave a throaty laugh and lit another cigarette. Stern could hear footsteps on the stairs, the creak of leather slippers drowning the faint squeak of Simon's trainers. The sounds steadily faded.

'Now, now, don't move.' She raised the gun. 'My husband won't be long. It's only forty-five minutes to the first interval. Then it'll be my turn.'

She puckered her dark-brown lips in the semblance of a kiss. Stern, feeling sick to his stomach, looked at the ceiling. The footsteps were directly overhead.

'Any moment now.' The lips twisted into a grimace that presumably stood proxy for a smile.

The next thing Stern heard was music – classical music. The paedophile was obviously an opera fan, because he recognized the strains of *La Traviata*. For the first time in his life, he wished Verdi had never written any arias for Violetta.

'Right,' said the woman, glancing at her watch. 'Let's make the most of our time and have a little chat. Come on, out with it. What are you really after?'

'Isn't that obvious?' Stern hoped she wouldn't notice the tremor in his voice. The soprano overhead was getting into her stride. 'You advertised for a boy. I delivered him.'

She was clever. She didn't make the mistake of coming any closer. At this range she could empty a whole magazine into him before he'd covered half the distance between them. The only weapons he could use against her were his voice and his intelligence, and both were threatening to give up on him.

Where the hell has Borchert got to?

'You can't be an informer – you're wanted by the police yourself. But you aren't one of us and you don't behave like a lawyer, so why did you respond to our advertisement?'

'I can explain the whole thing,' he lied. The truth was, he had no idea what to say or do to avert the danger. He could hear footsteps overhead again.

'I'm listening.'

Feverishly, Stern racked his brains for a plausible story while time was running out for Simon upstairs. He strove to remain outwardly calm. Inwardly he was programmed for escape, but there was no way out. If he stood up he was a dead man.

'Well? Cat got your tongue? It's a very simple question: Why did you abduct that child from a hospital and bring him to us?'

It struck Stern that the footsteps had fallen into a rhythm. The madman was dancing. A sudden thought occurred to him as he listened. He couldn't put his finger on it at first, but all at once it became clear. There *was* something he could do. Something profoundly repugnant and unnatural for which he would hate himself in retrospect. He nodded like someone who has had an idea and raised his hand. Slowly and cautiously, so as not to provoke a violent reaction on the woman's part.

'What are you doing?'

'Answering your question. Showing you what I'm after.'

She raised her left eyebrow far enough for it to show above the rim of her sunglasses. Stern had placed his hand on his chest. He proceeded to undo one of his shirt buttons, then another.

'What is this?'

'May I take off my jacket?'

'If you like . . .'

He not only slipped off his jacket, he undid the rest of his shirt buttons. Moments later he was sitting on the sofa stripped to the waist.

'What are you doing?'

In lieu of a reply, Stern ran his tongue over his lips and swallowed twice in quick succession. He hoped he looked lascivious. In reality, he was suppressing steadily mounting nausea.

'Oh, come on.' The woman had momentarily lowered her gun. She raised it again. 'You don't think I'll fall for *that*?'

'Why not? That's why I'm here.' Stern kicked off each off his leather slip-ons in turn and unbuckled his belt.

'You said it yourself: I'm not a cop. I'm not an informant either. I'm plain horny.' He pulled the belt out of his trousers and tossed it over to her.

'Come here and see for yourself.'

He couldn't see her eyes, so he didn't know if his theory held good, but experience had taught the lawyer in him that there was always some form of bait you could dangle in front of an opponent like a carrot in front of a donkey. With most people it was greed or lust that made them do things they regretted later.

The woman laughed. 'You're crazy,' she said, stubbing out her cigarette.

'Maybe, but I'll prove it if you like.'

He pulled off his socks. All he was wearing now were the thin trousers of his second-hand suit.

'How?'

'Come here and have a feel.'

'No, no, no.' She continued to stand there with the gun trained on his crotch. 'I've got a better idea.'

'Like what?'

Stern couldn't help smiling. He wasn't play-acting now. She'd taken the bait. Not completely as yet, but he could see her breathing faster and hear the note of excitement in her voice. He had struck some chord within her. But was it the right one?

'Stand up.' She backed towards the door, careful to maintain the distance between them.

He complied. It was good to move. In the right direction, too. Anything was preferable to sitting idly on the sofa and waiting for the soprano's voice to mingle with Simon's screams. At least, that was what he thought until the woman said, 'Let's see how *horny* it makes you to watch my husband in action.'

14

Carina was convulsed with panic.

What should she do? Drive straight on along Königstrasse? If so, how far? To Glienicker Bridge? Or turn off right towards the waterfront? She could also take one of the many access roads on her left.

The mobile on the passenger seat started ringing. It almost slid through her sweaty fingers when she tried to open it.

'Borchert?' she said, far louder than necessary.

'Cold.' Fear seemed to bite her in the throat when she heard the disguised voice.

'Who is this? What do you want?'

'Colder.'

Half demented with fear and concern for Simon, she strove to collect her thoughts. Endestrasse was coming up on her right. She nearly turned off. The name suited her situation.

'What is this?' she asked. 'Is it a game?'

'Warmer.'

She beat a wild tattoo on the plastic steering wheel with the fingers of her right hand. Could it be? Was this the voice Robert Stern had told her about, and if so, why call her?

'Am I heading in the right direction?' she asked, horrified, testing her suspicion.

'Warmer.'

It's true. The madman wants me to play blind man's buff.

'OK. I'm going to Potsdam, right?'

'Colder.'

So I turn off before?

'Here? Down Kyllmannstrasse?'

'Colder.'

'Do I turn left, then?'

'Warmer.'

She got into the outermost lane, almost overrunning the opposite carriageway.

'Am I nearly there?'

'Warmer.'

She looked round, but there were at least a dozen different cars and vans behind and ahead of her, not to mention two motorcycles. It was quite impossible to tell which of them was tailing her.

'Grassoweg? Do I go down Grassoweg?'

The distorted voice gave her another affirmative. Heedless of the oncoming traffic, Carina swung the wheel over and almost collided head-on with a florist's van. The driver slammed on his brakes and the van skidded, swaying precariously, into the other lane, which happened to be empty. The danger past, Carina sped along the narrow residential street, followed by a furious blare of horns.

'Is it here? In this street?'

'Colder.'

She took her foot off the gas. The street lighting was so dim, she found it hard to decipher the sign at the next fork.

'Am Kleinen Wannsee?' she said at length.

'Warmer,' the voice replied with an approving chuckle – the first time it had betrayed any emotion.

House number? What's the house number?

Carina debated what form her next yes-or-no question should take.

'Over a hundred?'

'Warmer.'

'A hundred and fifty?'

'Colder.'

It took her another seven goes before she came to a halt outside an imposing, four-storeyed house bearing the number 121.

15

The most important rule for winning a hopeless case against a superior adversary was something Stern had learned not at law school but from his father.

'Locate your opponent's weakness in his strength. Use his greatest asset against him.' That had been part of the old man's standard pep talk to Junior B, the local football team of which he was honorary coach.

Stern was wondering whether those maxims could help him today, when what was at stake was his life, not shooting or passing or marking your man. He analysed the situation while being shepherded out of the living room, barefoot and stripped to the waist. The woman had several advantages. The principal one, a 9mm pistol, she was holding in her hand. Moreover, as far as he could tell, the house was hermetically sealed. The doors and windows of an empty sale property had naturally to be secured against intruders. Even if he took advantage of his distance from the woman and fled along the passage to the back entrance, it was highly unlikely that he would find a door or a window unlocked.

She's keeping her distance with a gun aimed at my back and I'm shut in with her. Where's the weakness in her strength?

His neck muscles tensed as they always did when he was pondering an insoluble problem. When that happened at his desk it always and unmistakably heralded a migraine. A far more painful fate awaited him here, and he knew it.

The freshly stripped and polished oak floorboards creaked wearily as he started up the stairs. The music from above became more audible the higher he climbed, but the shuffling footsteps had ceased.

He's stopped dancing.

Stern forbade himself to speculate on what the man was doing instead. In that room. With Simon.

'Keep going,' the woman barked when he paused and started to turn his head. But he hadn't seen anything and couldn't tell from her voice whether she was following him up or had halted at the bottom. All he could see right then was a bright strip of light and some vague shapes, having been dazzled by one of the halogen spotlights that bathed the staircase in an unnaturally white glare, intensified by the bare, cream-coloured walls. He had to blink twice to efface the shadowy shapes dancing in front of his eyes . . .

And then, quite suddenly, he spotted the solution. Her weakness. Now about halfway up the curving staircase, he was nearing a very simple means of turning the tables on her. The only problem was, he couldn't be sure it would work. He could only hope so.

But he had to risk it, had to try something that might turn out to be his greatest – and, consequently, his last – mistake.

16

Carina got out of the car and scanned the building in front of her for signs of life.

'Is this it?'

She looked up. Painted wheat-yellow, the newly restored late-nineteenth-century house was surmounted by a hexagonal capped roof like a judge's wig. She could see no lights on any floor. All the blinds and shutters were closed.

'Hot,' the voice replied. Stiff-legged, she walked unsteadily to the wrought-iron garden gate. To her surprise it was unlocked.

And now?

She unzipped the bumbag that formed part of her runner's outfit. In addition to Simon's medication, some cash and one or two things Stern had asked her to keep for him, it contained Borchert's 'present': a Röhm RG 70.

'For emergencies,' he'd told her. 'Cute little gun. Perfect for a woman's dainty hand.'

A feeling of unreality crept over her as she walked up the gravel path. She had never held a gun in her hand before, still less been prepared to use it on someone.

'Is it open?' she asked when she reached the ornate front door.

For the first time she got no answer. Cautiously, she exerted pressure on the unyielding wood. It was shut and locked.

She turned round, but there was no one to be seen in the slumbrous light of the old street lamps. No passer-by. No pursuer. Nothing but the hum of traffic in nearby Königstrasse.

'How do I get in?' she asked the unknown man at the other end of the line. 'Around the back?'

Still no answer. Hoarse breathing, but that was all.

Looking at the entrance to the underground garage in the right-hand wing of the house, she could see tyre tracks in the wet leaves. 'The garage?' she said with her back to the front door. 'Is that it? Should I try to get in through the garage?'

The voice remained silent. The breathing had stopped too.

There's no time to lose, she told herself. *They may be hurting Simon inside there right now, and . . .*

She tightened her grip on the pistol butt and touched the brass bell push with her left forefinger. She wasn't a detective or a trained policewoman, and she was fighting a losing battle on this terrain anyway. She couldn't win. The most she could do was create a diversion.

'I'm going to ring the bell,' she said into the phone, and pressed the button.

'Colder,' said a resonant voice in her ear.

She felt a dazzling explosion right between her eyes, then nothing more.

17

Every step was torment, because every step brought him nearer to the possibility of extinction. But he himself was not the issue here. His death would rate no more than a brief report in the tabloids' local news section. The far more important tragedy was in progress in the room from which *La Traviata* continued to blare.

And it's all my fault, he thought.

Feigning a momentary loss of balance, he leaned against the wall on his left.

'What, weak at the knees already?'

OK, so you're just behind me. Only a few steps down. You probably don't want me diving around the corner and out of your field of fire when I get to the top.

He would have to be very quick, he realized, so he stayed on the left, away from the banisters. Only five steps to go.

The landing came into view. At the top of the stairs stood a terracotta urn containing an artificial fern. It looked bulkier and heavier the closer he got.

Another of his father's pearls of wisdom popped into his head: *The simplest tricks are often the most effective.* Whether or not his simple plan would succeed depended solely on four little plastic rectangles.

Another two steps.

Cautiously, he put out his hand. Like a wounded man whose tight bandage has been removed after several hours, he felt the blood rush into his fingertips. He would have preferred to use his right hand, but that would have been too noticeable.

One more step.

Now he could see the entire landing. There was no furniture apart from a mahogany side table with a property brochure lying open on it. No window either. *Luckily!*

Stern climbed the last stair as gingerly as if it were a crumbling ice floe. He fought the urge to look behind him and held his breath, totally focused on the next few seconds. He even faded out the man's voice, which was singing along to a Verdi aria.

Simon can't be far away.

'Down the passage, third door along on the right. You can hear the party's in full—'

The woman never finished her sentence. Spine-chilling in its suddenness, the shrill sound of a doorbell echoed around the bare walls.

Stern took advantage of this unexpected interruption to turn the tables in a final act of desperation, simply by hitting the shoulder-height row of light switches at the top of the stairs. That was the couple's Achilles' heel: they had deprived him of every potential means of escape, but the shutters also cut out any extraneous light. Once he had hit the switches, the ceiling lights would go out and plunge the entire stairwell into total darkness. He would then be able to pull the urn over and send the woman tumbling down the stairs in its company.

So much for the theory.

In practice, things looked rather different. Stern realized how wrong he was when he flipped the very first switch. Instead of getting darker, the whole of the gloomy upstairs passage was suddenly bathed in light. Instead of putting out the lights, he'd turned on a row of additional overheads.

Which made it easy for the woman behind him to take aim and fire with precision.

18

There were so many things about the room that Simon found surprising. For a start, the funny noise his trainers made on the shiny floor. When he sat down on the edge of the metal bedstead, he saw in the dim red glow that the whole expanse of parquet was covered with transparent plastic film.

The man removed the key from the door and went over to a black tripod in the corner. Mounted on it was a small digital camera, the lens of which was pointing straight at the bed on which Simon had been invited to sit. The man pressed a button and a little red light appeared beside the lens. Then he went over to the only window, which was covered with thick rubber curtains in army green, and turned on a miniature stereo system.

'Do you like music?' he asked.

'It depends,' Simon whispered, but the man in the dressing gown wasn't listening in any case. He was swaying in time to the music coming from the CD player. Simon wasn't sure he liked the song. He'd heard something similar in the matron's office at the children's home, and it hadn't appealed to him.

Meanwhile the man had shut his eyes and was looking dreamy. Simon wanted to get up and go. He'd heard of people like him. A policeman had visited his school one time and showed them pictures of the sort of men they shouldn't go with, although this one looked quite different somehow.

The music suddenly increased in volume. Simon coughed. Feeling a bit faint, he leaned back against the bedpost until the sensation subsided. As he did so, he noticed a number of medical instruments on a waist-high glass table beside the bed.

What is all this?

He experienced a sudden and quite unjustified pang of fear. This man couldn't harm him because of tomorrow morning. He would be meeting someone on a bridge at six o'clock. As long as he clung to that thought, he oughtn't really to feel afraid.

But when he saw the syringes he couldn't help it.

He'd seen syringes before, but only at the hospital and not as big. Another thing that puzzled him was the strip of silvery metal lying on the green cloth between a scalpel and a little saw. It looked like a miniature cycle chain with clothes pegs at either end.

'Come over here.'

The man must have been dancing by himself for several minutes, lost to the world. His voice sounded friendly. Simon, who had been resting his eyes, sleepily opened them. He looked away at once. The man had dropped his dressing gown around his ankles and was now wearing nothing but the latex gloves.

'Come on.'

'Why?' asked Simon, thinking of Stern.

'Be kind enough to bring me that thing on the bed.'

Simon saw what the man was pointing to. He coughed again, feeling even fainter than before, but he picked up what was lying on the stained mattress, which was devoid of bedclothes.

He got up and walked to the man on wobbly legs, feeling weaker and weaker with every step. His left hand was tingling again. He hoped Stern would come and get him soon.

'You're doing fine,' the man said breathlessly. He paused in the middle of a pirouette, stretched out the arm in which he'd been holding an invisible partner and patted Simon gently on the shoulder. Once, twice, three times. Then he laughed as if he'd cracked a good joke.

'You're a nice-looking boy. Did you know that?'

Simon shook his head.

'Yes, yes, but you could look even nicer.'

'I don't want to.'

'Yes, trust me.'

Simon felt the plastic bag wrenched out of his hand. Then he suddenly couldn't see a thing. He tried to take a breath but couldn't, the plastic went concave as he sucked it into his open mouth. Summoning up his last reserves of strength, he reached up and tried to tear the bag off his head, but the man seized his wrists, forced them behind his back and bound them together with something. He tried to scream, but he was too short of breath. All he inhaled was a little tuft of hair from his own wig, which had slipped off his head when the man pulled the plastic bag over it.

'There, *now* you look really nice,' Simon heard the naked man purr as he was forcibly dragged back to where he'd just been sitting. On the bed.

'Much nicer.'

Simon lashed out blindly with his feet. Although they occasionally connected with something soft, he quickly sensed that he was the only one sustaining any real damage.

He was steadily tiring, steadily growing weaker, and his lungs were threatening to burst, so he wasn't all that surprised by the loud report that abruptly drowned the music.

The man paused when he heard the shot ring out in the

passage. Then he grinned and tore off a long strip of duct tape, intending to wind it round the bag and the boy's neck. Only then would he have both hands free. And he needed them for what he had in mind.

19

When the shot sounded the world around him exploded. The pain that followed was unbearable, but it didn't make itself felt where he expected. Stern toppled forwards, cracking his head on the urn, although it was more of a reflex action than a physical necessity. He felt sure he'd been shot in the back and would see the exit wound in his stomach before death came. Instead, deafened, he found himself coughing his guts up. Every choking breath made him feel like he was on fire inside. After what seemed an eternity, and just before he thought he was going blind, he grasped what had happened.

Tear gas.

The pistol hadn't been loaded with lethal ammunition. The couple might be paedophiles but they weren't capable of murder. Either that, or they killed in some other way because a straightforward bullet wouldn't have enhanced their sexual pleasure.

Stern realized that he was quite wrong when the woman behind him started coughing too.

'Shit,' she said, but even that was almost inaudible. Her nose was streaming.

Stern rolled onto his stomach and peered down the stairs. His eyes felt like they'd been bathed in toilet cleaner, but he could just about see the woman a few steps below him. She was doubled up with her fists in her eyes. Like Stern, she hadn't been wearing a protective mask.

So she didn't know what the gun was loaded with, he concluded. The pair of them only acted blasé. They were new to the game. They couldn't have checked the pistol beforehand, and their premiere had just bombed.

Stern tried to stand. What happened next was as unintended as the cloud of chlorine gas. He lost his footing. Instead of stepping on to the landing, he went tumbling down the stairs.

A shaft of agony went through his back as he collided with the woman on the way down. For the second time in quick succession his head hit something hard, presumably a step, and blood spurted from his nose. As he was glissading down the stairs on his stomach, his left leg suddenly became incandescent with pain: his foot had got caught in the banisters and was supporting his entire weight.

Torn ligaments, severe tendonitis, broken ankle . . . He was suffering from all three, judging by the intensity of the pain, but he didn't care. Having gently freed his foot, he could see through a mist of tears that the woman was in a considerably worse state. She wasn't moving and one of her legs looked unnaturally contorted, as did the rest of her body.

Stern pulled himself up by the banister. He winced when he tried to stand on his left foot, so he hopped up the stairs on his good leg. His mucous membranes seemed to be dissolving, they were smarting so much.

Third door along on the right, the woman had said. Her directions were superfluous. In his present condition he could only be guided by his ears. *La Traviata* was still blaring through one of the massive oak doors. Stern rattled the handle.

Locked.

It took an instant for him to make up his mind. Ignoring the vicious pain seemingly caused by nails being driven into his left leg at every step, he hurried back to the urn. It was filled with heavy white pebbles, not soil. He could scarcely lift it, so he dragged it behind him along the passage. At the door he heaved the urn into the air, heedless of his creaking spine, and hurled it at the lock two-handed. It snapped off the handle and dented the lock. Stern charged the yielding oak panel with his shoulder. Once, twice. At last, drunk with pain, he staggered into the room.

The scene before him was worse than anything he'd ever seen, reducing his whole being to a single unspoken cry: *Too late!*

20

He saw the man first. Naked, bathed in sweat and paralysed with fear. His erection, subsiding only slowly, seemed to have numbed his reflexes completely. He shielded his face with his arms, but that was all.

Looking at the bed, Stern saw the faceless figure that was Simon lying motionless on the stained mattress with his hands bound behind his back and a cheap supermarket bag over his head.

'I can explain everything . . .' the man began. Blinded by tears, rage and pain, Stern limped swiftly over to the camera, gripped the tripod like a baseball bat, and shattered his jaw, sending the man over backwards, and the stereo rig to the floor. *La Traviata* died just as Stern made a dive for the bed and tore an airhole in the bag over Simon's head.

He felt like shouting aloud – with boundless relief. He had made one mistake after another, but at least he hadn't lost Simon. The boy was coughing and gasping like a shipwreck survivor newly plucked from the sea. He just couldn't stop, but to Stern the whistling intakes of breath with which he was sucking oxygen back into his lungs sounded better than any symphony.

'I'm so, so sorry,' he blurted out. Simon was sitting up on the bed now. Stern had torn off the rest of the bag and was holding the boy's head between his hands, careful not to bring him into contact with his grimy, bloodstained chest.

'It's . . .' Simon wheezed, 'it's all right.' He started coughing again and sniffed. Stern drew back a little. The cloud of tear gas had been contained in the stairwell, fortunately, but he was afraid that enough of it might be clinging to his hair to place an additional strain on the boy's breathing.

Unable to speak for coughing, Simon put out his arm and pointed to something. Stern turned in time to see the man with the shattered jaw making for the door.

'Stay here!' he yelled. He snatched up the tripod – the camera had already come adrift – and sideswiped him on the shin with it. The man doubled up and collapsed just short of the doorway, bellowing in agony.

'Don't move or you'll end up dead like that crazy wife of yours.'

Stern bent over the man, who was choking by now on his own cries of pain, and showed him the scalpel he'd taken from the side table. He felt like driving the end of the tripod into the man's foot or snapping off the scalpel blade under his fingernails, but he couldn't do that to Simon. The boy had witnessed enough violence. Worse still, he had *experienced* it. Thanks to him, Stern, he was going to need psychological therapy.

'Look, we can work this out,' the man mumbled, curled up on the floor in front of Stern. His expression had undergone a complete change attributable not just to the rearrangement of his teeth. 'I've got money. *Your* money. As agreed.'

'Shut up. I don't want any money.'

'What, then? Why *are* you here?'

'Simon, please look away,' said Stern, raising the tripod again. The man brought his knees up to his chin and buried his bloodstained face in his hands.

'No, please don't,' he begged. 'I'll do anything you want. Please.'

Stern let him tremble awhile in expectation of another blow. Then he asked, 'Where's the mobile?'

'What?'

'Your goddamned mobile. Where is it?'

'There.' The man pointed to the dressing gown lying beside the bed. Stern stepped back and picked it up.

'In the pocket. The right-hand pocket.'

Stern could barely understand the child abuser's plaintive whimpers. He found the phone and handed it to the man at his feet.

'What do you want me to do?'

'Call him.'

'Who?'

'Your contact. The person you spoke to in the living room. Go on, I want a word with him.'

'No, I can't.'

'Why not?'

'Because I don't have his number. Nobody has the Dealer's number.' The man said the penultimate word as if it were a name. Even in his situation, he couldn't disguise the awe in which he held the name.

'So how do you get in touch with him?'

'We email him and he calls us back. That's what happened with you. Tina sent him your name and ID number by phone in the car. Then he called us back.'

Tina. So the dying gorgon at the foot of the stairs now had a name.

'OK, give me his email address.'

'It's in the mobile.'

'Where?' The mobile beeped every time Stern pressed a key. He knew the model; he had used one himself for a short time.

'It's under "Bambino", but it won't be any use to you.'

'Why not?' Stern didn't even try to memorize the complicated entry: gulliverqyx@23.gzquod.eu. He would be taking the phone with him in any case.

'Because the address changes after every enquiry. That one's already defunct.'

'So what do you do the next time?'

'I can't tell you that.'

'Why not?'

'Because he'd kill me.'

'What do you think *I* plan to do to you? Tell me how you get the new email address or I'll send you to join your wife.'

'OK, OK, OK . . .' The man raised his arm defensively, staring wide-eyed at the tripod Stern was holding over his head. 'He's got various addresses. Thousands of them, but they only work once. Whenever we want to contact him we have to buy a new one.'

'Where? Where do you buy them?'

When he heard the answer, the scalpel slipped from his hand and stuck in the plastic-covered parquet.

'*What* did you say?' he gasped. His throbbing head, swollen ankle, wrenched back and burning lungs had combined to form a single, all-embracing pain.

'Say that again!' he bellowed.

'On the bridge,' the naked man at his feet repeated with tears streaming down his bloodstained cheeks. He was probably betraying the fraternity's best-kept secret. 'We buy the addresses on the bridge.'

21

Many scenes of one-time horror exude an aura capable of arousing contradictory emotions. But it is not the clearly visible signs of violence that attract and repel us. Not the splashes of blood or brains on the wallpaper above the bed or the severed limbs beside the chest full of clean laundry. It is the indirect signals that hold a morbid fascination for outsiders. A cordoned-off area in a normally crowded underground station exerts such an effect, as does a public square unnaturally ablaze with the headlights of several parked police cars.

'Shit,' said Chief Superintendent Hertzlich, rubbing his weary eyes without removing his gold-rimmed glasses. Grumpily, he beckoned Engler over from the Madison's entrance. In the gloom of the autumnal evening the brightly illuminated café on Mexikoplatz was acting like a lamp besieged by nocturnal insects. Numerous passers-by on their way to the S-Bahn station were having to be kept away from the police barriers. There really wasn't anything to see for once, as curious spectators were being regularly informed by a uniformed officer.

'This is a total fuck-up,' Hertzlich said loudly when Engler joined him. The whole case seemed to be getting out of hand, hence his wish to form an on-the-spot picture of the situation. He hadn't suspected it would look so disastrous.

'Let's have your report,' he said, eyeing Engler with distaste as the inspector extracted an Aspirin Plus C from its packet and chewed the effervescent tablet without any water. He wondered if it wouldn't be better to relieve him of responsibility for the case.

'Borchert's car broke down, that's how we happened to pick him up,' Engler began, 'and he directed us back here to Mexikoplatz. He firmly states that Robert Stern and little Simon Sachs have been abducted by a woman they met in this café. The licence number he claims to have seen isn't registered. The only clue we have so far is that email address.' Engler pointed wearily to the sign in the café window. 'It belongs to a smallish estate agent in Berlin-Stieglitz run by a man named Theodor Kling and his wife Tina. His secretary was just knocking off for the day, but she informed us that he was out viewing some properties with a client. She faxed us a list of the ones currently for sale. We're checking them at this moment.'

'How many are there?'

'Eight in the immediate vicinity. Not many, in other words. The only problem is, we can hardly gain access to all of . . . Just a minute, that could be Brandmann.'

Engler opened his mobile. A moment later he grimaced as if he'd bitten into a lemon.

Hertzlich raised his eyebrows enquiringly.

'Where the hell are you?' he heard the inspector ask. From the bewilderment in his voice, Engler clearly wasn't speaking to a colleague.

22

'An ambulance to 121 Kleinen Wannsee?'

Engler repeated the address, of which he'd heard only snatches from Stern. Hertzlich, who had also registered the information, stepped aside and took out his mobile.

'OK,' said Engler, 'wait there for us. Don't move from the spot.' The connection was so poor, he felt he was having to compete with a wind machine in the background.

Where in God's name is Brandmann when you need him?

'Can't . . . no time to expl—' Stern's voice was breaking up badly. 'The woman may be . . . the man is . . . You must detain—'

Engler didn't get the rest. He asked the most important question.

'How's the boy?'

'That's why I'm calling you.'

The lawyer must have left the dead zone, because he wasn't breaking up any more.

'Listen,' said Engler, 'this has got to stop. It's time you turned yourself in.'

'Yes, I will.'

'When?'

'Now. That's to say . . . Just a moment.'

There was a click on the line, and Engler thought he

heard Simon in the background. So Stern hadn't been lying. The boy was still alive!

'Give me another forty minutes or so, then we'll meet. Just the two of us, though. No one else.'

'OK, where?'

The inspector looked taken aback when Stern named the rendezvous.

23

The person you are calling is temporarily unavailable. If you wish to be notified by text message as soon as they . . .

Damn it. What was wrong? Why didn't Carina pick up?

And what has happened to Borchert? Why did he leave us in the lurch?

Stern silenced the mailbox's computerized voice. He felt like hurling the mobile out of the window and into the car park, which they'd reached after a wild drive across town. It profoundly disgusted him to think that, not many minutes ago, that filthy paedophile had held the same phone to his sweaty ear. But he still needed it. He'd made his most important call first and informed Engler, because he couldn't go on like this. He simply had to turn himself in, even at the risk of never learning what had really happened to Felix.

But that was secondary now. His insane pursuit of a phantom had to be brought to an end at last. Simon had almost been murdered. *That* was the reality, not his fantasies about Felix and the boy with the birthmark.

He felt a small hand on his shoulder.

'Feeling OK?' Simon asked.

Stern's eyes filled with tears once more. He'd left the boy alone with a grinning monster from hell, and Simon had asked how *he* was feeling?

'I'm fine,' he lied. The truth was, it was a miracle he'd made it out of the house at all without collapsing. Luckily, Simon seemed to possess incredible powers of recuperation and had descended the stairs unaided once Stern had secured the man to the bedstead with duct tape.

The woman hadn't stirred as they stepped over her at the foot of the stairs, but Stern thought he detected shallow breathing. Although every additional step and movement was agony, he'd gone into the living room and gathered up his scattered clothes before they left via the garage and the couple's car. He thanked God the American saloon was an automatic. His left foot was so swollen and painful, he could barely walk on it, let alone operate a clutch pedal.

'You don't look too good,' Simon said hoarsely.

Stern tried to laugh it off. 'And you sound like Kermit,' he retorted. Having lowered the sun visor and looked at himself in the vanity mirror, he had to agree. In the glove compartment he found some wet wipes for the windscreen. With a shrug, he took one from the packet and wiped some of the blood off his face.

'But how are *you* feeling?' he asked as he gingerly dabbed at the throbbing bruise on his forehead.

'OK.' Simon gave a muffled cough.

'I'm so sorry, so terribly sorry,' Stern repeated for at least the eighth time since leaving the house. 'But I'll make it up to you, I promise.'

'Nothing really happened,' Simon said wearily.

Stern turned on the roof light for a better look at the boy. Simon's eyelids were quivering and he couldn't repress a yawn. After the day's events, Stern had no idea whether that was a good or a bad sign.

'Need anything? Some water? Your medication?'

'No, I'm just tired.' Simon coughed again. His left leg

was twitching slightly, not that Stern had noticed it during the drive.

'Can you make it by yourself?'

'Sure.' Simon opened the passenger door, then hesitated. 'I'd sooner stay with you, though.'

Stern shook his head, and even that hurt. 'I'm sorry.'

'But you'll be needing me later, won't you?'

'Come here.' Stern pulled the boy towards him. Ignoring his aching back, he hugged the child as hard as he could. 'Yes, of course I will. Very much so. That's why it's important you do exactly what I told you, OK? You're to go into the hospital and report to your ward at once, you hear?'

Simon nodded. 'All right. What are you going to do now?' he asked, his voice muffled by Stern's shirt.

'I'm going to solve the case.'

Simon sat back and looked up at him. 'Really?'

'Really.'

'Does that mean I won't have to hurt anyone tomorrow after all?'

'It does.'

'Because I don't want to.'

'I know that.' Stern brushed a strand of hair behind Simon's ear and gave a weary smile. 'Can you really manage on your own?'

'Yes, I'm fine. My throat's sore, that's all.'

'And that twitching leg?'

'It's not bad. Besides, they'll soon give me something for that.'

Simon had one foot on the ground when Stern caught him by the shoulder.

'Remember what you told Dr Tiefensee when he asked you to imagine the most wonderful place in the world?'

'Yes.' Simon smiled.

'We'll go there when this is all over. You and me and

Carina. We'll go to that beach and buy ourselves the biggest ice-creams in the universe, OK?'

Simon smiled even more broadly and waved before he set off across the car park. Although it wasn't far to the hospital entrance, Stern watched him almost as if hypnotized every step of the way. He started the engine, but not in readiness to drive away; he wanted to be able to reach the boy's side within seconds in an emergency. The grounds of the Seehaus Clinic did not, of course, hold any dangers of the kind Simon had been exposed to in the last few hours, but Stern's anxiety didn't subside until the automatic doors slid open and the boy disappeared into the hospital building.

He glanced at his watch and reversed out of the parking space. It was six forty-six. He would have to hurry if he didn't want to be late.

24

'OK, he's here. What do you want me to do?'

The bearded man in the canteen stirred the froth on his latte macchiato as he watched Simon making for the lifts.

'I guess he's going straight to his ward,' he said into his mobile. He took the long coffee spoon from his glass and was about to lick it when he stiffened.

'Just a moment,' he said, interrupting the voice on the other end of the line. 'They've spotted him. A doctor's talking to him. I reckon all hell will break loose in a minute.'

He removed his huge paws from the fluted coffee glass and stood up for a better view of the doctors and nurses clustering round the boy. Voices were raised. The hospital was buzzing with activity.

'Really? You're sure?'

The agitated voices of the group in front of the lifts increased in volume. So much so that the man had difficulty in concentrating on the instructions he was receiving over the phone. He asked the other party to speak louder. Eventually he got the message and grunted an affirmative.

'All clear. Will do.'

Picasso hung up, leaving his coffee untouched.

25

'Teeeeeeeee pleeeeeeeee . . .'

To her ears, the unnaturally drawn-out words could have come from a tape recorder playing at half speed. They were quite unintelligible.

Where am I? What happened?

Carina felt as if she were in a washing machine in the final phase of its spin cycle. The hard surface beneath her was jolting violently. Now and then she was pitched forwards by some invisible force, only to be flattened a moment later against the equally unyielding back of the seat.

She blinked feverishly, feeling sick. It was only now, as if breathing through her eyes, not her nose, that she registered the all-encompassing stench of alcohol and vomit.

She strained to keep her eyes open but couldn't see a thing. Nothing, at least, that offered a plausible explanation of what had happened to her.

A thin man with a moustache and a cinnamon-brown side parting was bending over her. He held out a plastic card as though proffering his ID.

'W-what'sh . . . what'sh *happened to me*?' she tried to say, but her own words sounded even more incomprehensible than those of this stranger with the stern expression. He raised his voice, sounding rather brusque, and this time she grasped what he was saying.

'Tickets please.'

'Eh? W-what?'

With an immense effort, Carina turned her head and looked past the conductor at the bench seat opposite. Its only occupant was an elderly woman who stared at her in disgust and rolled her eyes contemptuously before reimmersing herself in a magazine.

'I, er . . . I remember being . . .'

Carina discovered that she herself was the source of the smell. Cheap red wine. Her tracksuit was spattered with it.

I don't understand.

The last thing she could remember was that horrible voice. *Cold . . .*

That plus the certainty that she was falling into an everlasting, dreamless sleep.

But now?

She clasped her throbbing head. To her surprise, she couldn't detect an injury of any kind. Not even a bump.

'Better get a move on unless you want to spend the night in a cell.'

As the seconds ticked by, more and more details of her surroundings combined to form a peculiar totality. The scratched windows, the flickering neon tube above her head, the grab handles. She grasped where she was but couldn't fathom why. She might as well have woken up on an Antarctic ice floe. The S-Bahn carriage in which she was rattling through nocturnal Berlin seemed just as unreal to her.

'I thought I was dead,' she said to the conductor, who couldn't help grinning faintly.

'No, you only look like it.'

He grabbed her right hand before she could snatch it away and removed something from between her fingers.

'It was there all the time.' He checked the stamp on the ticket, which evidently satisfied him.

'That's a new one on me. Drank yourself silly, but not too silly to buy a ticket.'

The inspector returned the ticket, advised her to take it a bit easier next weekend, and moved on.

The train slowed down and dived beneath the roof of a dimly illuminated station, the signboards of which were still adorned with its name in Gothic script: S-Bahnhof Grunewald.

We're only two stations from Wannsee.

Carina got to her feet – the other passengers made way for her as if she had an infectious disease, she noticed – and tottered out on to the platform.

Her head was buzzing like a beehive. The voice must have put a stun gun to it, poured cheap plonk over her and abandoned her on the S-Bahn like a down-and-out.

But why?

The fresh air not only revived her but intensified her anxiety. It didn't matter what had happened to *her*. What mattered was what had happened to Simon. And to Robert Stern.

Halfway to the stairs she paused beside the deserted waiting room and let the handful of passengers who had also alighted walk past.

She was feeling just as helpless as she had a good hour ago, when she hadn't known which way to go to rescue Simon and Robert, except that she was in a considerably worse condition. Her skull was splitting, she felt sick, and her stomach was rumbling so much it seemed to be vibrating incessantly. The hand she put to it landed on her plastic bumbag by mistake. Now her fingers were vibrating too. Simultaneously, something started beeping.

She managed to unzip the bag at the second attempt. It surprised her for a moment to find that everything was still there: money, Simon's medication, even the gun Borchert had given her. Then she took out the beeping personal organizer Robert had asked her to keep for him.

She opened the leather case and stared at the flashing entry. An appointment. The beeping was meant to remind him of an appointment he'd made only on Thursday. At her request.

Carina turned off the alarm, realizing that it couldn't be a coincidence. The chain of events that had begun on that derelict industrial estate beside the expressway was continuing to take its course. She hugged herself, shivering, and rubbed her upper body with her hands as if that could snap the strings with which the invisible puppeteer was guiding her through this lunacy.

After a while she set off, shuffling wearily along. She could make it if she hurried. The place wasn't far.

26

When the plasticuffs were secured around his wrists in the car park on Clayallee, Stern was reminded of something he'd been told by a client years before: *It's like handing your life to a cloakroom attendant.*

Although the female forger hadn't been wrongfully arrested, like him, Stern had to admit that her description of that initial moment of impotent despair was extremely apt.

'Why there?' Engler looked at Stern in the rear-view mirror. 'Why did you insist on meeting me at a fairground?'

The inspector was seated at the wheel of his unmarked police car, a grey saloon.

'So I could see if you'd keep to our agreement.' Stern forced his eyes to stay open. He was longing for merciful oblivion to put an end to all his aches and pains, but it was still too soon for that. 'I had to be sure you'd come on your own.' He jerked his head at the big wheel, the flashing lights of which were gradually receding as they drove away. 'The view from up there is really fantastic.'

He had called Engler from a gondola and told him to turn on his hazard lights. Having located him in the visitors' car park in that way, he had remained on the wheel for three more turns before deciding to risk it. And, sure enough, no plainclothesmen had jumped him when he got into the inspector's car.

'I see.' Engler nodded approvingly. He broke off for a sudden sneeze. 'But your fears were groundless,' he said once his nose had settled down. His cold sounded just as bad as it had been at their very first interview. Incredible to think it was only three days ago.

'We're being tracked by GPS,' he went on hoarsely, 'so headquarters always knows where we are. Besides, I think you're an arsehole, not dangerous.' He grinned at the rear-view mirror. 'Or at least, not so dangerous I couldn't cope with you single-handed.'

Stern nodded, looking at his left wrist. The rough edges of the plasticuff were already leaving marks.

'But why did you want to meet *me*? We aren't exactly best buddies.'

'That's just it. Always do business with your enemies, my father used to say. They can't betray you like your friends. Besides, I'm not too keen on Brandmann. I don't know him.'

'Smart guy, your father. So what's this deal of yours?'

'I'll give you information that will enable you to arrest at least two criminals: a trafficker in children and the avenger. In other words, the man responsible for those human remains I found.'

Their surroundings grew suddenly darker. No more houses were visible through the car's streaming windows. They had left the illuminated part of Hüttenweg behind and were driving along a link road that took them across the Grunewald forest.

'OK, what do you want in return?'

'No matter what evidence against me you think you've got, and no matter what I'm about to tell you, you must put my ex-wife's children under police protection at once.'

'Why?'

'Because I'm being blackmailed. And that brings me to my second request: you must let me go free until six o'clock tomorrow morning.'

'You're crazy.'

'Maybe, but not as crazy as these two.'

'What's that?' Engler glanced at the passenger seat. Despite the cuffs, Stern had managed to fish a tiny videotape out of his jacket and toss it across to the policeman.

'It's a tape from the estate agent's bedroom in Wannsee. Take a look at what he and his wife were planning to do to Simon Sachs – *if* you've got the stomach for it.'

'Is *he* the one pulling the wires?'

'The estate agent? No.'

As quickly as he could, Stern told Engler what he'd discovered in the last few hours.

'A baby is due to be sold tomorrow morning. Simon has a recurrent vision in which he kills the so-called Dealer. In revenge.'

'And you believe *that*?'

'No. If there's any truth in the story at all, another avenger will appear on the bridge tomorrow morning, and he'll shoot the Dealer at the first opportunity.'

Engler slowed as he approached the Hüttenweg-Koenigsallee intersection. The lights were red.

'All right,' he said warily, 'let's assume there's something in your fantastic theory. How does the boy come to know about it?'

Stern looked to see if they were being followed, but apart from a motorcycle ahead of them, which was disappearing in the direction of the Avus, they were temporarily on their own at the lights.

'How can your client, Simon Sachs, see into the future as well as the past?'

'No idea.'

The rain was getting heavier. Engler turned the windscreen wipers up a notch.

'"No idea" is a bad answer if you want me to let you go. How do I know you aren't involved yourself?'

As they drove on, Stern was briefly puzzled by a change in the engine note. It sounded as if Engler had filled the tank with low-octane petrol.

'That's why you can't afford to lock me up. I'll prove it to you tomorrow morning. On the bridge.'

'What bridge?'

'I'll tell you when we've got a deal.'

Just a minute. What is that?

Stern leaned forwards. He'd been mistaken. There was nothing wrong with the car's engine. The motor-mower sound was coming from outside. It was growing louder, too.

'Does anyone else know about our meeting?' Engler asked suddenly. He sounded nervous, and his tension transmitted itself to Stern.

'No, no one,' Stern replied.

'What number was it?'

'What do you mean?'

Stern felt for the mobile in his jacket pocket. It was still turned on. *That meant . . .*

'The number you called me from. Who does the mobile belong to?'

Engler was sounding more and more edgy. He glanced over his shoulder.

'The estate agent, why?'

The wiper blades swept the rain aside, momentarily transforming the windscreen into a magnifying glass and enabling Stern to see him clearly.

The motorcyclist. He had doubled back, cut his headlight

and was heading straight for them with one arm extended.

The lights turned green. Engler engaged first gear.

Hell and damnation! Andi Borchert expressly warned us all. Any fool can trace a mobile—

Something went bang. And Stern's train of thought snapped.

27

The three shots sounded innocuous, like the popping of half-ignited firecrackers. But the muffled reports were deceptive. They pierced the windscreen with lethal force and sent safety glass showering inwards like confetti.

Stern couldn't have said which shot was the first to hit the inspector, whose head slumped forwards on to the steering wheel. The lights were still green. When they changed to amber, the car's interior light came on. Not that Stern noticed this in his initial state of shock. His brain was far too busy processing a succession of horrific images: the motorcyclist, the shattered windscreen, the inspector's convulsively twitching fingers.

Stern's teeth were chattering. He was shivering with shock, pain and panic – and because a sudden gust of rain-laden wind was blowing into his face. He realized only now why the overhead light had come on: the door beside him was open. Someone had wrenched it open.

'You didn't keep to the agreement,' a man's voice snarled at him out of the darkness. Something cold prodded his temple. It was the muzzle of the motorcyclist's automatic.

'Best regards from the voice. You wanted to know whether a person could be reincarnated.'

Stern squeezed his eyelids even tighter together. He knew

then that none of the stock descriptions of your last few seconds applied to him. His mind's eye saw no personal biopic in the face of death, not even a still. Instead, for nanoseconds at a time, he could feel every single cell in his body. He was conscious of the dull thuds with which adrenalin was flowing into the maelstrom of his circulation from the adrenal medulla. He heard his bronchioles dilate and perceived the intensified contractions of his heart like minor explosions beneath his breastbone. His external perceptions underwent a change at the same time. He did not feel the wind as a totality, but as a stream of countless oxygen atoms sandblasted separately on to his skin in company with the raindrops.

He heard himself cry out, more afraid than he had ever been in his life. At the same time, he also experienced every other emotion more intensely than ever before. It was as if someone were trying to prove what emotions he would have been capable of if only he had given life a chance. Then, just before the end, he felt that he was dissolving – that the Robert Stern made up of atoms and molecules was trying to disintegrate into its separate components in order to facilitate the bullet's penetration of his skull.

And, just as a feeling of profound sadness enveloped him like a cloak, the fatal shot rang out.

The bullet found its intended mark. Right in the middle of the forehead, where it drilled a hole in the skull the size of a fingernail. Blood oozed from it like ketchup from a bottle.

Stern opened his eyes. Incredulously, he clasped his head and felt where the killer had held his gun only moments before; it was still hurting from the pressure of the muzzle. Then he looked at his hand, convinced that he would see, smell and feel blood on his fingertips. Nothing of the kind happened.

At last he looked straight ahead. And heard Engler's gun fall into the footwell with a thud. Half of the inspector's face seemed to be steeped in blood. Stern only realized later that this was the reflection of the traffic lights, which had turned red again.

He saved my life! With his last ounce of strength he managed to draw his gun . . .

For a moment Stern hoped Engler wasn't too badly wounded after all. The inspector was sitting sideways like a father making sure that everyone's seat belt was fastened before driving off. He even seemed to be regarding Stern amiably for the first time. Then blood trickled down his chin. He opened his mouth in surprise, blinked for the last time, and fell forwards over the wheel. The hand that had been holding the gun went limp, as did the rest of his body.

Jolted out of his trance-like state by the blare of the horn, Stern regained control of his body. The white noise in his head disappeared and life flowed back into his limbs. So did the pain. He undid his seat belt and slid sideways out of the car. He retrieved Engler's gun from the footwell and trained it on the long-haired man lying in the gutter; the rider's eyes were wide with disbelief. The last remnants of his life were seeping out of his head and on to the asphalt. Stern had never seen the clean-shaven face before, yet it somehow looked familiar.

Engler saved my life. Engler, of all people.

He only meant to walk a little way to the cycle path, but he stumbled after a few steps and rolled down an embankment. He landed on his plasticuffed hands and got a mouthful of damp earth and leaves before he found the courage to raise his head and stand up.

I must get away from here.

He swayed, put his weight on the wrong foot by mistake and leaned against a tree, groaning. But not even the fiercest physical pain could displace his rampant fear. Further up the slope a vehicle sped past, but no one got out to help him. Or arrest him. Not yet, but squad cars were bound to be on their way.

They'll never believe me. I must get away from here.

He groaned again, this time in a fit of mental agony worse than any physical pain he'd experienced. Then he staggered off into the trees. Only two days ago he had hated his messed-up life with all his heart. Now he wanted it back.

28

Eight-seventeen. That meant the skunk was seventeen minutes late, and if there was one thing he detested, it was lack of punctuality. And being inconvenienced. That was even worse. What were people thinking of? No one was immortal, yet everyone behaved as if there were a lost property office where you could retrieve the hours of life you'd squandered.

The coffee had gone cold. He tipped it into the sink with an angry splash, furious at the waste. And at himself. He'd known the boy would fail to turn up again, so why had he made any coffee in the first place? It was his own fault.

A spoon tinkled against a cup in the room next door. 'Would you like some tea for a change?' he called in a hoarse voice, stubbing out the filterless cigarette that had almost burned down to his fingertips. 'I'm just putting some more water on.'

'No thanks.'

Unlike him, his unexpected visitor seemed to have no problem sacrificing minute after wasted minute on the altar of death. Perhaps you had to develop piles – perhaps your teeth had to fall out and your toenails turn yellow – before you would refuse to wait even half an hour for someone to turn up. Or not, as the case may be. That was how long the said visitor had been sitting on his upholstered pinewood bench, the last piece of furniture he and his wife had bought together.

Maria had always been punctual. In fact she usually turned up too early. That was something she had in common with the lung cancer that had killed her. Ironical, considering that, unlike him, she'd never smoked in her life.

Huh?

He turned off the tap before the kettle was full and went over to the kitchen window, where he cocked his head and listened for a recurrence of that scratching sound. Perhaps he hadn't closed the dustbin properly. If so, and if he didn't want his nice lawn dug up by a marauding wild boar, he would have to venture outside again on this foul night.

The small, wooden-framed window was rear-facing. Normally, he could look out across the terrace to the little landing stage where he kept his rubber dinghy, but the contrast between the brightly illuminated kitchen and the inky darkness outside was so great that visibility was almost nil. He was all the more startled when a battered face suddenly appeared, pressed up against the glass.

What the—

He shrank away and almost fell backwards over a kitchen stool. The face had disappeared behind the film of condensation its breath had left on the pane. All the old man could now see were two bound hands hammering on his window.

He gave another start and tried to remember where he'd left the spear-gun he kept for self-defence in an emergency. He didn't realize his mistake until he heard someone call out.

'Hello? Are you in there?'

Even though he found it hard to associate the familiar voice with that grimy, battered face, the fact remained: the man out there was no stranger. On the contrary.

The old man shuffled out of the kitchen and made his way to the back door.

'You're late,' he growled when he had opened the door at last. 'As usual.'

'I'm sorry, Dad.' The battered face came closer. Its owner was dragging one leg and holding the upper part of his body curiously stiff.

'What happened to you? Run over by a bus?'

'Worse than that.'

Robert Stern hobbled past his father into the living room. He couldn't believe who was waiting for him in there.

29

'What are you doing here?' It was all he managed to ask before the floor rotated anticlockwise beneath him. The last thing he heard was a startled cry and the sound of china smashing. Then he collapsed beside the fragments of the coffee cup Carina had dropped in her alarm at his sudden appearance.

He recovered consciousness to find her bending over him, her eyes wide with anxiety. A strand of her curly hair was brushing his forehead like a feather, and he wished its gentle touch could embrace his whole body. Instead, the pain he felt when he tensed his neck muscles and tried to raise his head was a vicious reminder of all that had happened in the last few hours.

'Simon?' he asked hoarsely. 'Do you know . . .'

'He's safe,' she whispered. A tear trickled down her pale cheek. 'I called Picasso. They've posted a guard outside his room.'

'Thank God.' Stern started to tremble all over. 'What time is it?'

He heard a kettle whistling in the kitchen. That was a good sign. If his father was still making tea, he couldn't have blacked out for long.

'Nearly half past eight.'

She brushed away her tears with the back of her hand, picked up a knife she must have got from the kitchen and severed the plasticuffs.

'Thanks. Heard anything from Sophie? Are the twins all right, do you know?' His tongue felt like a tennis ball.

'Yes, she sent me a text. Some neighbour must have spotted us this morning and informed the police. They're searching her house.'

Stern's stomach muscles relaxed a little. At least the children were safe.

'We can't stay here, it's—'

He broke off. Two grey-green felt slippers had entered his field of vision and halted beside his head. Gritting his teeth, he heaved himself into a sitting position on the worn carpet.

'That's right, first you turn up late and then you push off.' A coin inserted in the old man's furrowed forehead would have lodged there. Georg Stern had overheard his son's last words as he entered the room carrying a pot-bellied teapot. He slammed it down angrily on a metal coaster. 'To be frank, I'm not surprised in the least.'

Stern turned to Carina, who was also looking the worse for wear. What was more, she smelled like a taproom.

'You haven't told him anything?'

'No, not in detail. Only that we were in trouble and needed a bolt-hole.'

'But how did you know—'

'Yes, trouble,' the old man broke in angrily. 'It's always the same old story, Robert, isn't it? You'd hardly have come to see me if there was something to celebrate.'

'Please forgive me, but . . .'

Stern pulled himself up by the bench while Carina faced his father with a defiant air.

'Your son has been through hell, can't you see that?'

'Oh yes, I can see that perfectly well. I'm not blind, young lady – unlike him. He doesn't seem to see I'm not an imbecile.'

'What do you mean?'

'I mean there's such a thing as television. You may think I'm senile, the two of you, but I can recognize my boy when he appears on the evening news in the role of an escaped criminal. What's more, I've had an Inspector Brandmann bending my ear on the phone. It'll only be a question of time before he turns up here too, so Robert's right for once. You can't stay here.'

'Then I don't understand,' said Carina. 'If you know what he's been through, why be so mean to him?'

'But that's the whole point, young lady.' Georg Stern clapped his hands. 'Of course I know Robert's in trouble – he has been for the last ten years, and now, from the sound of it, he's acquired some additional problems. But what am I supposed to do? He never really talks to me, just drops in and chats about the weather, the football results and my visits to the doctor. My own son treats me like a stranger. Even now, when he badly needs my help . . .'

Stern detected a hint of moisture in his father's eyes when the old man turned to face him.

'I know I go on at you, son. It happens every time we speak on the phone or see each other, but you're inscrutable. I don't understand you, much as I'd like to . . .'

He cleared his throat and readdressed himself to Carina, who was standing forlornly in the middle of the low-ceilinged room.

'But maybe you can do something with him, my girl. I knew at once you had guts three years ago, when he brought you here for supper that time. You contradicted me when I talked nonsense, and now you're doing it again. Good for you.'

He opened his mouth as though he had something else

of importance to say, but clapped his hands again and turned away.

'Enough of that,' he muttered to himself. 'This is no time for sentimentalities.'

He shuffled out of the room, to return only a few moments later with a small brown sponge bag.

'Here.'

'What is it?' Carina asked, holding out her hand.

'Maria's medication. She was swallowing painkillers like Smarties towards the end. I'm sure the Tramadol has passed its expiry date, but it may still work. Robert looks as if he could use a dose of something strong.' He gave a wry smile. 'And this is for the two of you.'

Stern caught the key his father tossed him.

'What's it for?'

'A camper van.'

'Since when have you—'

'I haven't. It belongs to Eddie, a neighbour of mine. He's abroad, and I have to move the thing when the heating oil supplier needs to gain access to his property. Take it. Find yourself somewhere safe for the night.' The old man knelt down and pulled a suitcase from under the bench on which Stern was sitting. 'And here are some clean things, sweaters and so on, for you to change into.'

Stern got to his feet. He didn't know what to say. He felt like giving his father a hug, but he'd never done that in his life. They had always parted with a handshake for as long as he could remember.

'I'm innocent,' was all he said.

Already halfway out of the room, the old man swung round as if he'd been shot.

'Who the hell do you think I am?' he demanded, sounding almost as irritable as before. 'You really think I doubted you for an instant?'

Long after the sound of the camper van's diesel engine had died away and its rear lights had disappeared around the corner, Georg Stern continued to stand at the door of his cottage and stare into the darkness. He didn't go inside until the wind veered round and blew rain into his eyes. Back in the living room he collected up the fragments of broken china and swabbed the table with a damp cloth. Then he retired to the kitchen, where he emptied the cold tea down the sink. Taking his mobile from the charger, he dialled the number the policeman had given him for emergencies.

30

In view of the short time they had left, the rest area behind the Avus Motel was their best available refuge for the night. There beside the exhibition centre and the busy urban expressway, large numbers of trucks and camper vans availed themselves of the free parking at all times of year. One vehicle more or less would hardly attract attention.

'It's a trap,' Carina said as she pulled into a parking space two slots away from a small removal van. They had scarcely managed to discuss the bare essentials on the short drive there. 'You mustn't go there tomorrow morning. Not on any account.'

Grimacing with pain, Stern climbed out of the passenger seat and made his way to the rear. He had swallowed several of his mother's pills, and their anaesthetizing properties were gradually making themselves felt. Utterly exhausted, he lay down on the bed in the back of the van, which proved to be surprisingly comfortable. After turning off the engine, Carina came to join him.

'I've no choice.' Stern had already been through all the options. 'I can't turn myself in, not now.'

'Why not?'

'It's too late for that. I should simply have waited in Engler's car instead of running off – with his gun, too! – but

I was so shocked that was all I could think of to do. I thought they'd never believe me if I said I'd met him on my own and then become the sole survivor of an assassination.'

'You could be right.'

'Besides, there must be an insider. The voice knows every move we make. If I go to the police now, he'll change his plans. He'll call off the meeting and go to ground, and I'll never know . . .' *what happened to Felix*, Stern thought disconsolately.

'Perhaps he already has.'

Carina sat down beside Stern on the bed and undid the top button of his shirt, then told him to sit up.

'Cancelled the meeting, you mean? It's possible. He's bound to know I'm still alive, but he doesn't know I've discovered where the bridge is. Besides, he'll want to confront the avenger at all costs. He'll go through with this thing as long as he isn't warned off by his police informant, and there's no reason why he should be. Engler was the only person I spoke to, and he's dead.'

Stern peeled off his sweaty shirt like a snake sloughing off its skin and turned over on his stomach. He heard Carina's intake of breath as she saw the massive bruises on his back. Then he experienced a sudden, unpleasantly cold sensation at the base of his spine.

'I'm sorry. The ointment feels cold at first, but it'll soon warm you up.'

'I hope so.'

Reluctant though he was to display any weakness in her presence, he would have winced if a butterfly had landed on his back.

'But let's talk about you, Carina. You're wanted for abducting a child. Your fingerprints are on the door handle of that paedophile's lair and your car is parked outside. And, until I can prove otherwise, you're on the run with a man who has killed a policeman. We must work out how you can turn yourself in without—'

'Ssh!' she said, and he didn't know whether she was soothing or silencing him. 'Turn over.'

He gritted his teeth and rolled over on his back. He was already finding it a little easier to move. The analgesics were taking effect.

'. . . without them pinning something on you too.'

'Not now,' she whispered as she brushed a blood-matted strand of hair off his forehead. He breathed deeply, enjoying the gentle touch of her practised hands. Working in concentric circles, her fingers transferred their soothing pressure from his neck to his shoulders and from there to his naked chest. They lingered over his rapidly beating heart, then slid further down.

'We don't have much time,' he whispered. 'Let's use it sensibly—'

'We will,' she broke in, and turned out the light.

This is crazy, he thought. He wondered what was anaesthetizing him more, the medication in his bloodstream or the feel of her breath on his skin. Pain flared into angry life once more when he tried to deter her by sitting up. Then, like a sulky child, it withdrew to a distant corner of his consciousness, where it waited to re-emerge in company with his manifold fears and concerns.

Almost despite himself, Stern relaxed. With parted lips he tasted Carina's sweet breath and his own tears, which her tongue must have collected on its way to his. The whistle of the wind plucking at the camper van's outer skin became transmuted into a pleasant melody. He strove to think of Felix, of the boy with the birthmark and some plan that would solve their unreal problems, but he couldn't even bring himself to regret the mistake that had kept them apart for so long. For a few hours the van became a cocoon that shielded them both from a world in utter turmoil.

This deceptive state of security did not last long. When a clap of thunder yanked him back to reality just before 5 a.m., Carina was still struggling with some unseen adversary in her dreams. He extricated himself from her restless embrace, pulled his clothes on and, wincing with pain, got behind the wheel. By the time he pulled up in the Seehaus Clinic's car park twenty minutes later, she had got dressed and joined him in the front.

'What are we doing here?' she demanded, staring out of the window. She sounded as wide awake as if he'd chucked a glass of cold water in her face.

'This is where you get out.'

'No way. I'm coming with you.'

'No. There's no point in both of us risking our necks.'

'But what am I supposed to do *here*?'

After careful thought, Stern had come up with a plan so absurd it wasn't worthy of the name. He outlined it to her. She protested as he knew she would, but she ended by seeing that they had no choice. *If* they even had that.

Stern sensed her reluctance to submit to his farewell embrace. He knew that what repelled her was the significance of his kiss, not the kiss itself. Only hours after they had rediscovered each other at last, it set the seal on a parting that might last even longer than the lost three years preceding it. Maybe for ever.

The Truth

I am as certain as you see me here
that I have existed a thousand times before
and hope to return a thousand times more.

Johann Wolfgang von Goethe

. . . it is the lot of men to die once,
and after death comes judgement . . .

Hebrews 9:27

Forgiveness is between them and God.
My job is to arrange the meeting.

Denzel Washington in *Man on Fire*

This could be the end of everything
So why don't we go
Somewhere only we know?

Keane

1

Robert Stern had seen a great deal in the last few hours: dead bodies in cellars, doctors' surgeries and chest freezers. People had been beaten up, hanged and executed before his eyes. He'd had to endure the sight of a child desperately struggling to breathe through a plastic bag while a naked man danced around the room in front of him. His picture of the world had been ripped from its frame. The hard-boiled pedant had become transformed into a sceptic who no longer categorically denied the possibility of reincarnation now that Simon Sachs had led him from one inexplicable phenomenon to the next.

Murder, blackmail, child abuse, a police manhunt, excruciating pain – Stern had taken all these things upon himself to discover what had happened to his infant son. Yet some of the episodes in his weekend had not differed so widely from the activities of many other Berliners. He had gone to the zoo, danced at a club and had three rides on a funfair's big wheel. Even his present destination was regularly plugged by several Berlin tourist guides, although he wasn't taking any of the itineraries they recommended or visiting it during the opening times they advertised.

Stern's route an hour before sunrise was taking him through the rainswept, storm-tossed darkness of the

Grunewald forest. He had parked the camper van in Heerstrasse and was covering the remainder of the distance on foot. Sodden fir branches lashed him in the face, drawing blood. He made slow progress, careful not to slither into puddles, trip over roots or put too much weight on his bad ankle. That the pain was temporarily bearable he attributed to an adrenalin rush. He hadn't taken any more painkillers, not wanting to impair his ability to respond if he witnessed a transaction involving a child.

Or a murder.

Until then he had another potential danger to contend with: the wind, which was snapping off rotten branches left and right. At times it sounded as if whole treetops were being felled, and he was relieved when the feeble beam of his torch finally guided him on to an asphalt footpath.

Another few steps brought him to the lakeside road, the Havelchaussee. The *Brücke* – the 'Bridge' – was immediately ahead of him, rolling so heavily it made him feel seasick to watch. Sporadic gusts of wind tore at the two-masted vessel, yanked at the creaking rigging, and tried to wrench the floating restaurant away from its landing stage. The boat was in total darkness, discounting its two riding lights and the illuminated sign over the entrance:

'The Freshest Fish in the City', it proclaimed.

Stern had understood that slogan's double meaning since yesterday. To the uninitiated the *Brücke* was a popular and well-patronized restaurant, especially during the summer months. It was only on Mondays, when it was officially closed, that 'private parties' congregated aboard.

Photos, videos, addresses, phone numbers, children . . .

He tried not to think of the horrific transactions that went on there week after week. He knuckled the rain out of his eyes and looked at his watch. Another five minutes.

Then he concealed himself behind an empty boat trailer

and waited for the man of whom all he knew to date was his disguised voice. There was no sign as yet.

The Havelchaussee was still closed to normal traffic at this hour for environmental reasons, but Stern heard the deep, throbbing note of an eight-cylinder engine above the roar of the wind. It was slowly but steadily approaching from the direction of Zehlendorf.

A dark-coloured four-wheel drive, the vehicle was travelling quite fast with only its sidelights on. Stern almost hoped its occupant had taken a short cut along the lakeside and would drive straight on, but the driver extinguished the lights altogether and turned down the approach road leading to the *Brücke*. The bulky vehicle pulled up some fifty metres short of the gangway. A man got out. It was still too dark for Stern to see more than his vague silhouette, but what he saw seemed familiar: a tall, erect, broad-shouldered figure with a vigorous, punchy way of walking. He knew it and had seen it before. Often, in fact.

But where?

The man turned up the collar of his trenchcoat and pulled down the peak of his baseball cap. Then, opening the tailgate, he removed a little basket with a pale-coloured blanket draped over it.

The wind veered briefly in Stern's direction. He wasn't sure if his overtaxed senses were playing tricks on him, but he thought he heard the cry of a baby.

He waited until the man had unlocked the wrought-iron gate that gave access to the gangway, then reached in his pocket. He had often heard how reassuring it felt to hold a gun in one's hand, but he couldn't endorse this, perhaps because he knew to whom the automatic had belonged: a long-time adversary, but one who had given his life for him.

However, he didn't plan to exchange fire with an experienced killer. If Simon had really contrived to see into the future for some reason, a third party would very soon appear: the buyer. He might be a paedophile, but he might equally be the 'avenger', the man responsible for murdering several criminals in the last fifteen years. Either way, the police would have to be quick if they wanted to prevent bloodshed.

Stern checked his watch for the last time. It was just before six. If Carina had kept to their plan, the deserted road would be seething with squad cars in ten minutes at most. But in case something went wrong – if there really was a police insider who thwarted the guilty parties' arrest – he wanted to make sure of unmasking the voice and discovering the identity of the man who could tell him what had happened in the neonatal ward.

And whether my son is still alive.

He came out from behind the trailer. The time had come.

2

Bending low, he stole quickly along the cobbled approach road leading to the *Brücke*. Even getting to the four-wheel drive left him out of breath. He leaned against the spare wheel mounted on the tailgate until he'd recovered a little, then turned on his torch just long enough to examine the licence plate.

The short Berlin number was easy enough to memorize, but he took its falsity for granted. Peering around the back of the vehicle he saw a finger of light flit across the *Brücke*'s deck. Evidently, the voice was also finding his way around with a torch.

All right, move.

Stern's next objective was the gangway. If he was to catch a glimpse of the man's face, he would have to get as close as possible. His heart beat faster. Speed was of the essence now, he knew. The baby's putative buyer had yet to appear, so the voice might not be suspicious if he noticed someone moving in the car park.

Praying he would be able to withstand the pain, Stern prepared to make a dash for the gangway. He was just about to go when he saw the passenger door.

He stopped short. *Could it be?* Sure enough, it wasn't shut properly. He tried the handle. And froze in horror.

Goddamn!

The interior light had come on. Stern felt as if he'd fired a signal rocket into the sky. He got in quickly, shut the door and watched from the dark interior to see if the unknown man aboard the *Brücke* had noticed anything. The finger of light on deck had disappeared, but a small lamp in the deckhouse had come on. He could see a shadowy figure inside. So he hadn't been spotted.

Quick.

Sitting in the passenger seat, he looked round. TRAP! A warning light started flashing in his mind's eye when he saw that the key was in the ignition. He reached for his gun and suppressed all the instincts telling him to run. Then he clambered on to the back seat and looked over the head rests into the load space. Having satisfied himself that he was alone in the vehicle, he activated the central locking system.

So it isn't a trap after all?

He checked the rear-view mirror to see if another vehicle was approaching, but there wasn't the slightest sign of movement behind him apart from the trees, the branches of which were bending in the wind like fishing rods. He opened the glove compartment, which contained nothing but a plastic box of wet wipes. Then he folded down the sun visors and looked in the side pockets. Nothing. No clue to the driver's identity.

As his eyes got used to the dim light of dawn, Stern saw that the whole of the car's interior was as clean and uncluttered as that of a showroom model. There were no CDs, petrol receipts, street maps, or any of the other ballast motorists tend to drive around with. Not even a parking disc. He felt under the seats for hidden compartments, but in vain. Propping his elbow on the console between the two front seats, he had almost decided to get out again when it struck him.

The console!

Of course. It was far too wide for an ordinary armrest. He tried the wrong side at first, but then it opened with a faint creak. The compartment beneath the leather cover was as empty as all the others. With one exception. Stern fished out the sleeveless silver disc with two fingers. There was just enough light for him to decipher the date someone had written on the DVD with a green felt-tip pen.

It was the last day of his son's life.

3

Visitors to a hospital the size of the Seehaus Clinic passed unnoticed unless they attracted attention in some way, for instance by asking directions at the reception desk, polluting the entrance hall with cigarette smoke, or getting an outsize bunch of flowers stuck in the revolving doors. The young woman in the grey tracksuit might almost have been invisible as she hurried to the lifts, even at this early hour.

Carina knew that breakfast preparations were already in full swing and the night shift was about to knock off. The weary doctors' and nurses' attention threshold was consequently at its lowest when she opened the glass doors leading to the neurological department. For all that, she was so anxious not to be recognized that she concealed her face beneath the hood of the sweatshirt Stern's father had lent her last night.

Emerging from the lift, she glanced at the big clock at the end of the corridor. Two more minutes to go. Another hundred and twenty seconds before she roused the staff. That was the most important feature of the plan.

'Just before six, go to your ward and sound the alarm,' Stern had impressed on her. 'I want as many of your colleagues as possible to hear when you report to the guard outside Simon's room.'

There was to be no doubt that she had turned herself in

of her own free will, then the police couldn't pin anything on her later. She'd also had to promise him something else.

'As soon as you've turned yourself in, tell the police where I am. But not until six on the dot, not a second earlier.' His words came back to her as she hurried down the corridor.

'Why not?' she'd asked him. 'Help won't arrive for at least five minutes.'

'Exactly. I'll need that much time to find out what happened to my son, and if someone really is selling a baby aboard the *Brücke*, a longer delay would present too much of a risk to the child.'

'But if the police turn up too late, you'll be dead.'

He had shaken his head wearily. 'I don't think the voice means to kill me. He's had plenty of opportunities to do so in the last few days.'

'So what *does* he want?'

Instead of replying, Stern had kissed her goodbye and driven off to find out.

Carina stopped short.

The frosted glass door of the nurses' room was normally open, but it seemed that some of the female staff had retired there for an early coffee break. She heard a high-pitched laugh. The voice sounded unfamiliar, and she assumed that it belonged to someone from another ward who had temporarily taken over her shift.

Click. The second hand of the clock ate another minute of her schedule. She raised her hand and was about to knock when she froze.

But this is impossible . . . She hadn't risked a glance in the direction of Room 217 when she emerged into the corridor, not wanting the policeman outside the door to notice her until she accosted him, but she'd glimpsed something out of the corner of her eye that shouldn't by rights have been there.

Nothing!

She slowly turned and looked down the long, antiseptically swabbed corridor.

It was true: there was no one there. No man. No woman. No policeman.

He could have sneaked out for a smoke, of course.

She walked slowly back along the corridor.

OK, perhaps he's gone to the bathroom. Or maybe he's looking in on the boy. But shouldn't there be a chair outside?

Rooms 203, 205, 207. Her footsteps quickened the more doors she passed.

Surely they haven't dispensed with a personal protection officer? Not after Simon's abduction, surely? Today of all days?

She passed Room 209 at a run.

'Hello? Carina?' a woman's agitated voice called out behind her. Her replacement's, probably. It sounded familiar, unlike the laugh she'd heard before, but she didn't turn round. This couldn't wait.

Reaching the door of Room 217, she flung it open – and stifled a cry because she saw what she'd feared. Nothing. No child. No Simon. Just a newly made-up bed awaiting a patient.

'Carina Freitag?' the voice asked again, right behind her this time.

She turned round. Sure enough, it was a new nurse. A redhead – they'd once shared a table in the staff canteen. Magdalena, Martina – something like that, but who cared? Only one name mattered to Carina right then, and its owner had disappeared.

'Simon – where is he?'

'They've transferred him, but I—'

'Transferred? Where to?'

'The Kennedy Clinic.'

'*What?* When?'

'No idea, it's down in the log. My shift has only just started. Look, please don't be difficult, but my instructions were to call the medical director as soon as you showed up.'

'Do that. And you'd better call the police as well.'

'Why?' The nurse, who had picked up the house phone, lowered it again.

'Because Simon has been kidnapped. The JFK doesn't have a neuroradiological department. It's a private hospital for internal medicine.'

'Oh . . .'

'Who approved the transfer? Who was on duty before you?'

Completely thrown now, the red-haired nurse reeled off some names until asked to repeat one. Carina nearly tripped over her own feet as she dashed past the girl and out of the room.

Picasso? Since when has he been back on night duty?

4

Stern turned the ignition key far enough to power up the four-wheel drive's onboard entertainment system. The DVD player swallowed the disc with a greedy, slithering sound. No longer watching out for movement on board the *Brücke* to his front, he focused his whole attention on the screen. He felt like a student who couldn't find his name on a list of successful examinees, except that this examination concerned his son's life. Or, more probably, his death.

He thought at first, when the picture took shape, that he was only watching a copy of the DVD he'd already seen. Like that one, it opened with some greenish shots of the neonatal ward at night. Felix was lying in his cot once more. Once more he stretched out his little fist and spread his tiny fingers. Stern wanted to turn away and shut his eyes, but he knew how pointless this was because the ensuing image was permanently imprinted on his mind's eye, as it had been ever since he saw it for the first time on the old television set at his house: the motionless infant with the far-too-blue lips and the expressionless eyes that still seemed, a decade after the event, to reproach his father for failing to prevent his death. Stern clasped his hands together, clenched his teeth, and prayed to be finally roused from this nightmare.

He hadn't come here to watch another video of his son's death.

But why? Are you really stupid enough to believe in another explanation?

'Yes!' he said, voicing his thoughts aloud for the first time. 'Felix is alive. I don't want his heart to stop beating. Please don't let him die. Not again.'

It was more of an entreaty than a prayer, and although he hadn't named the recipient of his despairing plea, his words seemed to be having an effect.

What is this?

All at once, the sequence of shots began to differ greatly from that of the first DVD. A shadow fell across the cot. The camera zoomed in and the images became grainier. Then something incomprehensible happened. A man's hands came into shot. First one, then the other. Bare, rough hands, they reached for Felix and cupped themselves around his frail little head. Stern blinked feebly, afraid that what followed would be even more horrible than what he'd been compelled to endure hitherto. He tried to command his fingers to turn off the DVD, but although his heart longed to blot out the scene by pressing a button, his brain resisted the impulse. In the end, so that his journey of exploration in that dark car park beside the lake could reach its final destination, he bowed to the inevitable, however terrible it might be. As the DVD continued its merciless rotation, he saw the man move his hands apart. Oh, Felix! One grasped his neck, the other his body. The muscular forearms tautened, and the unknown man . . .

Dear God, help me . . .

. . . took hold of Felix and . . .

No, this is . . .

. . . lifted him out of the cot.

. . . *impossible!*

Only seconds later the little mattress was occupied once more. By another infant. Same sleepsuit, same size, similar build. There was only one perceptible difference: it wasn't Felix.

Or was it?

The new baby looked so incredibly like his son, but something about his appearance had changed.

His nose? His ears?

Stern simply couldn't tell, the quality of the video was too poor. He rubbed his eyes and rested both hands on the dashboard with his face as close as possible to the screen. It was pointless, the baby's image only became more blurred. All he could tell with any certainty was that this infant was also alive. Weirdly enough, its movements seemed even more familiar to him than those of the newborn baby that had just been lying in its place.

But that would mean . . .

Stern looked at the date line.

And was utterly mystified.

With almost autistic concentration, he focused all of his senses on trying to fathom the meaning of the pictures. He failed.

Exchanged? It wasn't possible. Felix had been the only male infant in the ward and he'd seen him die. Which of the two DVDs was authentic?

Stern's breathing came and went spasmodically as he watched the deception being completed. Another close-up of the baby's face was followed by a shot of the man's hirsute, disembodied hands slipping a numbered ID bracelet over its right wrist.

It was all over. The video recording was at an end. The screen went dark and Stern looked down at his mobile, which had been vibrating in his hand for a considerable time.

5

'Good morning, Herr Stern.'

Robert Stern thought he'd long ago plumbed the ultimate depths of despair. The sound of that disguised voice told him how wrong he was. The lights in the floating restaurant's bar went off and on again. A shadowy figure came over to the big window facing the car park.

'What did you do with my son?' Stern managed to ask.

Although the reply accorded with his dearest wishes, he could hardly believe it.

'We exchanged him.'

'Impossible.'

'Why? You saw it for yourself just now.'

'Yes, and three days ago you sent me a video in which he died!' Stern shouted. 'What do you want from me? Which of the DVDs was genuine?'

'Both.'

'You're lying.'

'No. One baby died, the other survived. Felix is ten years old and living with an adoptive family.'

'Where?'

The voice remained quiet, like an orator reaching for a glass of water. Although the timbre was still metallic, the artificial distortion was less pronounced than it had been when he first made contact.

'You really want to know?'

'Yes,' Stern heard himself say. Nothing could have been more important to him at that moment.

'Then open the glove compartment.'

Like a remote-controlled toy, he did so. 'What now?'

'Take out the box and open it.'

With trembling fingers, Stern picked up the box of wet wipes. Air escaped with an angry hiss as he tore open the plastic lid.

'I've done that.'

'Good. Now pull out a wet wipe and put it over your mouth and nose.'

'No,' he replied instinctively. He needed no death's-head sticker to tell him how potentially lethal was the substance the fumes of which were already filling the car.

'I thought you wanted to see your son again.'

'Yes, but I don't want to die.'

'Who says you'll die? I'm merely asking you to put it over your face.'

'What happens if I refuse?'

'Nothing.'

'Nothing?'

'No. You can get out and go home.'

And never find out where my son is.

'It would be a mistake, though, now you've come this far.'

'You're lying. Those DVDs are fakes.'

The voice sighed deeply. 'You're mistaken.'

'Then tell me how you did it. You say there were two babies.' Stern's voice cracked. 'Why didn't we notice? Who did the other child belong to? Why did you exchange it?'

And why didn't anyone miss it after it died in Sophie's arms?

'All right, I'll tell you. But then it's your turn.'

Stern shut the lid and shook his head.

'You can't understand the whole story unless you know how I earn my living.'

'You traffic in children.'

'Among other things. We engage in many business activities, but dealing in newborn babies is one of the most lucrative.'

Stern swallowed hard. It was two minutes past six. He looked in the rear-view mirror, but the avenger had yet to appear.

'My business is based on the baby depository – a wonderful invention. Are you aware that certain Berlin hospitals maintain containers in which mothers can dump their unwanted offspring instead of abandoning them elsewhere or even killing them?'

'Yes.'

But what has that to do with Felix?

'When was the last time you heard of a baby being dumped in one? It's said to happen very, very rarely, but that's a lie. The fact is, it happens all the time.'

The voice clicked his tongue.

'As soon as a mother inserts her baby in the compartment, a silent alarm goes off inside the hospital and a member of staff comes and takes charge of the foundling. In two cases out of three, that member of staff is a nurse on my payroll.'

'No,' Stern gasped.

'Oh yes. That's the advantage of the silent alarm, nobody hears it. Data protection legislation prohibits the installation of CCTV cameras outside these depositories, so the hospital administrators don't know how many babies actually get dumped. All I have to do is collect them when their mothers abandon them of their own free will. The best part is, most of them are German babies, and childless couples pay top prices for those. It's a very simple business, really. Or would be, if someone didn't persist in killing my associates.'

Stern felt unutterably sick. It was the perfect crime. Child-traffickers didn't even have to risk a charge of kidnapping. The babies were 'voluntarily' surrendered to them, and no missing infants were subsequently sought by heartbroken parents.

'I still don't understand what this has to do with *Felix*.' Stern was feeling bereft of energy. The wind, which continued to buffet the car with undiminished ferocity, could have blown him away.

The voice paused briefly. Stern waited with bated breath. Then the dam broke.

'Your Felix was in the wrong hospital at the right time. A day before his birth, another very cute little baby was left in the hospital's depository. I informed my impatient customers of that fortunate occurrence. Unhappily, it transpired from a preliminary examination conducted by one of my doctors that the foundling had a terminal heart defect.'

An iron band seemed to enclose Stern's chest.

'It was doomed from the first. An operation would have been pointless and was out of the question in any case. No one could be allowed to know of the child's existence.'

The band tightened.

'I was in a difficult position, you must understand. It was one of my first transactions. I couldn't renege on the deal, nor did I want to. On the other hand, I didn't want to supply damaged goods.'

'So you switched the babies?'

'Exactly. As luck would have it, the foundling actually resembled your Felix. But even if he'd been bigger, fatter or uglier, you'd never have spotted the difference between such newborn babies. You only noticed the little birthmark the second time you saw your son, and by then we'd made the switch.'

Stern nodded despite himself. The voice was right. Immediately after the difficult delivery, the wet, bloodstained baby had been handed to Sophie wrapped in a blanket, and because Felix was the only male infant on the ward, they would have had no cause for concern when he was carried out of the room for postnatal attention. After all, why should anyone have wanted to do anything so cruel to them?

'Have you caught on at last? Discounting the first few moments after birth, it was always the foundling you fondled and caressed.'

The unsteady pictures of the neonatal ward flashed through Stern's mind once more.

'And the other baby . . . ?'

'It died as expected, two days after the switch. You saw the CCTV shots yourself.'

'Just a minute. Don't tell me those pictures—'

'Were taken by a fixed surveillance camera?' said the voice, sounding amused. 'Why not? Because of the cuts? The blurring, the close-ups, zooms and other digital effects? You've no idea what modern photo-editing software can do. Like scan a birthmark in the shape of Italy on to the shoulder of a ten-year-old boy. Ironical, isn't it, that I had to lie to you to induce you to believe me?'

'What if you're lying to me again?' Stern shouted.

'Find out for yourself. That's as much as I'm going to tell you. Make up your mind. Either put one of those things over your face if you want to see your son again' – Stern stared at the plastic container in his hands – 'or it's goodbye.'

All the lights on the *Brücke* went out, plunging the car park beside the storm-tossed lake into gloom. Stern clamped the mobile even harder to his burning ear, but the line was dead.

And now?

He looked at the ignition key. *But where would I drive to?* Back to a life the emptiness of which would, from now on, be filled with agonizing doubts? He suspected that he'd just been listening to a madman's cleverly concocted lie, but that no longer mattered. All that mattered was how much he wanted to believe that lie.

He opened the box and paused for a moment before extracting a wipe. It lay in his hand, heavy with moisture and steeped in a substance that, although it might not kill him, would assuredly bring him nearer to death. Involuntarily reminded of a shroud, he draped it over his face. Then he held his breath and thought of Felix. When his lungs reached bursting point, he breathed in deeply through his mouth and nose. He got as far as three deliberate breaths before utter darkness and silence engulfed him.

6

There was a smell of sweat and vomit. Carina feared the worst as she entered the restroom, used by hospital staff for snatching some sleep when their thirty-six-hour shifts permitted.

'He was going in there the last time I saw him,' the red-haired nurse called in a low voice. She had remained outside in the corridor. Carina didn't even bother to try the switch. The ceiling light in the cramped little room hadn't worked for ages and no one had told the maintenance man. Nurses who retired there for a nap didn't need a light in any case, which was why the blinds were always lowered as well.

But even the meagre light from the corridor revealed enough to make Carina shudder.

Picasso!

He was lying in a pool of vomit beside the narrow couch, having either fallen off it or failed to make it before he collapsed.

'What . . . Oh, my God!' The nurse had followed Carina in by now. She covered her mouth with a trembling hand.

'Fetch a doctor and call the police at once,' Carina told her as she bent over her motionless colleague.

The redhead didn't appear to understand. She stood rooted to the spot, her lower lip trembling uncontrollably.

'Is he . . . is he . . . ?' she asked, too shocked to utter the word.

Dead?

Carina knelt down beside Picasso. Gripping him by one muscular shoulder, she turned him over onto his back. The smell became even worse. She felt sick until it struck her that this was a good sign. She could detect urine, sweat and vomit, but no blood.

She sighed, her suspicions confirmed. 'Fetch a doctor! Fetch a doctor at once!' she shouted, loudly enough to jolt the other girl out of her inertia.

Picasso's eyelids flickered, then opened. Despite the dim light, Carina saw that his eyes looked far more alert than she'd expected in view of his poisoning symptoms.

'Can you hear me?'

He blinked.

Thank God.

She reached for his hands, meaning to soothe him by holding them, and found that he was clutching a sheet of paper.

'What's this?' she asked, as if he were in a condition to answer. His hands relaxed a little, enabling her to withdraw the sheet.

It was a computer printout. In the light from the corridor she made out the clinic's data table. Picasso had used the hospital computer to print out the bed layout of the intensive care ward.

But why?

She saw two names underlined in red. And was horrified.

Surely not!

She rechecked the date of the layout, which was several weeks old. But there was no doubt.

All at once, a hand descended onto her shoulder. She

spun round as if she'd been shot. A doctor and another nurse had hurried to the scene.

'Hey, hey, take it easy. You'd better come with us and wait for—'

Carina shook off the doctor's hand and thrust him aside, then unzipped her bumbag and pulled out her gun.

'He's been drugged,' she said, looking at Picasso, who was struggling to haul himself on to the couch unaided. Whatever it was that had been slipped into his coffee to facilitate Simon's abduction, the dose had been too low to fell a bear of a man like him.

'Don't dare follow me. Call the police and tell them to send all available units to Havelchaussee.'

'But, Carina . . .' the doctor called after her half-heartedly. None of the nurses ventured to follow her either, now that she was holding a gun.

What now?

The gun was of little use, but she couldn't wait here for the police to arrive. She had to help Stern, but how? She'd left her own car outside the house.

'You can't get away,' called the doctor.

He was right. *Unless . . .*

She rushed into the nurses' room and grabbed Picasso's leather jacket. On her way back along the corridor she paused briefly outside a room immediately opposite the smoking room. To be on the safe side, she opened the door, confirming her worst fears. It was empty.

Even while racing downstairs to the main entrance she felt in the pockets of the jacket. Wallet, chewing gum, keys.

Bingo.

Carina sprinted past the feverishly phoning receptionist and out into the car park. She knew where Picasso left his low-slung sports car.

'It'll do 280 kph max,' he'd boasted once, when trying to persuade her to come for a spin. She doubted whether even that would be fast enough to avert disaster.

7

Stern regained consciousness to find that the 'shroud' over his face had changed. It was thicker, denser and made of a coarse material that scratched his skin unpleasantly, like a cheap woollen sweater. His nausea was almost unbearable. It stemmed not only from the chloroform, which had yet to leach from his body, but also from the thing in his mouth. The gag tasted simultaneously sweet and salty, as if it had been rolled up and shoved beneath his tongue by a pair of sweaty hands. He started to retch, and even that minimal contraction of his throat muscles unleashed a wave of pain that spread from the nape of his neck to his forehead. He'd never had such a headache in his life. Nor felt so scared.

He opened his eyes and the darkness seemed to become even more intense. At least there had been streaks of light behind his closed eyelids. Now even those had vanished. His heart stopped beating for one scary moment. Then another.

I'm paralysed, it flashed through his mind. *From the neck down. I can't even move my lips.*

He tried to open his mouth but failed. He was relieved to find that his jaw muscles were still working until he realized to his horror why he could only breathe through his nose.

They gagged me, then pulled a sack over my head.

'Where am I?' he grunted, as well as the duct tape over his mouth permitted. Stark panic lodged in his nervous system like ticks in a dog's fur. He thought he was going to suffocate.

Suddenly a little light came on above his head, and he wished they'd blindfolded him as well. His head wasn't inside a sack after all. Even when his eyes had got used to the faint light source and the flashes on his retinas were gradually fading, it still took a while to grasp whose eyes were staring at him through the ski mask. His own!

He blinked twice in the rear-view mirror, then turned his head. Slowly and cautiously, avoiding any sudden movement that might cause him to vomit with the gag in his mouth.

Was this really . . . ? Yes, no doubt about it. He was sitting in an empty car. In the passenger seat. And he knew who the Mercedes belonged to. Him.

But where am I?

The greyish-black streaks beyond the windscreen slowly took shape. At first he mistook the swaying masts for an optical illusion, another of the anaesthetic's side effects. They proved to be trees bending before the wind. Between the Mercedes and the edge of the woods lay an expanse of open ground the size of a car park.

Cautiously, Stern leaned forwards to take the weight off his wrists, which were bound behind his back. Eyes narrowed, he tried to remember why this godforsaken spot seemed familiar. The truth was just beginning to dawn when he was distracted by a sound behind him. Someone coughed into a handkerchief.

'Good, so you've woken up. Almost half an hour before time.'

Stern recognized the voice. It sounded distinctly more human without any electronic distortion.

Cold air streamed into the car as the man got out. The yellowish light of the reading lamp had illuminated his distinctive profile for only a moment, but that was long enough for Stern to recognize him in the rear-view mirror. The sight of the man reduced his capacity for thought to zero, for what he had seen was a sheer impossibility.

'Well, *now* do you believe in reincarnation?' Engler laughed as he opened the passenger door and hauled Stern out like a sack of potatoes.

Stern stumbled forwards. Unable to save himself because his wrists were cuffed, he fell headlong on the muddy ground. His fall was cushioned by a layer of wet leaves and soil – much to his regret, because it didn't knock him out.

Engler of Homicide? How could it be?

A pair of strong hands hauled him to his feet again. Two things suddenly occurred to him: he recognized the place and knew why he was here.

'You shouldn't believe everything you see or hear,' the inspector said as he set Stern on his feet. Highly amused, he imitated the charade he'd staged at the psychiatrist's practice. 'Hello? Dr Tiefensee? Are you there?' He held a plastic device to his lips and went on, in a disguised voice: 'See those surgical scissors? Stab him in the heart.'

Engler stepped back and slammed the passenger door, which was still open. The sound reminded Stern of the doors slamming in Tiefensee's practice. It struck him only now that the two voices had not overlapped. Whenever Engler had used the voice scrambler he was in one of the treatment rooms. He had spoken in his normal voice only in the passage outside.

'It was a lot of fun, getting my associate off the hook when you surprised him at Tiefensee's place.' Engler laughed. 'Nearly as much fun as that staged shooting. Jesus Christ, man, everything was going according to plan, and all at once you wanted to turn yourself in? I had to put a stop to that. Lucky you're so gullible. All it took to deceive you was three gunshots, a shattered windscreen and some stage blood. OK, maybe a DVD as well.'

His laughter sounded almost hysterical now. He calmed down a little and spat on the muddy ground.

'How did you like the episode with the motorcyclist? Imagine, he wanted five hundred euros to shoot out the windscreen and hold a gun to your head. Don't worry, though, he's no great loss to humanity. The fellow had a taste for children, and besides, he also had Tiefensee on his conscience. He was the long-haired type you chased down the street, remember?'

Stern took a step backwards and came up against the boot of his Mercedes. He felt he would soon need something to lean against if he didn't want to fall over again, here in the middle of the car park of the deserted Wannsee Lido.

'That reminds me.' Engler acted as if he'd just remembered something important. 'Too many people knew about the *Brücke* for my taste, so I've arranged a new rendezvous with the man who plans to kill me. I've also postponed our appointment for forty-five minutes. Still, I'm sure we won't get bored, waiting for our surprise visitor to arrive.'

8

Nothing. No lights, no car. No sign of life. The absence of something can sometimes be just as palpable as the presence of a noisy crowd. To Carina, standing by herself in the car park beside the *Brücke*, her solitude felt overwhelming.

Where are they? Where's Robert? Simon?

The car she'd driven here was the only one outside the floating restaurant. The rustle of leaves, the creak of rigging and the splash of the waves might be drowning other sounds in the vicinity, but her instincts told her there were none to drown. She was alone.

She took out her mobile to give the police another call, as she had done on the drive here. There was no point in trying Stern again. His phone was either turned off or out of range.

With the little automatic in her hand she made her way once more to the locked gate leading to the gangway and wondered whether to try to climb over it. The wrought-iron grille was topped with spikes and enough barbed wire to rip an intruder's stomach open.

She couldn't help thinking of movies in which the hero would grab a rope and haul himself aboard, but her feeble arms transmitted a very explicit message: 'Not a chance.'

Behind her, the sound of a car speeding by mingled with

the angry roar of the autumn gale. She felt blindly for the redial key on her mobile, meaning to call emergency again, then propped her back against the gate. And that was when she felt it – just as she shut her eyes.

She was so startled, she dropped her mobile. It hit the ground, shedding its battery, and fell over the landing stage into the dark, choppy water. Carina slowly turned round, too distracted to mourn the loss of her only means of communication.

Sure enough, it had been there all the time: the big laminated cardboard sign that had dug into her back as she leaned against the locked gate. She had overlooked it because it was so obvious. Until now she had taken it to be a list of opening times or a health and safety warning to those who went aboard that they did so at their own risk.

On closer inspection, however, it looked far too unprofessional for an official notice. It appeared to be a home-made computer printout haphazardly attached to the bars of the gate with four lengths of wire. Carina was also puzzled by the big, beaming smiley at the foot of the sheet – the only thing she could decipher in the faint light of the moon.

She produced a lighter from her bumbag. As its yellow flame illuminated the wording, her last remaining hope died.

To all late arrivals!
Just for once, today's morning walk
will start from Wannsee Lido.
Please turn up at 6.45 on the dot.
Robert has arranged a little surprise.

9

Nothing made sense any more, yet he suddenly felt he could see things quite clearly. Here and now, in the slowly paling light of dawn.

The DVDs, the fake assassination by the biker, his own Mercedes, beside which he was standing in a state of collapse – all these could mean only one thing: Engler's sadistic plan certainly didn't include telling him the truth about Felix. On the contrary, the policeman would derive the greatest pleasure from sending him to his death in ignorance. Stern nodded in bewilderment like someone who has finally acknowledged a grave mistake. Little by little, the pieces of the jigsaw were fitting together to form a picture that would ultimately feature his corpse.

'Don't look so horrified.' Engler was still chuckling as he strode round the car. 'You've brought all this on yourself.'

He took a canvas bag from the back seat of the car and tossed it on the ground in front of Stern.

'First Harald Zucker, then Samuel Probtyeszki. You simply couldn't let the dead rest in peace.'

Stern felt a gust of wind pluck at his trouser legs. He wished it would turn into a hurricane and blow him away. Away from this nightmare.

'I discovered the bodies of my associates years ago. If it

had been up to me, they would still be rotting in their hiding places.'

'Why?' Stern grunted uncomprehendingly. It sounded like the groan of a wounded animal, but Engler understood it in spite of the gag and looked at him as if he'd just asked the stupidest question in the world.

'Because I didn't want to investigate myself.'

Oh God.

A floodgate seemed to open in Stern's brain, releasing a whole host of realizations at once. The murdered men had all been Engler's associates. As long as they were only thought to be missing, no one had needed to go looking for them. Everyone was glad the scum had disappeared until Simon turned up and their bodies were found. Now everyone was looking for their killer. Engler had to find the avenger before someone else did. And before someone found out that Engler's own name was on his hit list.

Stern shivered when it dawned on him what role he'd been assigned in the final act of this drama.

The inspector looked at his watch and gave a satisfied nod. Whatever he had in mind, he seemed to have it well in hand.

'We still have fifteen minutes. I want to use the time to thank you for warning me. I still can't understand how Simon got to know of this morning's rendezvous aboard the *Brücke*, but it doesn't really matter. Once you'd tipped me the wink, I realized that the buyer's order from me – a very convincing one, I might add – was a ruse, so he had to be the avenger we're expecting in a minute or two.'

And you'll sacrifice me to him in your place. I'm to be your scapegoat.

Stern strained at his plasticuffs and tried to cry out when he grasped the truth: all that he'd done in the past few hours was sign his own death warrant. He had gone to the slaughter of his own volition. He was to be murdered in the course of a child-trafficking transaction, having previously done all he could to be mistaken for a paedophile capable of such depravity.

He swallowed involuntarily, tasting blood. Engler had clearly been less than gentle when he inserted the gag.

How could I have been so stupid?

He had thought the whole time that he was tracking down the voice. In fact, he'd merely been following a trail the latter had laid for him, which had ultimately lured him into this trap. First he had cast suspicion on himself by finding those bodies and making wild statements about reincarnation; then he had abducted a little boy from a hospital and left his fingerprints at Tiefensee's surgery and in a paedophile's lair; and finally, to crown everything, he had personally handed Engler a video of himself stripped to the waist and rushing into a room in which a child was being tortured.

Carina's car was parked outside the estate agent's house of horror and her fingerprints were on the door handle. Being in charge of the investigation, Engler would find it easy to brand him and his lady friend a pair of paedophiles – and his only witness for the defence was a former producer of porn films who had once been charged with rape. It was diabolical. Engler was laying the blame at his door. Worse still, he, Stern, had opened that door and taken delivery.

'Don't be too hard on yourself,' Engler growled at length. He hawked and spat a blob of phlegm on the ground beside the canvas bag. 'You didn't do everything wrong. All I really wanted from you at first was the name of the avenger. You had access to the source, to Simon Sachs. Jesus, you nearly drove me crazy at that first interview. For years you'd been representing one shitface after another. Then along comes a potential client who could be useful to me and you turn him down. So I brought some pressure to bear the next day.'

The first DVD.

'That, by the way, was the only stroke of fate in the whole affair: the fact that you, a lawyer whose child had been switched by my people ten years ago, could be the key to the solution of my biggest problem.'

Stern looked up at the stormy sky – the nocturnal darkness was turning a dirty shade of grey. It reminded him of the walls of the police interview room.

Engler, the voice, gave another laugh. He bent over the bag and proceeded to unzip it. As he did so, Stern developed an unbearable stitch.

'A shame you didn't bring your girlfriend along, she could have kept you company. But let me guess: you got her to call the police at a prearranged time, didn't you? Well, like to know why I couldn't care less?'

Engler removed a grey plastic bag from the canvas one. It seemed light despite its bulk, like a pillow.

'Because the police are already here. Three mobile units.'

Stern turned on the spot and peered into the gloom.

'Twenty men or so, but all keeping well out of sight so as not to blow the stake-out. They're waiting for my signal.' He tapped a radio on his hip.

'The road to the lido is a dead end. The roadblocks won't be set up in preparation for the snatch until I signal the buyer's arrival.'

He carried the plastic bag over to the boot of the Mercedes.

'Don't look so sceptical. I gave official notice of this undercover operation after my enquiries disclosed that you intended to meet the child abuser today and at this very spot.' He grinned broadly. 'I'm not here for my own amusement, I've come to arrest you. My one fear is that I'll be too late to prevent the tragedy that's about to take its course . . .'

So saying, Engler opened the boot of the Mercedes. Stern gasped when he looked inside. The gag in his mouth seemed to swell until it forced his jaws apart and his skull threatened to explode. With a single twitch of the hand, the inspector yanked off the green hospital gown that had been draped over the unconscious boy's body. In the dim glow of the boot light, Simon looked as if he was already dead.

10

The boy was lying curled up like a discarded winter tyre. Stern couldn't tear his eyes away.

'Keep still!'

Engler had stepped behind him – Stern could feel him pressing up against his back. He thought the inspector was going to dislocate his wrists, he was twisting them so painfully. Then came a sudden click and his hands were free to move. Engler had severed the plasticuffs.

'No false moves,' he hissed. Stern could feel Engler's breath through the thick material of the ski mask. 'Now turn away.'

He felt dizzy. It took an immense effort to obey instructions and lose sight of Simon. Engler now stood facing him, his left hand holding a pistol with a halogen light mounted on the barrel. The other hand was clasping a baby to his chest.

Stern's eyes widened, and it was a moment before he grasped that the flesh-coloured head was that of a doll. It was the only part of its body protruding from the white linen cloth in which the life-sized dummy was wrapped. 'It can even speak,' Engler said with a sarcastic smile, and pressed its midriff.

So that was it. Stern remembered the whimpers he had heard beside the *Brücke*.

Engler shut the boot. No groaning or twitching. Nothing. Simon didn't appear to have stirred at all.

'I'm going to give you your final instructions. Then I shall sit in the back of your car and watch you. If you take it into your head to deviate from my instructions for any reason, I shall get out, open the boot, and smother your little friend. Is that clear?'

Stern nodded.

'Do everything to my satisfaction and Simon will be found unconscious beside your dead body. He's anaesthetized, so he won't remember a thing. I'm not bluffing – I can afford to let him live. Believe it or not, I thoroughly detest killing children, unlike Probtyeszki. No good trafficker destroys his wares willingly. But it all depends on you.'

The sweat under the ski mask seemed to burn like acid. Stern felt as if he were slowly suffocating in a woollen vice. Once he had run through Engler's instructions in his mind he was handed the doll in a little wicker basket that the policeman must have taken from the back seat of the car. Then he felt an envelope being thrust into his hip pocket.

'What is it?' Engler had read the question in Stern's eyes. 'I keep my promises,' he said in a ironical undertone. 'I've written down your Felix's address. Who knows, you may be able to do something with it in another life.'

Engler's laughter stopped abruptly as the car's heavy door clicked shut.

Stern had to summon up all his willpower not to hyperventilate. He tilted his head so as to accustom his eyes more quickly to the prevailing gloom, but he still couldn't make out any headlights through the trees bordering the approach road.

But that would soon change. Death was on its way and would get here in a few minutes' time. He tensed the upper part of his body in expectation of the pain that would soon transfix him. Then, reluctantly, he set off.

11

It never ceases to amaze me how much strength God can bestow on a person determined to fight evil, thought the man. He cleared his throat, then coughed and quickly took his foot off the gas when he saw that his moment of inattention had caused him to exceed the speed limit. Sweat was trickling down his wrinkled brow into his bushy eyebrows. The truth was, his body was no longer up to the stress to which he intended to subject it today. He had overtaxed himself too much in the past, during his long years as a self-appointed avenger of the innocent.

It had all begun with a short article on child abuse. He had written it for the religious weekly because the editor was sick and he was the only person capable of standing in for her.

Today he regarded it as a sign. It couldn't have been mere chance that *he* should have written about that terrible crime, given that his own brother had disappeared at the age of eight. When discovered six months later, his body was in such a dreadful condition that his parents had been advised not to look at it.

His article had expanded into a series and the series into the manuscript of a book, though the latter had never found its way to a publisher. He saw no point in publishing such a dark chapter in the history of humankind. It wouldn't help any child to forget the torments it had undergone or dissuade any paedophiles from indulging in their perverted activities. Nor would it bring his brother back. Everything would go on as before.

One Sunday, when he perceived this bitter truth as clearly as he saw the images that robbed him of sleep every night, he decided to act.

The first two murders were the hardest. The others died more easily, unlike Zucker. He hadn't meant to split Zucker's skull at all, but the man was strong and had defended himself fiercely. He even managed to grab the gun. Fortunately God provided the avenger with another weapon when he needed it. Although the factory was a burned-out ruin even in those days, the axe was still hanging on the wall beside a soot-stained fire extinguisher. He had never been able to eat nuts after that. The sound of shells cracking was simply unbearable.

The old man mopped the sweat from his brow. He thought of turning on the radio but refrained. Although fond of music, he preferred to await the last act in silence.

His car, which had faithfully accompanied him on his baleful missions for many years, passed the Hüttenweg exit. Only a few more kilometres.

We'll soon be there.

As usual before it happened, he was faintly aware of a call of nature. Pure nerves. He would forget the pressure on his bladder as soon as he was looking evil in the face. The preparations for today had taken months. Not for the first time, he'd had to don a disguise and assume the worst of identities: that of a paedophile. It was quite a while – two and a half years – since he'd last eliminated such a blot on humanity's landscape. Many of his former contacts had dropped out and others were suspicious of his sudden reappearance. In the end, however, he had succeeded in contacting the man known as 'the Dealer'. Via the Internet. And today, at last, they were to meet in person. Of course, he couldn't be certain he would really get an opportunity to tear out the evil by the roots, nor did he know what to make of the fact that the rendezvous had been changed at the last minute and postponed for three quarters of an hour. He knew only that his fate was in God's hands. He was old. Unlike the children, he had nothing to lose.

The man turned off at Spanische Allee. He patted the revolver lying beside him on the passenger seat. It went without saying that he often wondered if he was doing the right thing. He communed with the Almighty every Sunday and asked for some sign, some little indication of whether he should stop. Once, when told about Simon, he'd thought that was it: a divine omen. But he'd been mistaken.

And he'd gone on. Until today.

He turned on his headlights when he reached the gloomy road through the woods. The dead end that led to Wannsee Lido.

12

Another forty metres.

Stern put one foot before the other. First the good one, then the swollen one. He kept heading straight for the headlights, just as Engler had told him to.

The wait in the cold and rain had seemed like a fear-stricken eternity, but it was only a few minutes after Engler had left him alone that the car turned off the access road and drove into the deserted car park, its headlights blazing. He wondered one last time whether there was any possibility of delaying the inevitable, but nothing occurred to him. Like a lamb to the slaughter, he walked step by step towards the gradually slowing car and, thus, to meet his own death.

His heart beat faster as the elderly Opel came to a sudden stop.

The wind carried the metallic ratcheting of a worn handbrake to his ears. Almost simultaneously the driver's door opened and an ungainly figure got out.

Who is he?

At every other step, Stern's spine was traversed by flashes of pain so intense, he half expected them to light up the rainswept car park. He looked in vain for some indication that he knew the man who rounded the front of the car with dragging footsteps and came to a halt between its headlights. He felt like someone dying of thirst in the desert who makes his way towards a mirage. That was how unreal the whole situation seemed. The closer he got to the lights, the more indistinct the man's figure became. Only one thing was certain: he wasn't young and might even be old. The slow movements, the short steps, the slightly stooping posture – Stern tried to discern even more about the shadowy figure now standing motionless between the headlights. Obscured by the heavy overcast, the meagre light of the rising sun invested the unknown man with a weird aura. *Like an angel of death complete with halo*, thought Stern, blinking a raindrop out of his eye.

Another thirty metres.

He walked even more slowly. As far as he could recall, that was the only course of action still open to him. It did not break any of Engler's lethal rules.

Just walk straight ahead, Engler had told him. *Not to the right, not to the left, and don't make a run for it.*

He knew the consequences, and he also grasped the nature of the plan he was carrying out. Every step he took shortened his life.

He hugged the basket to his chest. Engler had removed the doll's batteries for safety's sake. Nothing could be allowed to distract the newcomer's attention or warn him that he was confronting the wrong man. Engler had devised a duel in which Stern had to participate unarmed. The avenger, if such he really was, would assume he was the child-trafficker and shoot him. In a few seconds' time.

Twenty metres.

Stern was well within hailing distance, but the gag in his parched mouth, which seemed to be expanding every moment, precluded any form of communication. He was assailed by the feeling of utter impotence that had last overwhelmed him at Felix's funeral.

Or the funeral of some other baby?

All hope was gone. There was no way out. Anything he did would endanger Simon. Anything he failed to do would end his own life.

Another fifteen metres.

He realized how unlikely it was that Engler would leave anyone alive after engineering his execution. As soon as he had a bullet in the head, the inspector would shoot the avenger and Simon. He would then take a minute to arrange the bodies before giving his men the signal to close in. Stern could visualize his official report:

> Child-trafficker (Robert Stern) attempted to hand over boy (Simon Sachs) to paedophile (?).
>
> An exchange of shots ensued, in the course of which all three persons sustained fatal injuries.
>
> The concealed witness (Inspector Martin Engler) was unable to prevent this development without endangering his own life.

Another ten metres.

Who knows, though? Stern experienced an irrational flicker of hope. *Simon is anaesthetized, so he isn't a potentially dangerous witness. The more dead bodies, the greater the risk.* Would Engler kill more people than absolutely necessary? Would he let Simon live after all?

The man's shadowy figure was becoming more distinct. Stern's vague feeling that their paths had crossed before intensified.

'Are the goods healthy?'

He gave a start and almost stopped short. Although Engler had told him of this 'password' in advance, it felt as if his executioner had asked whether he had anything to say before he was dispatched.

Seven metres.

Stern came to a halt. As instructed, he slowly squatted down and deposited the basket on the muddy surface of the car park as carefully as possible. Next, he was to straighten up and make a V-sign with his left hand.

'That'll clinch the deal,' Engler had said.

And turn me into a target, thought Stern. He remained bending over the doll for a second longer than necessary.

That second made all the difference. Perhaps because the glare of the headlights was refracted differently from that angle, or perhaps because of his proximity and the light of the rising sun. To Stern, it didn't matter why he suddenly recognized the man whose tousled, thinning hair was fluttering in the wind, even though he had seen him only once before in his life.

He pulled himself together and rose slowly to his feet.

What do I do now?

The sweat was collecting beneath his scratchy woollen mask.

How do I give him a sign without arousing Engler's suspicions?

He raised his arm, which suddenly seemed to dangle from his shoulder like an uncontrollable lead weight.

There must be some way. You must be able to do something.

He longed to tear off the mask and the duct tape, but that would sentence Simon to death.

The other man's arm was already halfway to waist height. Stern sensed rather than saw him take something from his pocket. *An automatic? A revolver? No matter. Another two seconds and you're history.* He gagged, feeling certain, although he couldn't see the avenger's hands, that a gun was aimed at his head.

A guttural sound, so soft that he alone could hear it,

issued from his parched throat. That finally dissolved his mental block.

Of course. That's it.

It was idiotic, banal and probably doomed to fail, but at least he wouldn't meet his end in a state of total inactivity.

Click.

Only seven metres away, the man he recognized had cocked a revolver. Despite this, Stern raised his arm, shut his eyes and started to hum. Six notes only, the simplest melodic sequence he knew but the only one fraught with special meaning.

Money, money, money . . .

He hoped that the elderly ABBA fan would recognize it. Prayed that this hint would belie the V-sign he was making with his left hand – prayed that it would be enough to give pause to the man whose wheelchair he had blundered into when visiting the hospital two days ago.

Money, money, money . . .

He hummed the phrase again, then screwed up his eyes in expectation of a lethal explosion inside his skull.

Two seconds later, when nothing had happened, he blinked convulsively. His hopes revived a little, his heart beat faster. Jubilant at the possibility that his sign had been interpreted correctly, he opened his eyes. At that precise moment the first shot rang out.

13

Engler, who had circled round behind the other two, saw Stern topple over backwards. He leaped at the gunman even before the lawyer's head hit the ground. The force of the impact dislodged two of the old man's vertebrae and fractured a rib. The inspector kicked his moaning victim's gun out of his hand. Then he turned him over on his back and sat on him, pinning his arms to his sides, before holding an automatic to the man's head.

'Who the hell are you?' he shouted.

The beam of the torch attached to the barrel of Engler's handgun lit up a wrinkled face he'd never seen before in his life.

'Losensky,' gasped the man. 'My name is Frederik Losensky.'

He spat some blood into the inspector's face. Engler wiped his cheek on his sleeve and forced Losensky's jaws apart. He was about to insert the muzzle of his automatic into the man's mouth when he paused.

'Who are you with? Who are you working for?'

'Him.'

'Him who? Who's your boss?'

'The same as yours. Almighty God.'

'I don't believe this!' Engler jabbed his gun into the underside of Losensky's lower jaw. 'Don't tell me we've been fucked around for years by a retired religious maniac.'

His laugh developed into a bronchitic cough.

'OK, I've got some good news for you,' he said hoarsely. 'Your boss has just invited you to an important meeting, and I'm to send you on your way. He's in a bit of a hurry, so—'

'Drop your gun!'

Engler raised his eyebrows and turned to look. A figure had just emerged from behind a clump of fir trees.

'Welcome to the party,' he said with a laugh when he recognized Carina. 'Better late than never.'

She took a couple of steps towards him but remained at a safe distance.

'Drop your gun and get off him.'

'Or else what?'

Engler had to shout to make himself heard in spite of their proximity. The wind was blowing even harder now.

'I'll shoot you.'

'With that thing in your hand?'

'Yes.'

He laughed. 'Is that the pea-shooter from the bumbag you were wearing yesterday?'

'So what?'

'Do me a favour and pull the trigger.'

'What do you mean?'

Carina, who had been holding the gun in one hand, clasped the butt with the other hand as well. She might almost have been praying.

'Only asking,' called the inspector. The old man beneath him was breathing heavily. 'You don't have to aim it at me. Just fire in the air.'

'Why?'

Carina's arms had started to tremble as if the gun in her hands were growing heavier by the second.

'Because you'll find the fucking thing isn't loaded. You really think I'd give it back without emptying the magazine first?'

'What makes you think I didn't fill it again?'

'The look on your face, Fräulein Freitag.'

Engler removed his automatic from Losensky's lower jaw and levelled it at Carina's chest. 'Bye-bye,' he said.

There was a click as Carina squeezed the trigger. Click, click. The fourth futile click was drowned by Engler's chesty laughter.

'Too bad.'

He aimed the laser pointer straight at Carina's forehead. His finger tightened on the trigger.

When the shot rang out like a whiplash over the Wannsee, the gale seemed to hold its breath for one brief moment. Then, with a renewed roar, it swallowed up the lethal sound.

The Beginning

It is no more remarkable
to be born once than twice.

Voltaire

This is attested by the accounts of people
who have undergone a near-death experience.
Nearly all of them sensed that their soul detached
itself from their body before they were resuscitated.
What is more, some even say they knew, while dying,
what new body their soul would migrate to.

Carina Freitag

1

The voices were overlaid by a metallic hiss that made them sound as if they were coming from audio headphones with the volume turned up too high. The more the vehicle lurched around, the louder and more distinct they became. They eventually tugged so hard at Simon's consciousness that he couldn't remain asleep any longer and opened his eyes for the duration of one overexposed snapshot. It was just long enough to reveal that two men were sitting beside him in the back of an ambulance.

'Cryptomnesia?' said a hoarse voice. He recognized it at once.

Borchert!

'Yes,' replied Professor Müller. 'Reincarnation is a thoroughly controversial field of research, of course, but cryptomnesia is currently regarded as the most plausible approach to explaining suprasensual rebirth experiences in a logical and scientific manner.'

Simon wanted to sit up. He was thirsty and his left knee was itching beneath the thin pyjama trousers. Used to being alone when he woke, he needed a little time to himself – to clear his head, as Carina put it. Whenever she said that, he was reminded of those 'snowballs'. Glass globes you shook and then watched the polystyrene flakes drifting slowly down.

He sometimes thought his head must look exactly like that when he woke up. For the first few minutes of the day he liked to wait until the pictures and voices in his head drifted back to where they belonged. That was why he decided to pretend to be asleep for a bit longer while he sorted out his thoughts and listened to the two men's low voices.

'Do I need a university degree to follow this?' Borchert was asking.

'Not at all. It's really quite simple. Until recently scientists assumed that the human brain possessed a built-in filter. It's capable of processing innumerable items of information simultaneously, but not all of them are important. At the moment, for instance, your main concern is to listen to me, follow what I'm saying and, at the same time, prevent yourself from slipping off your seat when the ambulance goes round a corner. But it's totally unimportant to you what examiner's number is stamped on this medicine chest or whether I'm wearing lace-up shoes.'

'They're slip-ons.'

'Quite so. Your eye has been registering that all the time, but the filter in your brain sifted it out until I drew your attention to it. A good thing, too. Think what it would be like if you counted every leaf on every tree when you walked through a forest. If we were talking together in a café, you'd be unable to fade out the conversations going on at neighbouring tables.'

'I'd probably wet myself.'

'You may laugh, but you're right. Without a filter your brain would be so busy processing an unimaginably vast influx of information, you'd probably be incapable of the simplest bodily functions.'

'But you just said this filter theory is old hat.'

Simon felt an invisible force propelling him forwards, which meant that he was lying with his head pointing the way they were going and the ambulance had just pulled up.

'Not exactly,' said Müller, 'but there's a new and very plausible theory based on research into savantism.'

'What's that?'

'Autism is the term you're probably more familiar with.'

'*Rain Man*?'

'Yes, for example. Let me think of the best way of explaining it to a layman.'

Although his eyes were shut, Simon could clearly visualize the medical director thinking hard, the corners of his mouth turned down. It was all Simon could do not to grin.

'All right, forget about the filter and think of a valve instead.'

'OK.'

'Thanks to the brain's almost limitless ability to store data, there is much evidence to suggest that our first step is to store everything it registers, but only on a subconscious level, and that a biochemical valve prevents our long-term memory from becoming overloaded by releasing only the data we really need.'

'So everything is filed away in a filing cabinet, but we have a tough job opening the drawers?'

'That's one way of putting it.'

'But what's all this got to do with Simon's reincarnation?'

'That's quite simple. Ever fallen asleep in front of the television?'

'All the time. I was watching some boring documentary on burning witches the other night. That did it.'

'Good. You stored all the information but the valve has prevented you from actively remembering it. However, a specially trained therapist could stimulate your subconscious under hypnosis.'

'And open the drawer.'

'Precisely.'

Simon heard a click followed by a faint, irregular scratching sound not far from his right ear. He guessed that the medical director was giving Borchert a graphic illustration of what he meant by drawing a diagram with his ballpoint.

'In the case of most regressions in which the patient is put into a trance or hypnotized, that's exactly what happens. People believe their spirit is roaming around in a previous existence. In reality, they're only recalling something they quite unwittingly stored in one of their brain's deepest levels of consciousness. If you underwent a regression of that kind, Herr Borchert, it's possible you would remember that television documentary on the Middle Ages and believe you were a witch being burned at the stake. You would even be able to quote authentic dates and places because you'd been told them by the programme's presenter.'

'But I didn't see any pictures.'

'Yes, you saw pictures in your own imagination, which are often more vivid than actual impressions. You probably know that from reading books.'

'Hm, sure, from way back. And that's called crypto-whatsit?'

Simon sensed that the ambulance was steadily putting on speed. It reminded him of the way Carina had driven to the ruined industrial estate where he'd met his lawyer for the first time.

Robert and Carina. Where are they?

'Cryptomnesia. That's the technical term for representing knowledge you've subconsciously absorbed from other people as your own. Are you still with me?'

'Just about. But Simon didn't fall asleep in front of the television, did he?'

Simon was tempted to blink. He screwed up his eyes. The harder the pressure on his eyeballs, the clearer the picture he'd just been dreaming of.

The door with the number on it. Number 17.

'No, not that,' Müller replied, 'but something similar. I think you're aware that we discontinued his radiotherapy a month or so ago?'

'Yes.'

'Because of the side effects. He was placed in intensive care with a temperature of forty-one, suffering from pneumonia. Another patient was admitted at the same time.'

'Frederik Losensky.'

'Exactly. A sixty-seven-year-old journalist. Suspected minor heart attack. Chest pains but fully conscious. He was placed in intensive care for observation.'

'Don't tell me: he was in the bed next to Simon's.'

'That's it. As you must have read in the press, Losensky was a serial murderer of paedophiles.'

'The so-called Avenger.'

'And a very God-fearing man. Even at that stage he was already in touch with the head of a child-trafficking ring. I think it was no accident that he suffered his heart attack shortly after receiving confirmation that the Dealer wanted to meet him face to face.'

'And Losensky talked to Simon that night in intensive care?'

'Not exactly. Simon wasn't capable of holding a conversation. His temperature was so high, we didn't expect him to survive. But for all that, or for that very reason, Losensky talked to him.'

'Like a television presenter?'

'In a manner of speaking. We suspect that Losensky regarded his proximity to a young, terminally ill child as a divine omen. He had burdened himself with guilt for the sake of children, after all, so he took advantage of that night in intensive care to confess. He told Simon of his murders one by one. Being their author, he could give a vivid and detailed description of them.'

'He was deranged.'

Borchert coughed. Simon would have done likewise, but he didn't want to draw attention to himself prematurely. Not before he had understood what the two grown-ups' conversation had to do with the hotel room in the dream from which he had just emerged.

'Deranged, yes, but we ourselves might be unbalanced if we'd seen the child cruelty Losensky had. Whatever, Simon unexpectedly recovered and events took their course. On his tenth birthday he was put into a hypnotic trance and underwent regression. It was as if Dr Tiefensee had pricked a certain area of his subconscious with a surgical needle. The memory blister burst and Simon remembered something that had found its way through the fog of his feverish dreams and into his brain a month earlier.'

'Losensky's confession.'

'Logically enough, he didn't know *how* he had acquired these memories. See what I mean?'

Borchert uttered a bark of laughter. 'I reckon it's like finding some cash in an old pair of bell-bottoms and being unable to remember ever wearing the ugly things.'

'Good example. You find the money and spend it because you're bound to assume it belongs to you. Simon found a recollection of these terrible murders in his head and was firmly convinced of his own responsibility for them. That's why he passed the lie-detector test.'

'But how could he know about the future?'

'Losensky finished his confession by asking Simon . . . Here . . .'

Simon heard the dry rustle of newspaper.

'It's in every scandal sheet. They found Losensky's diary in his bedside cupboard and printed extracts from it.'

Müller proceeded to read aloud:

'"So I told Simon about my last great plan. I said I was going to carry it out on the *Brücke* at 6 a.m. on November 1st. 'Simon,' I said, 'I'm going to shoot the evil one after he's handed over the baby, but I'm not sure if I'm doing the right thing. That's why I'm asking one last favour of you. Very soon, when you enter the presence—'"'

'" '—of our Creator, tell him I killed them all with a pure heart.' "'

To Müller's and Borchert's astonishment, Simon had opened his eyes and completed the last few words of Losensky's confession.

'" 'Ask him if I'm doing wrong. If I am, he must send me a sign and I'll stop at once.' "'

'You're awake.'

'Yes, I have been for quite a while,' Simon admitted. He cleared his throat, looking sheepish.

Borchert bent over him. 'So it's true?'

'I couldn't understand everything you've been saying, but I can remember the voice. It sounded very . . . very kind, somehow.'

The ambulance was slowing. Simon made a feeble attempt to sit up.

'So I didn't do anything bad?'

'No, not at all.' Borchert and Müller spoke almost simultaneously.

'I didn't kill anyone?'

'Certainly not.'

'But why aren't Robert and Carina here?'

'The thing is . . .' Müller rested his long, warm fingers on Simon's forehead. 'You've spent most of the last three days asleep.'

'And during that time,' Borchert added, 'certain things have, well . . . happened.'

'Like what?' Simon was puzzled. The two grown-ups sounded odd, as if they were keeping something from him.

'Did I do something wrong? Don't Robert and Carina like me any more?'

'Nonsense. Don't even think it.'

'Can you really not remember anything?' asked Borchert.

Simon shook his head. He had woken up numerous times in the last few nights, but only briefly and always on his own.

'No. What's wrong?'

The sun seemed suddenly to go down behind the vehicle's frosted glass windows, and the hollow sound of its diesel engine reminded Simon unpleasantly of the moment when the ugly woman drove her car into the underground garage.

'We're there,' called a voice from the front of the ambulance. Someone got out.

'Where are Robert and Carina?' Simon asked again. The rear doors opened.

'Well,' said Professor Müller, taking him gently by the hand, 'I think you'd better hear that from someone else.'

2

Skewed and devoid of a soundtrack, the black-and-white shots were of cheapest home video quality. The car's headlights were dazzling the camera, which lent them a resemblance to overexposed ultrasound pictures.

'Is it a boy or a girl?' the district attorney had quipped when shown the tape for the first time. Brandmann himself had taken a while to make out the figures of the two men standing in front of the car.

'There, you can see Losensky draw his gun.' He cleared his throat and tapped the relevant spot on the screen with the edge of a throw-away lighter.

'You're in the light.'

'Oh, sorry.' Brandmann stepped out of the projector's beam. 'There, look: the old man seems to be hesitating. Now he raises the gun a little, and: bang!'

The muzzle flash left a bright yellow streak on the screen. As if struck by a wrecking ball, Stern went over backwards in the lido car park, hitting his head, and lay motionless.

'Engler filmed this himself. His camera was lying on the parcel shelf of the car he was hiding in.'

The inspector cleared his throat, as he did after almost every sentence he uttered. He refrained from asking if he could smoke and paused the tape briefly.

'It would have made perfect visual evidence. An abortive child-trafficking transaction. A pair of scumbags eliminating each other. Engler was a video freak. We assume he simply left the camera running in order to be able to sell the tape as a snuff movie later on. Or for home use, who knows? Of course, we were never meant to see the shots that follow.'

3

'Where are you taking me?'

The wheelchair's footrest left a black mark on the wall as it was manhandled up the stairs from the underground garage. Simon looked over his shoulder at Borchert, who was hauling away at the handles and sweating. 'You're due for some rehab,' he panted.

The ambulance driver, pushing from below, was also breathing somewhat faster as they neared the top.

'What sort of rehab?'

'Special treatment for specially difficult cases like you.'

'But where are we?'

They had reached the top step. Simon looked down at Professor Müller, who was still standing at the foot of the stairs.

'A private clinic,' Müller said with a smile.

'Without a lift? Funny sort of clinic, isn't it?'

'You'd best take a look round yourself. Wheeee!'

Simon couldn't help giggling. All at once it felt like being in a fairground dodgem car. Borchert propelled him violently forwards, then backwards, then spun him on the spot like a top.

'Please stop,' he cried between gusts of laughter, but

Borchert spun him twice more before pushing him out of the stairwell and along a passage with bare walls.

'I feel sick,' he groaned. The wheelchair came to rest at last, unlike the images whirling before his eyes. The faces of Borchert, Müller and the ambulance driver gradually stopped revolving around him.

'What . . . what's *this*?'

Experimentally, Simon felt his head. He always removed his wig and deposited it on his bedside table at night, but no, he wasn't dreaming. He could distinctly feel the wig beneath his tingling fingers. So the whole scene couldn't be a dream, much as it looked like one.

'Well, what do you think?'

Simon's look of mute amazement was answer enough. Very slowly, as if he'd just taken his medication, he folded up the white hospital blanket on his lap and draped it over the armrest.

He couldn't have explained why he did this. Perhaps it was just to occupy his trembling hands before the flood of glorious impressions totally paralysed him. Then his face broke into an irrepressible smile and the leaden armour that had seemed to encase his limbs fell away.

He turned, hesitated and scanned his companions' faces with an unspoken question in his eyes. They smiled at him encouragingly. Borchert, whose own eyes were strangely moist, was grinning even more broadly than the other two. So Simon stood up and took two paces into the room, which seemed incredibly spacious. Although there was so much else to discover, he couldn't detach his gaze from the palm trees flanking the doorway. He shut his eyes, afraid that the mirage would have disappeared when he reopened them. But a moment later everything was still there: the sandy beach; the bamboo hut, brown as sugar cane; the ceaseless, muffled roar of the surf; and, a little way off, the smiling young woman with flowers in her hair.

'Hello, Simon,' said Carina, coming towards him slowly.

He was pervaded by a pleasurable sensation of warmth.

'May I?' he asked shyly, wondering why his voice sounded so different. And, as the men broke into laughter and applause, he planted one bare foot awkwardly on the creamy white sand, like a young puppy.

4

Brandmann pressed 'Play' again and the frozen image lurched into motion. On the screen, Losensky was overpowered by Engler, who abruptly turned his head.

'This is the moment when Carina Freitag enters the equation,' Brandmann explained. 'Not that she ever appears on camera. Her gun wasn't loaded, unfortunately.'

'Or fortunately.'

'Yes. Depends which way you look at it.'

The screen showed Engler raising his automatic and aiming at an invisible Carina. Then, from behind him, came a muzzle flash. The bullet hit him squarely in the back of the head.

'Yes,' said Stern, 'that's the way it was.' He removed his little finger from the cigarette burn in the worn leather sofa and struggled to his feet. Then he started humming.

'ABBA, eh?' Brandmann smiled. 'I honestly believe Losensky interpreted it as a divine omen and fired a warning shot in the air when he heard you hum "Money, Money, Money".'

'That's pretty much what I was gambling on. It was only fright that sent me over backwards, not a bullet. I realized I wasn't hurt, so I knew I mustn't try to break my fall or he'd know I was still alive. When you come down to it, I beat Engler at his own game. He tricked me by playing dead and it worked for me too. Mind you, it did get me these.'

He pointed to his flesh-coloured cervical collar and the bandage around his head. Although concussed, he had managed to worm his way across the car park and reach the revolver Engler had kicked out of Losensky's hand. However, if Carina's intervention hadn't gained him a few vital seconds, he wouldn't have had time to raise the gun, take aim and fire.

Stern limped over to the special investigator.

'I thought you were my enemy all the time, that's why I confided in your partner instead of you.'

'That's understandable.' Brandmann cleared his throat for the twentieth time at least and flicked the flint wheel of his lighter with a thumb. 'But Engler wasn't my partner. Officially I'm a criminal profiler employed by the Federal Police Bureau, but that's just camouflage. I really work for Internal Affairs. Engler had long been suspected of involvement in criminal activities. There were indications that he owned a clutch of holiday homes in Mallorca and other assets unaffordable on his salary, but no one had guessed the full extent of his activities, least of all me.'

Brandmann's reproachful expression was presumably aimed at himself.

'So you weren't supposed to be investigating my case at all?'

The inspector shook his massive head.

'Not from the very first, no. We didn't believe there was any connection between Engler's corruption and Simon's dead bodies.' He cleared his throat and licked his dry lips. 'Our strategy was to make him nervous by means of my clumsily intrusive interference in his work. If we exerted sufficient pressure and put him off his stroke, we hoped he'd get careless – send an unencrypted email or use an insecure mobile number. Anything that would lead us to his sources of income. But when the Simon Sachs case became more and more convoluted, the chief superintendent thought it wouldn't do any harm to bring in a man of my experience. So I helped the team out a bit – organized Simon's lie-detector test, collected witnesses' statements and assisted Engler in his scene-of-crime work.'

'And gave Picasso your phone number?'

'Yes. Your father was given it too, by the way. The two of them were to call me as soon as they spotted anything suspicious. Picasso was neutralized before he could see that the police guard on Simon's room had been withdrawn. We already know who slipped an overdose of rohypnol into his coffee, by the way.'

Stern raised his eyebrows.

'The police guard himself, an accomplice of Engler's. According to his statement, Herr Stern, you overpowered him. Too bad he didn't know of Engler's death at the time he was interviewed.' Brandmann couldn't hide a smile. 'The whole thing was meticulously planned. I reckon Engler thought he was fireproof after all those years of leading a double life. He lured you, Carina, Simon and even his own prospective murderer to the lido car park – right under the eyes of the police.'

'Where were you all the time?' Stern's question sounded rather more abrupt than he intended. 'If it was your job to keep an eye on Engler, why didn't you get wind of his last major operation?'

Brandmann cleared his throat and made an apologetic gesture.

'Chief Superintendent Hertzlich withdrew me when the situation escalated. I was only there to investigate financial irregularities, as I told you. From that time on, my work was temporarily suspended so as not to interfere with further investigations. I was already packing my bags.'

'And now? What happens now? What about Engler's associates? Somebody must have been helping him, surely?'

Brandmann gave an affirmative grunt after each question, his Adam's apple jerking up and down.

'Yes, worse luck. Losensky had considerably thinned the ranks of his psychopathic associates in recent years, but Engler was always able to replace them in short order. As head of the murder squad he was well placed, after all. Nevertheless, we've confiscated a mass of material that should help to smash the remainder of his gang. Hard disks, files, tapes, DVDs – not forgetting Engler's car. The boot was crammed with the latest video technology . . .'

Stern was reminded of how Engler had filmed himself and Brandmann at the animal cemetery. He had thought the pictures were live, but they'd merely been played after the event. A cheap trick like the performance at Tiefensee's practice.

'The only nice thing we found when we searched Engler's home was his dog. Charlie the Labrador will be living with me from now on.' Brandmann chuckled.

'Didn't you discover anything else?' Stern asked hesitantly.

'Not what you're alluding to, no. To be honest, I wouldn't get your hopes up too much in that respect.'

Stern's heart raced. At the same time, the left-hand side of his body went numb as if someone had sprayed it with coolant from the inside. He had almost been expecting the news, but having his worst fears confirmed at first hand was something else.

'We're still evaluating the evidence, but so far we haven't found anything that points to your son. No documents, no photos or films of him, either as an infant or more recently. As for the baby depository theory . . .' Brandmann ahemmed.

To judge by his husky voice, he really did have a lump in his throat. 'Well, we're naturally following up that lead and checking hospitals nationwide to see if such an eventuality might be possible. To date, however, we haven't turned up anything that would corroborate what Engler told you.'

Naturally.

Stern put all his weight on his right-hand crutch and drove it into the cellar's concrete floor as hard as he could. With his free hand he felt for the crumpled envelope in his hip pocket. Engler's parting gift to him had been a photo of the ten-year-old boy in the act of blowing out his birthday candles. Written across the cake in capital letters were the words APRIL FOOL!

So he'd been hoodwinked on that score too. He blinked as if something had flown into his eye. It might sometime transpire how Engler had got hold of the CCTV footage and managed to manipulate it so convincingly. It might even prove possible to find the birthday child whose features had been modified to resemble his own with the aid of some kind of ultra-modern picture-processing software. The boy's whole figure might be a bogus, computer-generated illusion.

Stern relaxed his furious grip on the photo when he heard the blood roaring in his ears. None of this altered the fact that the video of that ten-year-old boy had simply been a cheap trick. Felix was dead and always had been. He was glad he'd never shared his irrational hopes with Sophie.

'We shall follow up every possible lead and check to see if your son—' Brandmann broke off and stared at the ceiling. Muffled reggae music was drifting down into the cellar from upstairs.

'What's that?' he asked in surprise.

'That? That's our cue.'

Stern hobbled to the door.

'Thanks a lot for showing me the tape, but I'm afraid I must now ask you to remove your shoes.'

'Why on earth . . . ?' Brandmann looked as if Stern had tipped a glass of iced water over his crotch.

Stern opened the door and the Caribbean strains increased in volume.

'Because that concludes the official part of the proceedings and I want to keep a longstanding promise.'

5

'There you are!'

Laughing, Simon plodded towards Stern across the man-made beach. A dozen operatives from an events agency had spent the previous night spreading fine sand all over the living-room floor. That done, the walls were quickly decorated with tropical motifs and a host of artificial palm trees, banana fronds and torches distributed around the dunes. Even the hearth was filled with driftwood and now resembled a campfire *à la* Robinson Crusoe. What really put the finishing touch to the island scenery, however, was a genuine bamboo beach bar. Installed behind it, Andi Borchert was busy mixing non-alcoholic cocktails.

Stern experienced a sudden urge to run away, to head in the direction his dark thoughts were trying to propel him – to go anywhere, as long as it was away from this place he no longer recognized as his home. Not because of the coral sand and the palm trees, but because it was filled with sounds he had banished from it for years: laughter, music, happy voices. Looking around, he saw Simon, Carina, Borchert, Brandmann, Professor Müller – even his father. Familiar faces all, and all belonging to people whom he himself had invited but now felt somehow disconnected from.

And then, as Simon drew nearer and his urge to flee became almost irresistible, a change came over him. It was as if the boy were carrying an invisible torch that lit up his surroundings. Stern realized only now how much he had missed him.

When Simon was standing in front of him at last, smiling with a sincerity of which most grown-ups are incapable, he understood for the first time why Carina had summoned him to that derelict industrial estate. The boy had never really needed his help. It was the other way round.

'Thank you so much,' Simon said, and his laughter momentarily silenced the nagging questions in Stern's mind.

'Thanks, this is really cool!'

At the touch of his soft hand, Stern had a vague feeling that the answers he'd been seeking in the last few days weren't crucial at all. As the boy led him to the beach bar, he saw for the first time what his open but unseeing eyes had ignored until now: Simon, Carina, the twins, himself. They had all survived. No longer tormented by inexplicable, murderous fantasies, the boy at his side could laugh, eat an ice-cream, dance the lambada and enjoy this moment, even though the thing running riot in his head was far more destructive than any bad thoughts.

If he can do it, so – perhaps – can I, Stern told himself. *Not for ever, not for long, but maybe for today. For now. For this moment.*

Leaning against the bar, he nodded first at Borchert and then at Carina, pleased that his friends understood him without the need for words – and that they treated him to one of the ice-creams he'd promised Simon.

The party went on for two hours or more. They lit the campfire, improvised a beach barbecue, and ended by dancing. Once the excitement had passed its zenith and subsided a little, Stern joined Simon and Carina, who abruptly fell silent when he sat down beside them on the sand.

'Well,' he said, 'what have you been talking about behind my back?'

'Nothing,' Simon replied with a mischievous grin. 'It was just that I couldn't believe this is really your house.'

'Yes, Carina's right for once.'

'You actually live here?'

'When I don't have to sleep in a camper van, yes.'

Stern smiled at Carina, who smiled back just as broadly.

'But where's all your furniture?'

'Oh, don't worry about that,' Carina said with a laugh. She knew only too well that Stern's home had never been more comfortably furnished than it was right now. She got up and went over to the bar for something to drink. Stern watched her go, his eyes lingering on the dainty little footprints she left behind in the soft sand.

'Listen,' he said to Simon, who had stretched out on the sand beside him and was gazing up at the net filled with genuine coconuts that had been suspended there in place of a chandelier. 'Professor Müller just told me he may try radiotherapy again. Those CT scan pictures of the brain can be deceptive sometimes. Tomorrow he wants to check how far the tumour really has grown into the other half of your brain, and then—'

He broke off.

'Simon?'

'Yes?'

'What's wrong?'

'I . . . I don't know.'

Simon had sat up and was staring at his left foot. He looked as dismayed as Stern himself.

'Carina?' Stern called, getting to his feet. 'Don't worry, it's only a touch of epilepsy,' he said, more to himself than the boy. The tremor in Simon's foot had transmitted itself to his leg, but it looked different from the twitching Stern had witnessed before. Although it hadn't yet spread to the rest of his body, it looked considerably more ominous.

'Make way,' called Carina, who had hurried over to them with Professor Müller. The lorazepam drops were already in her hand.

'It's all right, everything'll be fine.'

Simon's wig came away when she brushed the hair off his forehead.

'We must take him back at once,' Müller said in a low voice.

Stern nodded. He was feeling like the victim of a car crash. They had all been laughing together a moment ago, and now he had to watch a sick child being carried out of the room by Borchert.

'Bring the ambulance round to the front, quickly,' he heard Carina call as he hurried after the others. The warm sand beneath his feet had become a morass that clung to his ankles and prevented him from walking fast enough. It seemed an eternity before he reached his front garden. He strode swiftly across it to the waiting ambulance and knelt beside the stretcher.

'Listen,' he said softly, for fear the boy would hear the anxiety in his voice if he spoke any louder. 'Don't be scared, OK? You're going to be fine.'

'Maybe.'

'No, listen to me. As soon as Professor Müller sorts you out we'll go to a proper beach, OK?'

He squeezed Simon's hand but felt no answering pressure.

'You mustn't be sad,' said the boy.

'I'm not sad.' Stern was weeping now.

'It was so lovely. We had a lot of fun.' Simon was sounding more and more tired. 'I've never had such a good time. The club, the zoo, watching that video with the twins, and then this brilliant party . . .'

'Don't let's talk about the past.'

'But I want to.'

Stern sniffed. 'What do you mean?'

'Time to go,' the driver called from up front. Carina put her hand on his shoulder. Stern shook it off.

'What did you want to tell me, Simon?'

The boy's eyelids drooped like withered leaves.

'The light in the cellar.'

'What?' The engine started just as something died in Stern's innermost self.

Click.

'It flickered again. Earlier on, when I was asleep all that time.'

No, no, no, cried the worsening pains in Stern's head.

Click. Click.

'It was even darker this time. Awfully dark. I could hardly see.'

No, please not. Don't let that nightmare begin all over again, thought Stern, and he felt an icy poison flooding through his veins as Simon told him one last thing. Then the boy lost consciousness.

Ten Days Later

The Park Inn

Ask to see our weekend offers

It must have been an age since someone had slid the faded letters into the grooves in the brown felt board above the reception desk, but it was obvious that no one was expected to comply with their injunction at this time of year. The lobby of the cheap motel was as deserted as the streets of the little town they'd just driven through on their way to it.

'Hello?' Stern called. He looked around for a bell, but the counter was empty save for two little perspex stands with some advertising brochures wedged in them.

'What are we supposed to do, chuck them at the wall?'

He turned and shrugged at Carina, who had perched on her overnight bag for want of any other form of seating.

'Hello, you've got guests!' Stern called as loudly as he could without actually shouting. The only response was the sound of a nearby toilet being flushed.

'About time too,' Carina muttered. Moments later a woman built like a wardrobe pushed a louvred door open and squeezed in behind the desk.

'What's all the rush?' she demanded breathlessly.

Ignoring her ungracious reception, Stern gave his name and deposited his ID on the counter.

'We booked.'

'Yes, yes, but you needn't have. They're all vacant.' The woman indicated the board on her right with a calloused forefinger. It was bristling with room keys. 'I can quote you a good price for the suite.'

Stern could imagine what the suite looked like. Unlike the other rooms, it probably boasted a television set.

'No, we want *that* room. I explained that on the phone.'

'Really? Number 17, eh? Hm, it's not our nicest.'

'I don't mind,' Stern said truthfully. They wouldn't be staying the night in any case. 'Number 17 or nothing.'

'If you say so.'

His fingers brushed the woman's bone-dry skin as he took the key from her. He started as if he'd driven a splinter into his hand.

'On your honeymoon?' she asked, leering suggestively at Carina.

'Yes,' said Stern, this being the shortest answer that occurred to him.

'Out of the door and follow the signs,' she called after them. 'It's the one at the far end on the right.'

The rain of recent days had stopped and the wind was playing billiards with the clouds overhead. It was only midday, but it felt much later. Even now, another wall of dirty grey cloud drifted across the sun and darkened the concrete walkway.

Room 17 was the motel's only detached building. The lock on the door didn't look as if it would welcome the key, which Stern managed to turn only at the second attempt.

'Shall I wait outside?' Carina asked.

'No, but please don't touch anything.'

He reached for the light switch and the heavily curtained

room was illuminated by a shadeless electric bulb. It was surprisingly neat and tidy.

Carina gave a noisy sniff. Stern was equally surprised by the complete absence of the smell of dust and damp he'd been expecting.

'She knew we were coming, after all,' he murmured, and set to work.

First, he examined the wardrobe. He gathered up the hangers and tossed them on to the bed beside Carina and her bag. Then he tapped the plywood back for hidden cavities.

Going into the bathroom, he was disappointed to find that it only contained a toilet and shower. He had been counting on a bathtub with enclosed spaces behind and beneath it. The water simply drained away through a small hole in the tiled floor.

'Well?' said Carina when he returned to the bedroom five minutes later, after examining the cistern and drainhole for concealed clues.

'Nothing,' he said, rolling up his wet sleeves. 'As yet.'

He lay down and looked under the bed. Carina got up at his request. While he was probing the mattress with a knife in various places, she examined the concrete floor for dents or grooves – anything that might conceal a hidden door or other form of access – but she couldn't detect the smallest irregularity.

Meanwhile Stern had taken a yellow handspray from the bag – the kind normally used for misting houseplants – and proceeded to spray the floor with a colourless reagent.

'Don't be alarmed,' he said when he'd finished. Moments later the overhead light went out, plunging the curtained room into total darkness.

'What do we have to look for?' Carina asked when the ultraviolet torch in Stern's hand was bathing their faces in a ghostly, lunar glow.

'You'll soon see.'

He turned clockwise on the spot.

'Or not, as the case may be,' he added after a while. Some hotel guest might have had a nosebleed at one point, but the UV light did not indicate that attempts had been made to remove any substantial traces of blood.

'What now?'

Stern turned on the light again. He stretched out on the mutilated mattress, breathing heavily and staring up at the ceiling.

'Now I suppose I'd better call him.'

He took his mobile from his jeans and dialled a number scribbled on a slip of paper.

'Robert Stern,' he said.

'You're late. Your special permission for this call runs out at 1 p.m.'

'And it's twelve forty-seven now, so kindly put me through to him.'

The surly voice at the other end of the line was replaced by another. Although it sounded far friendlier and more civilized, its owner differed from the supervisor of the prison hospital in having committed several murders.

'Losensky?'

'Yes.'

'You know why I'm calling?'

'Yes, because of Room 17.'

'What can you tell me about it?'

'Nothing, I'm afraid.'

'You didn't give the boy this address?'

'No, the place means nothing to me. I never told Simon about it and I've no idea why he should have directed you there.'

Stern heard the old man cough in an agitated fashion.

'Why would I lie to you?' Losensky went on. 'I already

gave the police a full confession and took them to all the crime scenes Simon hadn't already identified. Seven dead bodies in fifteen years. Why would I keep quiet about one more?'

I don't know.

'I'm in a prison hospital and I'm going to die here anyway. What have I got to gain by lying, young man?'

'Nothing,' Stern conceded. He thanked Losensky briefly and hung up.

'All right if I have a shower before we go and pay her for the damage?' Carina asked.

Stern just nodded mutely. When he heard the sound of water running in the bathroom he got up off the bed and drew the curtains back, then opened the sliding door to the terrace as wide as he could. Fresh air streamed into the little room.

He went outside and gazed into the distance. The beach flanking the Park Inn Motel stretched away for kilometres in both directions. The waves, which had been pounding the shore when they arrived, had subsided a little. Stern shut his eyes and felt the wind on his face, soft as silk, then a pleasant sensation of warmth. Opening them again, he was dazzled by fingers of sunlight tentatively feeling their way through the tattered overcast. All at once the dirty blanket of cloud was rent open and the sun shone down as if it were the first day of spring.

He was about to call Carina when something bumped gently into his leg.

Looking down, he saw a rubber beach ball lying at his feet. The sunlight was growing steadily brighter, and he had to shield his eyes with both hands as he peered in the direction from which it must have rolled towards him.

'Please may I have it back?' The voice was unbroken and very youthful. Stern stepped forward. And the warmth inside him became almost unbearable. The boy was standing on the sandy shore only a couple of arm's lengths away, licking a lemon ice-cream. At that moment, although he understood nothing else, Stern grasped why he was there.

Recognition dawned. The boy's crumpled photograph, a snapshot of a television screen, was still in his hip pocket.

And, when the ten-year-old smiled at him, Robert Stern felt he was looking into a mirror.

Acknowledgements

Well, where are you at this moment? In an armchair, on the sofa, in the Underground, in bed? Or are you still standing in a bookshop and wondering whether you really ought to invest in a thriller, especially one by an author with such a bizarre name? No matter. Thank you anyway. You're holding my book in your hands and dipping into it, even if you're only glancing at the end to see if the person who wrote this story has any friends to thank. Strangely enough, he has.

I'll start with the ones who would give me the most trouble if I forgot to mention them, given that our paths cross almost daily:

Manuela. Please go on taking plenty of exercise and stick to a healthy diet. If you ever fell by the wayside and stopped organizing my life, I'd be done for.

Gerlinde. My thanks for all your help, support and love. All else apart, this manifests itself in the fact that you always dump my meals on the desk when I'm in the thick of writing. If you didn't, I'd have starved to death by now.

Clemens and Sabine. I'm sure you're beginning to wish I would sometime write a story in which illnesses and psychoses don't play a central role. Unfortunately for you, you're going to have to act as my medical advice team in the future as well. You're simply too good at your job.

Patty. Many thanks for the impressive account of the regression you underwent, and for allowing me to use your experiences in this book.

Zsolt Bács. I took you to my heart even before I could pronounce your name properly. You're the best brainstormer there is!

Ender. Thanks for repeatedly introducing me to remarkable people who inspire characters in my books, e.g. Borchert! (But please tell him I'm really OK and he isn't to break my thumbs for me.)

Sabrina Rabow, Thomas Koschwitz, Arno Müller. Thank you for your friendly and professional support over the years, even though I always saddle you with my books in the form of manuscripts in ugly folders.

Peter Prange. You blazed the trail it's now my privilege to follow. If for that reason alone, you deserve a place of honour in any acknowledgements. Besides, it's always nice to be able to cite a bestselling author as a friend.

Roman Hocke. I don't know how you manage it all, but you're the best. If it weren't for your work as my agent, my books would never have been published in nearly twenty countries or filmed, and I'd still be writing purely for myself and my dogs. My thanks go also to your excellent team in the persons of Claudia von Hornstein, Christine Ziel and Dr Uwe Neumahr.

Still on the subject of agents, I'll say two words only: Britain and America. Thanks for everything, Tanja Howarth!

My thanks go also to the following representatives of the wonderful team at Droemer Knaur:

Dr Hans-Peter Übleis, for believing in me so much and for promoting me in your publishing house.

Dr Andrea Müller. Your wide-ranging comments have made me sweat yet again, and your unceasing efforts have got the best out of me. A thousand thanks for that and for laying the foundations of my career as an author.

Carolin Graehl. Our incredibly productive final spurt was fun. I look forward to the next editorial marathon!

Beate Kuckertz. Thanks for your unerring ability to sense which of my crazy ideas has the makings of a genuine thriller.

Klaus Kluge. Thank you for lavishing all your marketing skills on me and my books. Working with a professional of your calibre is an immense pleasure. The same goes for Andrea Fischer.

Andrea Ludorf. You keep me chasing all over the country, and a good thing too. Please go on organizing my public appearances and reading tours so efficiently.

Susanne Klein, Monika Neudeck, Patricia Kessler deserve my gratitude for jointly making waves in the press.

Dominik Huber. Although you're a master of the virtual world, I'm glad I've got to know you in reality.

I should also like to thank the booksellers who sell my books and the publisher's representatives who get them to where they belong. Standing in for a host of equally deserving individuals, the following merit my very special thanks: Iris Haas, Droemer's sales manager; Heide Bogner; Roswitha Kurth; Andreas Thiele; Christiane Thöming; and Katrin Englberger. Oh yes, and – of course – Georg Regis. It's easy to predict a favourable future for me as long as you continue to work so tirelessly on my behalf.

Who does that leave? Masses of people, for instance my father Freimut Fitzek, from whom I inherited more than just a love of literature; Simon Jäger; Dirk Stiller; Michael Treutler; Tom Hankel; Matthias Kopp; Andrea Kammann; Sabine Hoffmann; Daniel Biester; and Cordula Jungbluth. You all know why. If not, you owe me one.

I also welcome any visitors to www.sebastianfitzek.de.

Either drop in there, or write to me direct at fitzek@sebastianfitzek.de and tell me whether you liked the book. I promise to reply this side of the grave.

Sebastian Fitzek

Berlin, September 2007

PS. Thank you too, of course, Simon Sachs. Wherever you may be . . .